SHERLOCK HOLMES

AND

THE BARON OF BREDE PLACE

[Being a manuscript found in the tin dispatch-box of
Dr. John H. Watson in the vault of
Cox & Co, Charing Cross, London]

Book Two in the series,
Sherlock Holmes and the American Literati

As Edited

By

Daniel D. Victor, Ph.D.

Paperback ISBN 9781780927732
ePub ISBN 978-1-78092-774-9
PDF ISBN 978-1-78092-775-6

Published in the UK by MX Publishing
335 Princess Park Manor, Royal Drive,
London, N11 3GX
www.mxpublishing.co.uk
Cover design by www.staunch.com

Also by Daniel D. Victor

The Seventh Bullet:
The Further Adventures of Sherlock Holmes

A Study in Synchronicity

The Final Page of Baker Street
(Book One in the Series,
Sherlock Holmes and the American Literati)

Acknowledgements

For their patience and help, many thanks are once again in order to Sandy Cohen, Barry Smolin, Ethan Victor, Seth Victor, and my wife Norma Silverman. Without their support, the newly discovered manuscript of Dr. Watson would have remained hidden forever.

Here's another for Norma, Seth, and Ethan

Watson's accounts are as remarkable for those cases that they omit as they are for the ones that they relate . . . . Much of Holmes' work as an in-house detective to the English upper classes in the 1880s and 1890s has gone unrecorded, the victim of Watson's discreet censorship.

--Nick Rennison
Sherlock Holmes:
The Unauthorized Biography

If in telling the story I seem to be somewhat vague in certain details, the public will readily understand that there is an excellent reason for my reticence.

--John H. Watson, M.D.
"The Adventure of the Second Stain"

Some of this story is true.
--Paul Ferris
Headnote, *Cora Crane*

Preface

In the many years that I have narrated the adventures of my friend and colleague, Mr. Sherlock Holmes, I have always appreciated the forgiving nature of my readers. They have understood that the occasional alterations I've made to the historical record—excluding those cases Holmes has asked me to disguise or omit altogether—represent my best efforts to shield not only the identities but also the sensibilities of the guiltless personages involved. Even in those rare instances when I employed manipulation to swell a scene or render some action more engaging, a tolerant public generally turned the proverbial blind eye.

Yet even the best intentioned of authors can go too far, myself included. As difficult as it is for me to admit, the case I titled "The Adventure of Charles Augustus Milverton" serves as the most egregious example. Since the narrative first appeared in *The Strand* in 1904, it's taken me more than twenty years to summon the strength to set the record straight, to report the full extent of the emotional pain and cold-hearted criminality that I neglected to set down as I should have from the start.

Mea culpa.

To be fair, one cannot say, however, that I didn't offer hints of my obfuscation. Far from it. In the opening paragraph of the original narrative, I admitted to a "suppression" of certain details and even announced to the reader that I had intentionally concealed "any fact by which he might trace the actual occurrence". Not that I expected such

1

candour to stifle the harshest of my critics. For them, my confessions served only to raise new questions about what other facts I had distorted or failed to record. My detractors cited vague descriptions, inaccurate dates, and inconsistent characterizations often enough that many in the general audience began to doubt my oft-stated devotion to Truth.

The criticism has stung, and I am prepared to begin anew. With so long an interval having elapsed and so many lives having passed since I penned my initial account of the Milverton affair, I believe it is high time to correct the public record. As the following narrative will reveal, the long arm of the odious blackmailer, whom Holmes once called "the worst man in London", stretched far beyond the capital's boundaries, far beyond the shores of England. Because even America fell under Milverton's shadow, there exists a poetic justice in defending my apologia with the words of Supreme Court Justice Louis D. Brandeis. "Sunlight," he famously observed, "is said to be the best of disinfectants."

Such a belief has always guided me in making public the adventures of Sherlock Holmes. Howsoever far I may have strayed from the concept in my original narrative about Milverton, howsoever much I may have distorted and concealed, I still remain committed to Brandeis' premise. It is a commitment that has compelled me to resurrect with greater honesty the insidious crimes perpetrated by Milverton and— even worse—the emotional consequences that accompanied them.

John H. Watson, M.D.,
London 1927

Part I

The Americans

Daniel D. Victor

Chapter One

I stood upon a high place,
And saw, below, many devils
Running, leaping,
And carousing in sin.
One looked up, grinning,
And said: "Comrade! Brother!
--Stephen Crane

"Are you familiar with the American writer named Stephen Crane?"

It was a hot July afternoon in 1898, and I was returning to our rooms in Baker Street from a mid-day luncheon at my club. No sooner had I entered the sitting room than I heard the preceding question put to my friend, Sherlock Holmes. The voice was hoarse; the accent, American.

"Ah, Watson," exclaimed Holmes, "just in time. May I present to you Mr. Harold Frederic, the acclaimed novelist and London correspondent for the *New York Times*. He wants me to help him solve a problem."

Both men rose to greet me, and I was immediately impressed by our guest's imposing size. He was a giant of a man, his height eclipsing the tall, lean form of Sherlock Holmes, who was rather over six feet himself. Broad-shouldered with thick dark hair and a walrus moustache, Frederic gave the impression of one who was quite prepared for action. Indeed, his dark business suit appeared large enough to enable someone of his bulk to move about quite freely. He didn't look like a man accustomed to asking for help.

5

Given the heat then, I wasn't surprised at how much
Mr. Frederic was perspiring. Yet I also couldn't help noting
the effort, accompanied by an inhalation of breath and a
punctuating grunt, that he exerted in order to stand.
Admittedly, the armchair he'd occupied had deep cushions,
but as a physician I knew that a man of his relative youth
should not find rising so difficult.

"Whatever you wish to say to me," Holmes informed
our guest, "you may say to Dr. Watson. He and I have
worked together on many a perplexing problem."

"Yes, yes," said Frederic, waving Holmes off. "The
two of you are quite well-known among us pressmen." He
turned to face me. "Dr. Watson," he said and, catching his
breath, extended a hand—a large paw might be a better term
for it. "It seems hard to believe that I've been writing for the
New York Times here in London for close to fifteen years,
and yet this is the first time I've actually met you and Mr.
Holmes."

"You don't live nearby, I take it," said I, shaking his
hand. "If you did, our paths might more easily have crossed."

"No," Frederic smiled between his huffs and puffs. "I
live just south of Croydon. We have a beautiful residence
there called Homefield. Lots of trees. Rustic setting. Quite
different from all the mysterious activities that I can guess go
on here at Baker Street."

The big man paused to stroke his chin and catch his
breath again. Perhaps his discomfort seemed more noticeable
to me because I am a doctor; but one needn't have been a
medical man to observe the flutter of his eyelids and the
pauses in his speech.

"What's funny, Doctor," said he, "is that I've read so
many of the cases you've recorded . . . that I feel as if I've
known the two of you right along."

To my great embarrassment, I couldn't return the compliment. Although I knew of Mr. Frederic's works, I had to confess that I hadn't read any of them, not even his best-selling novel, *Illumination.*

Frederic took another short breath and tried again. "Perhaps you know the book by its name in the States, *The Damnation of Theron Ware.*"

I remained in the dark, but Holmes surprised me by interjecting, "A most apt treatise on religious hypocrisy, Watson. I highly recommend it."

Our visitor nodded in appreciation while I was left to wonder. Generally speaking, Holmes revealed little interest in fiction.

"Now, Mr. Frederic," said he, "let us return to the problem that brought you here." Holmes indicated that we be seated, and Frederic appeared all too ready to sink back into the soft chair.

"Stephen Crane, Mr. Holmes. Before Dr. Watson's arrival, I was asking if you've ever heard of him?"

"The author of *The Red Badge of Courage?* What member of the reading public is not familiar with that small but grand account of a Union soldier in the American Civil War? If I am not mistaken, so accurate are his descriptions that there are those who believe the young man himself actually participated in the conflict."

The writer allowed himself a nod and a chuckle, the brief laugh devolving into a small cough. "'Young man' is the very term, Mr. Holmes," said Frederic, clearing his throat. "Why, Steve's too young to have even *seen* a soldier during that war, let alone *been* one. He's just twenty-six—born in November of '71, more than six years after the war had ended. A good-looking fellow, though not very tall. About five-foot-six. He only weighs a-hundred-and-twenty pounds—about eight-and-a-half stone in your lingo."

Holmes smiled at the superfluous conversion.

"Steve may be small, but he's athletic," explained Frederic. "He played baseball at Syracuse University."

"Baseball?" Holmes queried.

"Oh, yes," said Frederic, who seemed to recover some of his energy in speaking of the game. "He had a strong throwing arm in his college days. Back then, he played catcher and shortstop."

"'Shortstop'?"

As I've noted elsewhere, Sherlock Holmes was knowledgeable in many areas; but sport—especially American sport—was not one of them. On this occasion, his ignorance put me in mind of the comment made to him a year or so earlier when he confessed to not recognising the name of Godfrey Staunton, the then missing three-quarter who played rugger for England. "Why, Mr. Holmes," Cyril Overton (himself a crack player) had observed, "I thought you knew things."

"The shortstop's like the bowler in cricket," I endeavoured to explain.

Frederic sighed, shaking his head. Maybe I too had got it wrong.

"Steve still loves the game. He'll play whenever he gets the chance. Why, he's told me how he and Ham Garland like to toss a baseball around when they talk about writing."

I knew of the American author, Hamlin Garland: he'd met with my agent Arthur Conan Doyle in the States a few years before. Conan Doyle had made a point of telling me of their meeting because he'd given Garland a collection of my Holmes stories. In fact, Conan Doyle boasted that to reciprocate for the gift, Garland had promised to teach the Englishman how to pitch.

Frederic took another short breath. "Steve wanted to be a professional ballplayer. You know, along the lines of 'Cap' Anson or 'King' Kelly—probably still does."

Unfamiliar with the references, Holmes got up to open a window. A wisp of warm air crossed the room, and we could clearly hear the clatter of horses and cries of vendors from the street below.

"Baseball's like rounders, isn't it?" he asked over his shoulder while adjusting the blinds. He drew them halfway, mitigating the bright sunlight that reflected off the yellow bricks of the house across the road.

"It's more like cricket," I corrected.

"Rounders is older than cricket, Watson," Holmes persisted as he returned to his seat. "That much I know. It dates back to the Tudors; it came *first.*" As testy as he was, one might have thought he was boasting.

During our banter, Frederic withdrew a handkerchief from his jacket and mopped his glistening brow. Then he proclaimed, "Baseball was invented in America, gentlemen. That's all you need to know." Our guest stared defiantly at us, breathing loudly through his nose.

Sherlock Holmes returned the stare. "Most interesting, I'm sure, Mr. Frederic, but I can't imagine you came to Baker Street on such a warm summer's day to discuss the athletic accomplishments of Stephen Crane."

"You're right about that, Mr. Holmes--though Stephen Crane remains the point of this discussion. The young man is in trouble, you see; that's why I've come here. From what I know of your reputation, I can't think of anyone better than yourself to ask for help in this matter."

Frederic blotted his forehead again with the handkerchief.

"Would you like some water?" I asked, indicating the carafe on the table.

In answer to my question, Frederic reached inside his coat and produced a cigar, which he held up for me to observe. He bit off the tip and, after soliciting a match from Holmes, brought the cigar to his lips and inhaled. He then leaned back and closed his eyes to preserve the joyous moment without distraction.

At the same time, Holmes reached for his briar and black shag. Almost immediately, the pungent aromas of duelling tobaccos filled the air.

Now I enjoy a good smoke as much as the next man, but watching Harold Frederic in his cigar-induced ecstasy, I couldn't help wondering if smoking might not be the best activity for a man who appeared so short of breath. In point of fact, as he blew a cloud, I was beginning to wonder if some serious condition might be afflicting him.

Seemingly unconcerned, Holmes drew in more of his own acrid tobacco. "Pray, proceed, Mr. Frederic," said he and nodded for our guest to continue.

"Simply put, Mr. Holmes, Stephen Crane's being blackmailed."

Holmes' grey eyes flashed at the word.

"A couple of months ago, Steve received the first letter demanding money. Then he got another. He's already paid out hundreds of dollars. If he doesn't give more, he's been warned that certain facts will be made public that would be quite damaging to his reputation. He's—"

"May I ask," Holmes interrupted, "why it is *you*, Mr. Frederic, who are bringing this matter to me and not the man himself? I know something about Mr. Crane's past, but I confess to not having kept up with his present. Where is he now?"

"Cuba!" Frederic announced with a burst of renewd energy. "He left England back in April to join the American navy and fight the Spanish. Joseph Conrad, a fellow writer

10

I'm sure you've heard of, raised the money to send him. Conrad put up his own literary advances as collateral for a loan."

"Well, well," Holmes mused, "Joseph Conrad. I know the man. In fact, we recently conversed. It speaks well of Crane if he's got the support of a deep thinker like Conrad."

"Funny. At first, Conrad didn't feel so good about anteing up the money. He said he was afraid he might be sending Crane off to die. As it turned out though, once Steve got to the States, the navy wouldn't take him. They were worried about his health. Pretty ironic, don't you think? He ended up reporting the war for a couple of local newspapers—first, Pulitzer's *World;* then, Hearst's *Journal.*"

"His health?" the doctor in me asked.

"Bad lungs," said Frederic, suddenly struggling through a wet, ropy cough of his own.

Talk about irony!

He raised a hand to ward off our concerns. "Steve and I are very close," he resumed at last. "I suppose our friendship started with my praise of *The Red Badge of Courage* in the *New York Times.* Maybe you read it. I'm the one who wrote that his battle scenes surpassed those of Tolstoy, Balzac, Hugo, and Zola." He ticked the names off on his large fingers as if he had repeated the list many times.

"High praise, indeed," observed Holmes.

I held my tongue. Unlike Frederic's *Theron Ware,* I had actually read some of the works of Stephen Crane, including *The Red Badge of Courage.* I was clearly not as enamoured with the war novel as was our current visitor, however. To be sure, the novel was well written and contained lots of rich military action; but as a soldier wounded in conflict myself, I could see little to praise in a story about a young military man called Henry Fleming who had run from battle. To those who point out that, by the story's finale, Fleming does indeed come to perform heroically, I would simply say that, had he not fled in the first place, there would be no need to highlight his conversion at the end. On that particular afternoon, however, I saw no advantage to be gained from interrupting Mr. Frederic's narration.

"When Steve arrived in London," our guest went on, "I steered him through the churning waters whipped up by the literary elite. He's a new and exciting personality, gentlemen; and many writers and critics have hungered to get their hands on him."

Sherlock Holmes puffed at his pipe more frequently now, a sign of his growing impatience.

For his part, Frederic pulled at his cigar; and when he resumed speaking, smoke trailed from his lips. "Since I first met Steve, our two families have become quite fond of one another. We spent part of last May together on the Irish coast. And even today he doesn't live far from us. His wife Cora is enamoured with our children."

Holmes arched a single eyebrow at the mention of Cora Crane. At the time, I didn't know why. Then he said, "See here, Mr. Frederic, we are all busy men. Might we return to the blackmail business you mentioned? You have already told us that it is responsible for your presence here."

"Quite so, Mr. Holmes," Frederic said, patting down his thick moustache and sucking in a couple of quick breaths. "Let's do just that. Steve wrote me from Havana at the end of May. He told me that a swindler right here in London has been demanding money from him."

Holmes leaned forward, taking his pipe from his lips. "A swindler, you say? Here in London?"

"That's right. A man named Charles Milverton."

"Charles Augustus Milverton?" At last, Holmes' keen eyes looked fully engaged.

"I guess," Frederic nodded. Despite the apparent drama of his pronouncement, he sounded tired, and he mopped at his brow again.

"Pray, continue," Holmes prodded.

"Well," said Frederic, "there's not much left to tell. As soon as Steve told me this Milverton fellow was headquartered in London, I immediately thought of bringing the matter to you. As I said before, I reckoned that Sherlock Holmes is just the man to help out my friend."

"I have, in fact, had dealings with this Milverton. He is, perhaps, the worst rogue in the entire city. He makes a habit of securing proof of people's weaknesses and then charges them great sums to prevent him from revealing these frailties to those who matter."

I myself had never met the scoundrel and knew of him only by his sour reputation.

"What is the nature of Milverton's hold over Crane?" asked Holmes.

Placing his cigar in the ash-stand next to his chair, Frederic took a few quick breaths. He seemed to be weighing his options. "I have a loyalty to my friend Steve," said he with a sigh, "but I guess I've known all along that by coming here to Baker Street, I'd have to make this information available to you."

Holmes gestured him on with an open hand.

"Mr. Holmes, Dr. Watson—it is evident that we are men of the world." Frederic was breathing deeply now, as if recounting this narrative required all the strength he could muster. "As painful as it may be, I'm sure that we can all imagine acts the public would call morally repugnant. And yet, however immoral or repulsive such an act might be, however offensive one might consider it——I hope we can also agree that such behaviour cannot justify some villain's foul exploitation of a man's poor judgement—or even his weak temperament. Am I not correct, gentlemen?"

Holmes didn't respond.

"I couldn't have put it any better myself," said I. Yet for the life of me, I couldn't imagine what sorts of indiscretions Stephen Crane might have committed that would have caused Harold Frederic such consternation.

Frederic picked up the cigar again and took another pull. Only after letting out a breath that was as full of suspense as it was of white smoke was he ready to announce: "Steve has taken up with a young man."

It required a moment for the words to register in my brain.

"'T-Taken up with'?" I stammered at last. "Do you mean to say that Stephen Crane is an invert? A Uranian?" As best I could remember of *The Red Badge of Courage,* Henry Fleming may have run from battle, but he was no Nancy.

Frederic held up his large free hand like a stop sign. "I don't know the details. I can only say that with a wild little wife like Cora, it's hard to imagine. What I *do* know is that, thanks to some damn snitch in New York or Cuba or both, Milverton has been made aware of Steve's entanglement with this man. Milverton has since written to Crane for large sums to prevent the information from being made public. Steve's been sending Milverton money for weeks now, money that Steve's had to beg his publishers for, money that could have been used to spare poor Cora from the harassment of their creditors here in England."

"Do you still have any of these letters Crane has sent you?" asked Holmes.

"No, I burned them—as Steve requested. There weren't very many—two or three—but you can't be too careful with a blackmailer running around."

"I see." Holmes' look of disappointment was obvious. Harold Frederic leaned over to extinguish his cigar in the ash stand. Even so small an effort seemed to tire him now, and it took a moment for him to regain his strength.

"To his credit, gentlemen," said he, "Stephen Crane has always been a friend to those some call the 'denizens of the underworld'. As you may know, he's written a novel called *Maggie* about a young woman forced by poverty into prostitution.

"Such a topic is not surprising, is it?" asked Holmes.

Frederic's eyes widened at the charge.

"Come now, Mr. Frederick. Regardless of your friendships, unless I am very much mistaken, Cora Crane, the woman he brought with him to England, is just such a type. Did she not oversee a brothel in Florida?"

"Really, Holmes!" I exclaimed as Frederic's face turned red. "Your allusions to the sensational have no bounds. Whatever one thinks of Stephen Crane, let us be considerate of his wife. Besides, if the woman had been employed as you described, why would he need—as Mr. Frederic so delicately put it—to 'take up with a man'?"

Frederic cleared his throat and changed the subject. "Steve hasn't written to me about the details of this alleged relationship. But I'm not worried. I'm sure there's some reasonable explanation. He's probably just helping some poor soul survive the way Steve's always done. Or, for that matter, he might simply be seeking material for a new book."

"Perfectly logical," Holmes said. "But if that's the case, why do you think that Crane would submit to Milverton's blackmail?"

We could all feel the heat now, and I too reached for a handkerchief. Sherlock Holmes drew on his pipe.

"The fact is, gentlemen," said Frederic, his voice growing hoarse again, "Stephen Crane considers himself quite the adventurer. Today, as a reporter, he faces enemy guns in Cuba. Before Cuba, he and Cora had gone off to Greece to cover the war against the Turks. He often carries around a six-shooter—usually unloaded, thank goodness—and still reminisces over his dreams of being a professional athlete. He has an eye for the ladies and with his good looks has reeled in many adoring worshipers. He's a man's man, if you get my drift; and he absolutely cannot abide Milverton's humiliating aspersions on his manhood."

"Yes, yes, Mr. Frederic," Holmes said impatiently. "I'm afraid we do—as you put it—'get your drift'. What I don't get is what you would you have *me* do?"

"Do?" Frederic exploded in exasperation. "*Do?* God's trousers, man! I want you to stop this son-of-a bitch Milverton! *That's* what I want you to do! I've gotten his address from Steve's letters. Go speak to the swine. You just told me that you've had dealings with him. I want you to convince him to stop blackmailing my friend. Threaten him if you need to."

The more agitated the writer became, the redder his face grew.

"See here, Mr. Holmes," he growled, "I'd do it myself, but I thought it was more in your line of work. On behalf of my friend, I'd be more than willing to pay you."

"Believe me, Mr. Frederic, were I able to rid the world of Charles Augustus Milverton, I would charge no fee at all. But understand this"—Holmes held his briar by the bowl and pointed the stem at Frederic to underscore the point—"there are but two ways to apprehend Milverton. He will cease to threaten people only when one of his victims denounces him in public and risks having a sordid tale exposed. Or when he is caught red-handed in an illicit act of burglary trying to get the so-called proof of some poor soul's ill-advised behaviour. But since he's too smart to be entrapped, and since as yet no victims have come forward to admit their own indiscretions, I fear the reptilian Mr. Milverton will continue his cold-blooded behaviour unchecked."

"God's trousers!" Frederic exclaimed once more. Breathing hard, his face red, he struggled to rise. "See here, Holmes—" he barked.

I got up to offer Frederic help; but he shook me off, preferring to stand, however unsteadily, on his own.

"—If you're not man enough to face this creature, then I shall take matters into my own hands. I will either go to his home in Hampstead or get him to come to mine in Hammersmith and—"

Now it was Holmes' turn to interrupt. "Mr. Frederic," he said, pointing the pipe stem again, "in dealing with Charles Milverton, one must be very careful indeed. Although he likes to promote exaggerated stories about his fearlessness, he is known to carry a loaded revolver, and he maintains a stable full of solicitors to defend his objectionable behaviour. In short, he is utterly ruthless. Nonetheless—"

"All humbug!" Frederic spat out, laying his great hands on the back of his chair to secure his balance.

"You didn't let me finish," Holmes said. "Nonetheless, I *will* go to see the man—not because you or Stephen Crane demands it, but because for years I've been seeking some way to shut down his nefarious operations. Since I have not yet arrived at the precise method, there is the hope that Crane's dilemma will provide me the opportunity."

Holmes's offer served to calm our visitor. Although Frederic appeared less interested in the larger picture Holmes was painting, the writer grunted his approval. With that final utterance, he seemed to have run out of words. Fatigue had got the better of him at last. Wavering as he stood, he produced a slurred farewell, his *s*'s sounding particularly wet. "Lemme know the results, Mr. Holmes. Now I must go." He issued a perfunctory nod in my direction and slowly made his way out the door.

Only after the sound of Frederic's heavy footfalls thumping down the stairs had dissipated did I turn to Holmes. "I'm glad he made it safely down the stairs," said I, "but I must ask how it is that a man so upstanding can accept behaviour in his friend that is so obviously unmanly, disreputable, and indecent?"

"Ah, Watson," Holmes chuckled drily, "ever the defender of the moral code—however hypocritical its nature."

"What do you mean by 'hypocritical'? The man seemed forthright enough."

Holmes smiled. "Did you not note, Watson, how he appeared to confuse the location of his home? He referred to it as Croydon when he first arrived and Hammersmith just before leaving."

"Of course I noticed, Holmes. But I attributed his mix-up to whatever physical malady is plaguing the man. You witnessed the effort it took for him to stand, his irregular breathing, his indistinct speech, how tired he seemed. All symptoms of a recent affliction—perchance some sort of minor apoplectic fit, if you'd like my medical opinion."

"Duly noted, Doctor. I myself observed how, even with Frederic's large frame, his clothes seemed to hang loose about him. I believe that a recent and precipitous weight loss would be consistent with your diagnosis."

I nodded solemnly. I hoped my expression would reflect an appreciation of collegial agreement rather than the annoyance I felt with myself in failing to recognize Frederic's baggy coat for the weakened physical condition it suggested.

Holmes, however, was back to the original point. "Apart from the medical issues, old fellow, the man really does maintain two houses."

And why not? thought I. "Quite fitting for a writer—a place like Hammersmith in London for work and a place well outside the city, like Croydon, for relaxation. Taken all together, I heartily approve. I wish I could afford two houses myself."

"My dear Watson," Holmes sighed, "you remain the epitome of blind British morality. Harold Frederic has two homes because he has two families. I checked my files after I learned he was coming to see me. His legal wife lives with their four children at Brook Green in Hammersmith; his so-called *other* wife and their three children live in Homefield near Croydon. He spends time quite openly with both."

"'So-called *other* wife'?" I repeated in disbelief. "Children?"

"Now you can see why he is not at all put off by whatever singular entanglements his friend Crane has got involved with in America."

Exasperated, I fell back into my chair.

"Modern writers," I groused. "Bohemians." If such sordid social attachments could occur in 1898, to what sort of debaucheries might we have to look forward in the rapidly-approaching twentieth century?

It was too hot a day to pursue an answer to that provocative question. I settled instead for a glass of water. For his part, Sherlock Holmes took down two scrapbooks from the shelves above his desk. The first showed the letter "M" on its spine; the other, the letter "C". When I retired for the evening, he was still immersed in his studies.

Chapter Two

Many red devils ran from my heart
And out upon the page.
They were so tiny
The pen could mash them.
And many struggled in the ink.
It was strange
To write in this red muck
Of things from my heart.

--Stephen Crane

I had finished Mrs. Hudson's serving of ham and eggs the next morning, but was still seated at the breakfast table when Sherlock Holmes produced a small visiting card from his "M" file—"One of the richest letters in my collection," he was fond of saying about the volume. *Charles Augustus Milverton*, the card read, *Appledore Towers, Hampstead.*

"I'm driving to Hampstead this afternoon," he said. "I must see if there's some way to influence Milverton in this Stephen Crane affair. What say you, Watson? Care to come along?"

"To the lair of one of the city's most vile inhabitants? How can I refuse?" I had no patients to attend that afternoon, so I could readily agree. "Before we go," I added, motioning for him to join me at the table, "I have some questions that concern your files."

Billy, our pageboy, removed the dishes. At my suggestion, however, he left us our cups, milk, and silver-plated coffee pot.

"Tell me," said I, pouring each of us some of the still-hot brew, "what you have gleaned from the "C" file you examined yesterday? I am particularly intrigued by the titbits about the so-called Mrs. Crane that Harold Frederic let slip."

Sherlock Holmes touched the cup to his lips. "Not Crane's legal wife, I'm afraid," said he matter-of-factly. Then he drank the coffee.

"Not his legal wife?" I cried. About to splash milk into my cup, I froze at Holmes' words, holding aloft the small porcelain pitcher.

"She may call herself 'Cora Crane', Watson; but she is, in fact, Cora *Stewart*—her current married name. Of course, it might just as easily be Cora *Taylor* or *Murphy* or *Howorth* depending on which previous life one chooses to highlight. But under the law, Cora Crane is simply the already-married woman with whom the writer Stephen Crane sailed to England, the already-married woman he encountered in Jacksonville, Florida, running a disorderly house—the 'Hotel de Dream'."

"And her true husband?" I asked, finally adding the milk.

"Cora Crane—as I trust we shall now call her—was, and still is, legally married to an Englishman, called Donald Stewart. He is the younger son of Field Marshall Sir Donald Stewart."

"Sir Donald Stewart!" I ejaculated, almost spilling the pitcher as I set it back on the table. "Do you mean to say that the hero of the Indian Mutiny and the former Commander-in-Chief of Her Majesty's forces in India is Cora Crane's father-in-law?"

"The same. A baronet, no less."

I was dumbfounded. I knew of the father. When I was with the Berkshires in Afghanistan, it was the departure of his troops from Kandahar that led to Ayub Kahn's massacre of the British at Maiwand. It had happened on the twenty-seventh of July in 1880, a date I would never forget. In fact, my hand instinctively inched upward to my shoulder as I recalled the horrific injury from a Jezail bullet I had received in the slaughter. It was the wound that invalided me out of the war the following year.

Aware of my personal history, Holmes said, "You have another link to the Stewart clan; for the younger Stewart—that is, Cora's husband Captain Donald—marched with Lord Roberts and his ten thousand from Kabul to Kandahar a few days later to clear out the very Jezailchees who'd overrun you and the rest of the British forces at Maiwand. The next year, Captain Donald was also wounded in Afghanistan."

I mindlessly rubbed my shoulder, nodding vacantly and remembering how lucky I'd been. Murray, my orderly, had thrown me onto a horse in the middle of the ferocious battle and led me to safety.

"It was this same Captain Donald who met Cora in Florida," Holmes went on. "They eloped to England and were married a short time later in London. But marrying into the British aristocracy carries with it much responsibility, in which Cora had little interest. When her husband was called upon to defend the empire once more—this time in India—Cora wanted no part of it. Instead of travelling with him, she insisted on remaining in London and having her own good times. In the end, she sailed off to Florida in the yacht of an heir to the Chase Bank money."

"My word," I exclaimed.

Holmes smiled again. "And that wasn't the worst of it. She wound up getting so angry with the man that she dived off his yacht into the Jacksonville harbour and swam to shore in her shift."

In her shift?

I had yet to touch my coffee. The stories Holmes was providing were stimulation enough!

"Surely," said I, "a man like Captain Stewart would want nothing more to do with such a woman. A party-goer, a former madam, an American uninterested in waving the Union Jack round the world—I should imagine he would desire nothing else but to get her out of his life."

"An excellent point, Watson. It is very strange indeed that the captain has not sought a divorce—especially since Cora Crane's been after him to get one. A divorce, you see, would grant her freedom. If she were divorced, she could marry Crane legally—although the two of them claim to have wed in Greece."

"Why do you think Captain Stewart has kept her on then?"

"The common answer is that, having been injured by her once when she refused to accompany him to India, he seeks to protect the family name from any additional scandal—like divorce."

"Seems a bit late to protect the Stewarts from scandal."

Holmes nodded, sampling his coffee again. "There is another explanation, of course. Due to all the grief she's caused him, the man simply hates her and actually enjoys denying her freedom. It's ironic, isn't it? She wants to get away from those British aristocrats while some of them—some even from her husband's own social circle—still insist on referring to her as 'Lady Stewart'."

"'*Lady* Stewart'!" I exclaimed. "Surely, Holmes—"

"I've never been one to sit in judgement, Watson. As far as I'm concerned, if Stephen Crane calls her 'Mrs. Crane', then 'Mrs. Crane' she is."

Holmes finished his drink and pushed away the cup. "You haven't touched your coffee, old fellow," said he.

I took a single sip, fully aware that I was too perturbed to enjoy the brew. "It's cold now," I said, hoping Holmes wouldn't notice how disturbed I was by all this information.

Just then I caught a glimpse of my bulbous reflection in the rounded base of the silver coffee pot. Though my features appeared comically inflated, I could see no humour in the pallor of my cheeks. Excusing myself, I went upstairs to my room to settle my nerves. Soon it would be time for our venture to Hampstead. No matter how devilish this Milverton rogue proved to be, however, I couldn't imagine hearing anything more shocking than the singular story of Cora Crane that I had just been told by Sherlock Holmes.

* * *

The warmth of the summer's afternoon provided a temporary respite from thinking about Charles Milverton or Mrs. Crane. The clear sky and warm breeze promised a pleasant enough ride; and soon a hansom was transporting us northward toward Regents Park. The green swards looked predictably inviting as we skirted the grounds by way of the Outer Circle. Numerous sun-worshipers—women in light-colour dresses and broad hats, men in white flannels and straw boaters—filled the walkways as we continued on our mission, rattling along Fitzjohn's Avenue and ultimately alighting in Hampton High Street. From there, it was but a short stroll up Well Walk to East Heath Road and the corner where Holmes pointed out the looming façade of Appledore Towers.

To some, I'm sure that the rustic, old house seemed charmingly traditional. As I have noted before, key to the design was a tiled outdoor gallery that ran the length of one side. This veranda was shaded by a line of tall laurels, and several windows and doors opened onto it. To me, however, with its overhanging eaves, darkened windows, murky shadows, and six-foot-high walls, the edifice looked gloomy and sinister, even menacing.

Holmes rapped smartly on a front door studded with brass nails. Milverton's secretary, a sallow-looking fellow with rheumy eyes, answered almost immediately and took Holmes' card; within minutes we were ushered into the study.

Overwhelmed by the pungent odour of stale tobacco, I found the room singularly oppressive. Thick velvet curtains of a muddy maroon colour covered the windows, allowing not the least hint of the sunny day outside. An equally heavy drape of the same hue comprised the *portière* that hung before the entrance to Milverton's private chambers. Two ponderous armchairs and a broad leather settee occupied most of the floor space. Between the wall and a high bookshelf stood a large green safe with brass knobs. So impregnable did the container appear that one could only assume that it must have held the very life-blood of the blackmailer, the revelatory correspondence employed to extort large sums from reluctant victims.

As for Milverton himself, not unlike a voracious spider at the centre of its web, he sat on a red-leather chair at a red-mahogany desk in the middle of the room. An electric chandelier bathed the man in a sour yellow light; and from atop the bookshelf with more than a little irony, a pale bust of Athene, Greek goddess of wisdom, stared down upon him.

As I suggested in my original narrative, everything about the man seemed designed to please—the smooth chin and plump form; the avuncular grin; the warm, ruddy face; the gentle voice. Indeed, as I noted before, had he donned a top hat, he would have borne a remarkable resemblance to the convivial Mr. Pickwick of Charles Dickens. And yet the darting grey eyes behind gold-rimmed spectacles suggested a less than amiable nature. The large revolver lying before him on the smooth surface of the shiny desktop confirmed it.

"So pleased to make your acquaintance at last, Dr. Watson," he said to me as if anticipating a life-long friendship. To Holmes, he announced unctuously, "And how nice to see you again, Mr. Holmes." Nodding at the gun, he quickly added, "As soon as my secretary announced your arrival, I prepared myself for whatever circumstances might occur. After all, Mr. Holmes, you *have* taken to threatening me in the past."

Despite the hostility, the smile remained.

"Yes, Milverton, that is true. In representing your victims—as I too often have had the sad occasion to do—you've left me little recourse. How fortunate for you that—so far, at least—they've all agreed to pay up."

Milverton flashed an even broader grin.

"Today, however, I'm not here on behalf of those victims, at least not directly."

"How refreshing," said Milverton with a hint of curiosity in his voice. Pointing to the armchairs, he added, "Please do sit down, gentlemen. May I offer you tea?"

"No!" said Holmes sharply as we seated ourselves. "I prefer to get directly to the point. I am here on behalf of Mr. Harold Frederic."

"Frederic? The American newspaper man?" The smile faded as Milverton raised an eyebrow. "I'm afraid you've made a mistake, Mr. Holmes. Harold Frederic's not one of my clients. I can see how you might think he would be; his bifurcated lifestyle with its two households makes him a prime candidate. Yet so many people know of his unconventional accommodations that there's no money to be made. No, I'm afraid he would hardly prove a profitable investment."

"He is best of friends with Stephen Crane," Holmes announced.

"Ah," Milverton ejaculated, "now I understand." And he leaned forward on both elbows to pay closer attention.

"Mr. Crane does not enjoy the financial resources that most of your victims do."

Milverton grinned voraciously. "That's true," said the rogue, sitting back in his red-leather chair. "I prefer my clients to come from the nobility—or at least the officer-class of the military. Such groups can more readily gain access to large sums. But I assure you, Mr. Holmes, that I accept payment from every level of society—including writers. After all, money is money; and you would be surprised to discover how much can be mustered by the very people who say they lack it."

It is difficult to barter with a cheat. Small wonder that the economic argument provided scant gain for Holmes. Hoping that a different approach might be in order, I took the liberty to appeal to Milverton's conscience.

"Harold Frederic's not a well man," I offered "We came in his stead to ask you to let go of Mr. Crane. Frederic should remain calm; he's quick to anger. Who's to say just how agitated he might become were you to deny his request to spare his friend and continue your pursuit of Crane? You have no quarrel with Harold Frederic, and I'm sure that you wouldn't want his blood on your hands. As I understand your history, Mr. Milverton, an assault on Frederic's well-being would mark a major escalation of your villainy."

Milverton chuckled at my feckless appeal.

"Harold Frederic's a giant of a man, Mr. Milverton," I warned, feeling my anger rise. "Who's to say just what he might do were you to ignore his pleas regarding Crane?"

Milverton shrugged his shoulders. "Do you know, Doctor, until now I had no idea that Stephen Crane was becoming uncooperative. Until now, I had considered him a most obliging client. But while I do appreciate your information, any threat to me on Harold Frederic's part should serve to raise your concerns for Mr. Frederic." Once more the smile left his lips. "I do not tolerate people who interfere with my transactions, Dr Watson. I may be only a simple businessman, but I can assure you that very bad things have a way of catching up to people who make me cross—if you take my meaning."

I stared down at the revolver. "You can't go round shooting people you don't like," said I.

"No, of course not," Milverton smirked. "As Mr. Holmes can attest, I am not a violent man. I don't conduct my business with a gun in my hand. Perhaps, a suggestion of how I *do* operate will help you see the position Mr. Frederic might find himself in."

I confess that he had my full attention.

"Do you remember Sir Nigel Chandless?"

I did not, but Sherlock Holmes immediately provided the answer. "The Assistant to Sir William Christie, the Astronomer Royal at Greenwich."

The blackmailer raised his eyebrows. "Impressive, Mr. Holmes, your ability to recall so arcane a piece of information."

"On the contrary, Milverton. One does not easily forget the second in command of the Royal Observatory at Greenwich—not at the time a deranged terrorist attempted to blow it up."

"Quite so," Milverton confirmed. "Strange that you should mention the explosion; for just before that unhappy occurrence, I acquired in what one could only be described as a curious coincidence some useful information from a servant in Sir Nigel's employ. The Assistant to the Astronomer Royal wasn't playing fair with his wife, you see. And when I informed him that I knew of his indiscretions, he seemed quite uninterested in paying to keep his dalliances quiet—even *after* seeing some of the incriminating letters I'd managed to acquire."

"Blackguard," I found myself muttering although I was sure that the scoundrel was used to hearing worse.

Save leaning forward to stroke the barrel of his revolver, Milverton went on as if I had said nothing. "Women are more forthcoming than men. Women will pay to hush up their activities; men often need to be helped along in making the decision."

"And am I to understand, Milverton," said Holmes, "that you were just the one to 'help Sir Nigel along'? That at last we have finally discovered the true cause for the attempted bombing of the Royal Greenwich Observatory? I've read much about it—the case has long troubled me though I was not in England at the time."

Holmes was referring to his three-year hiatus that followed his deadly encounter with Professor Moriarty at the Reichenbach Falls. It was the troubling murder of the Honourable Ronald Adair that had brought him back to London some seven weeks after the explosion at Greenwich.

"'*Read* much about it,' Mr. Holmes? Surely you are slighting your brother. I would be greatly surprised if he had not informed you first-hand of *all* that was known concerning the event—wherever you might have been."

Holmes ignored the charge; yet given the important but secret position that Mycroft Holmes held in the government, Milverton's arrow seemed to have struck quite close to the mark. As hard as it was to believe, the blackmailer may have had his paid informants in Whitehall as well.

"It was late in the afternoon of Thursday, the fifteenth of February, 1894." As definitively as he spoke, Holmes might have been repeating a news account verbatim.

"A powerful explosion in Greenwich Park tore off the left hand of a tailor called Martial Bourdin, a twenty-six-year-old Frenchman. Unfortunately for him, the blast from the package in brown paper he was carrying—a large can full of nitro-glycerine—also ripped a mortal wound in his stomach."

"The fool," Milverton mumbled, curling his fingers into a fist. "He's said to have tripped over the roots of a tree."

The details supplied by Holmes coincided with the inside information I'd learned directly from Inspector Lestrade. Even though I had presumed Holmes to be dead during my friend's long absence, I'd tried my best to continue following Scotland Yard's most provocative cases. Shadowing the battle against crime had seemed in some strange way a method of keeping alive my close intimacy with Holmes. Fortunately, the Inspector had been sympathetic to my concerns.

"It was Lestrade's belief," said I, "that the infernal machine had exploded *before* Bourdin could actually place the thing inside the observatory."

"Quite so, Watson," agreed Holmes. "Colonel Majendie, the Inspector of Explosives, maintained the same view. In point of fact, the inquest identified Bourdin's cause of death as '*Felo de se*'—that is, suicide."

"Lestrade told me that dozens of people reported to him what they'd seen. No one actually witnessed the blast, but they all described some fifty pieces of flesh and bone scattered along the blood-spattered walls. The police found the knuckles of Bourdin's left thumb on the pathway leading up to the building."

"Yet from all the police work," Milverton grinned, "your Inspector Lestrade still learned nothing about what really happened. Bourdin was dead thirty minutes after the explosion, and he never offered any explanation of why he did what he did."

"That's correct," said Holmes. "As I understand it, Bourdin was fully capable of speaking until he died, and yet he said nothing."

"And if he had confessed," Milverton persisted, "whom do you reckon he might have implicated? David Nicoll, the anarchist? The Rossettis and the radical press? Inspector Melville of the C.I.D.'s Special Branch—as some people fancy?"

"You may be full of provocative insinuations, Milverton," said Holmes, "but I see no connection between you and Sir Nigel in your ramblings. Most experts on the subject place the bombing in a political context, and you're no political animal. In 1894, officials were calling England the refuge of nihilists and anarchists—a veritable 'cave' of anarchism. Some unnamed activist still remains the most likely suspect for prompting Bourdin to act."

"That rings true," said I. "Bourdin carried a member's card for the anarchist's *Club Autonomie*. Lestrade allowed me to accompany him on a raid of their meeting place in Windmill Street in search of likely suspects."

"Where he had no success, of course," said Milverton.

"An unsolved crime is an itch," Holmes observed. "It continues to nag. When I learned that Bourdin was French, I thought he might have had links to Huret, the so-called Boulevard Assassin I helped track down in Paris. He didn't. Our dealings with Coram, the Russian, made me wonder if Bourdin might have associated with the Russian Brotherhood. But I found no connection there either."

"Of course not," said Milverton.

"Maybe not, but it was regarding just such conspiracies that Conrad spoke to me last March. He was hoping to write a book about the Greenwich affair after a friend had told him about Bourdin. He'd heard that I had contacts in the underworld that might have had some knowledge of the bombing. I didn't, of course."

"Joseph Conrad," Milverton growled. "Another writer snooping about for political conspiracies. And yet here I am suggesting an alternative to your anarchist radicals— someone trying to threaten Sir Nigel."

Holmes fixed Milverton with a glare of defiance. "You offer lots of innuendo, Milverton, but nothing to convince me that the bombing wasn't political. You can't have it both ways. You sound like a man who's trying to convince us you know a great deal about something you claim to have had nothing to do with."

Holmes flashed that look of keen interest he showed when he was on the hunt. Suddenly, I realized that Milverton had become his quarry—that he was hoping to prod the rogue into admitting his involvement in the singular affair at Greenwich. All this historical chatter about anarchists may have had precious little to do with Harold Frederic or Stephen Crane; but what an accomplishment it would have been if, while performing some service for the two American writers, we had got to the bottom of the Greenwich outrage!

"What about the gold sovereigns then, Mr. Holmes? You're forgetting the £13 the police found in Bourdin's pockets."

"I'm impressed you know the precise amount."

"Common knowledge," Milverton smirked. "But an ominous total, I'm sure you'd agree. Is it any wonder that the anarchists and nihilists disowned him? Not only did they believe that the result of his act would make England more inhospitable for their ilk, but they were greatly concerned about where all that gold had come from. Who paid him? For whom was he working? Having that much money on one's person doesn't seem typical of an obsessed extremist at war with the ruling classes, does it?"

"And you suggest that this gold is another link to Sir Nigel?"

As if he contained a valued secret, Milverton offered a Cheshire grin. "If I was asked to guess, I would say that the money was some sort of payoff—a financial reward for planting a bomb that had nothing whatsoever to do with politics. It makes perfect sense. The gold was for Bourdin's escape. The way I've heard it told, Bourdin was hoping to leave for France directly after completing his mission. To get away— that's why he was carrying the money."

It did seem that Milverton had his own inside knowledge. Or hoped to persuade us that he did. If the rogue had actually been the source of Bourdin's money, Milverton would surely have had access to the Frenchman's plans.

In fact, he had more to say. "Even Bourdin's brother-in-law—"

"Henry Samuels," Holmes inserted.

"—Thought that somebody had put Bourdin up to the job."

"An *agent provocateur*?" I offered.

"Exactly, Dr. Watson, except that the French term is too political. I meant that there was someone *else*—an outsider, as it were—who was using Bourdin as a catspaw."

"There are those within the anarchist movement," Holmes offered, "who lay such a charge at the feet of the brother-in-law himself."

"Samuels," Milverton snorted. "I know the man. A boastful anarchist who loves the feel of money—whatever its source—be it the police or even a humble businessman like myself."

"*You* paid him?" I cried.

"I said '*like* myself', Doctor."

"Just before Bourdin left for Greenwich," said Holmes, "he was observed conversing with a man near Berkeley Square."

I knew Holmes had purposely misnamed the location, and Milverton immediately took the bait.

"*Hanover* Square," Milverton corrected. "They met at Hanover Square and separated near Whitehall. Bourdin then crossed Westminster Bridge to catch the tram that would take him to the observatory."

Holmes smiled. "For all these years, Milverton, I'd assumed it was Samuels that Bourdin was seen talking to. But your familiarity with the logistics of the situation makes me think I might have been mistaken."

"No," Milverton smiled in return, "it probably *was* Samuels." It seemed as if he and Holmes were sharing the same unspoken knowledge. "I told you I know the man. Henry Samuels would be quick to work for anyone paying to get a bomb planted. The location wouldn't matter—even at the First Meridian. Anywhere a message might need to be conveyed."

Holmes leaned back and placed his fingertips together. Slowly, he examined the man sitting opposite him.

"Do you know, Milverton" said Sherlock Holmes, "I'm almost willing to believe that you really do have the solution to this mystery."

"I might," he grinned. "Then again, it might all be sheer conjecture."

If Milverton was going to say more than he had intended, I thought now would be the time. But the man simply went on smiling complacently—like the smug little schoolboy who, by however illicit the means, has come to possess the examination answers before the test is given.

"Scotland Yard," said Milverton, "were content to let people believe that anarchists had been responsible. That way, the government didn't have to publicize a scandal involving one of their own irresponsible toffs."

"Which, I presume," observed Holmes, "brings us back to Sir Nigel, the man you're insinuating that—what exactly?—you or Bourdin's brother-in-law offered thirteen pounds to have murdered."

"Bah!" Milverton ejaculated. "A dead Sir Nigel would have been of no use to me."

"But an *intimidated* Sir Nigel would."

Just then I realized the error of my earlier conclusion. It wasn't the solution to the Greenwich outrage that Holmes was seeking. Rather, it was a much longed-for confession from Milverton that he'd used the threat of murder to extort money from a British gentleman. With such an admission before the two of us, perhaps a case against the miscreant could be established once and for all and any demands on Crane could be forgot—demands on all his victims could be forgot.

"The explosion occurred at 4:45," Holmes prodded, "well after most of the staff, including Sir Nigel, were gone. The bomber—or whoever was directing him—knew just the right time it would be safe to enter the observatory and discharge a device that would harm no one—but might well frighten a person who worked there."

Milverton smiled broadly. "You've done your research, Mr. Holmes; I'll give you that. Let us just say, that according to the rumours *I've* heard, had the device not blown up in the hand of the poor fool who was carrying it, the bomb would have ended up exploding *after* work-hours in the office of Sir Nigel Chandless."

"In the *empty* office of Sir Nigel Chandless," Holmes stressed, "thus eliminating the possibility of killing the man—or should I say, killing the goose that you hoped would soon be laying golden eggs"?

"Exactly my point," replied Milverton with a chuckle.

The impudence of the man!

Milverton was lucky he had that revolver in front of him. His calm demeanour in hinting at his own involvement in an act of such terror was not only difficult to listen to—but also, after so many years, next to impossible to prove. The man needed a sound thrashing.

"Whoever was responsible," Milverton said, his duplicitous smile frozen on his lips, "I am happy to report that Sir Nigel paid up not long after the affair at Greenwich. Once the hint of a conspiracy against his life was suggested to him, his resistance to my offer crumbled. Whoever was responsible, it all worked out quite splendidly. I got my money, and Her Majesty's government could offer Scotland Yard's crackdown on radicals as proof that England would no longer remain a haven for malcontent anarchists."

We had reached a blind alley, and I could no longer tolerate another moment in the vile man's company. Such a remorseless creature could never be tricked into admitting any guilt. I made ready to rise, and Milverton slid his hand over the butt-end of the revolver.

"Do you know, gentlemen," he grinned, "this little conversation of ours has been most helpful. Sir Nigel's acquiescence makes me think that Stephen Crane might also profit from additional encouragement—encouragement provided by his friend, Mr. Frederic. I am certain that when I apprise Mr. Frederic of the terribly bad luck that almost struck Sir Nigel at the observatory, Mr. Frederic will willingly give up the rather unhealthy notion of attempting to get me to leave Mr. Crane alone. More to the point, I might even convince him to persuade his friend to be more forthcoming."

How foolish we'd been! How easily we'd been duped! Holmes had hoped to evoke a confession from Milverton; instead, the discussion about Greenwich and Sir Nigel was now to be the impetus for Milverton's harassment of Harold Frederic.

I knew Holmes shared my realization. In his silence I could sense his growing fury.

Yes," Milverton said, rubbing his palms together, "thanks to you both, I believe I shall schedule a visit between myself and Mr. Frederic."

"Enough!" shouted Sherlock Holmes, springing to his feet. "You have not heard the last of me, Milverton! Though the wheels of Justice may grind slow, they grind exceeding small."

I stood in support of Holmes, my face flushed in anger. With full appreciation of his dramatic exit-line, I couldn't wait to leave Milverton's den and its noxious stench of evil.

Chapter Three

Two or three angels
Came near to the earth.
They saw a fat church.
Little black streams of people
Came and went in continually.
And the angels were puzzled
To know why the people went thus,
And why they stayed so long within.
                              –Stephen Crane

Come quickly, the telegram read. *Harold has suffered a paralytic stroke.*

Though signed "Mrs. Frederic," the wire had been dispatched from Croydon by Kate Lyon, who, as Holmes had explained, was in reality Frederic's common-law wife.

The attack had occurred on Friday, 12 August 1898; and though the telegram arrived at Baker Street early Saturday morning, we didn't receive the news until later that afternoon, more than a fortnight after our confrontation with Milverton. True to Holmes' word, just after we had visited Appledore Towers, he had telegraphed Frederic about the futility of our meeting with the blackmailer. But not until Saturday's dire telegram did we receive any communication at all from Homefield.

Had we been in our rooms on the morning the telegram arrived, we could have reached Homefield, Frederic's residence outside of London, later that same afternoon. But while Milverton and Frederic may have been in our thoughts, the solution to two murders had also been demanding our attention. At the moment the telegram from Homefield was delivered to Mrs. Hudson, Holmes and I had been in the Norfolk countryside, resolving the untimely death of Hilton Cubitt at Riding Thorpe Manor. The mystery involved yet more Americans and a bedevilling code made up of stick figures called the "Dancing Men." At the same time, Holmes was also dealing with the Amberley murders in the case I recorded as "The Retired Colourman."

It was not until early Sunday, therefore, that we set out for Homefield in hopes of ministering to the stricken Harold Frederic. My friend said nothing to me as we journeyed by hansom to Charing Cross Station. From there, via the Brighton line, we would travel fourteen miles south—just past Croydon near Kenley—to Oxted, the nearest station to the Frederics' house. Holmes maintained his silence as the railway began to move. Once it began its rhythmic swaying and clattering and I realized that he still had no intention of speaking, I picked up a discarded copy of a morning paper lying next to me on the empty seat-cushion.

The lead article immediately caught my attention. It reported the signing of the Protocol of Peace by the United States and Spain, the agreement that made official the American victory in Cuba and effectively ended hostilities there.

I dared to point out to the taciturn Holmes the article in question. "How do you reckon the new Protocol might affect Crane?" I asked him. "I should imagine he's still in Havana writing about the war."

Holmes didn't respond; he simply stared out the window.

I knew my friend well enough to recognize he was quietly fuming. I also knew him well enough to suspect what was agitating him. Although I had no information, I was sure that he perceived a link between Frederic's attack and some sort of contact on the part of Milverton, the villain whom Holmes himself had alerted to Frederic's concerns. However spontaneous a stroke of paralysis might be, I felt certain that Holmes regarded himself as the indirect cause. There was no point in trying to distract him with the news of the day, so I put down the newspaper and for the rest of the journey contented myself with watching the undulating green hills of the English countryside fly past.

At the station in Oxted, we engaged a trap. For an additional fee, the driver agreed to wait for us at our destination until we'd completed our business. The cart transported us down a tree-lined road into Caterham Valley and ultimately to the two–storey residence of Harold Frederic. Surrounded by pale-purple lilacs and emerald-green lawns, the house belied the tragedy taking place within.

We came to a halt beside a dogcart, its tethered sorrel horse impatiently stamping a foot in the dust. Reminding our driver to wait, we were about to walk up the flagstone path when we noted a tall, thin gentleman emerging from the front door. He was wearing a brown bowler and sported a brindled goatee.

Sherlock Holmes broke his silence at last. "The doctor in attendance," he observed, eyes fixed on the black bag the man was carrying. "No doubt the occupant of the empty dogcart."

Not only a fellow physician, thought I, but one with a vaguely familiar look. Although I thought I'd seen the man before, I was still more than a trifle surprised when, after glancing in my direction, he exclaimed, "Dr. Watson. Dr. John Watson, if I'm not very much mistaken."

My raised eyebrows and parted lips revealed my puzzlement.

"Pray, forgive me, sir. I'm Dr. Malcolm Playfair, don't you know? We met briefly at a conference in London a few years ago. A medical convocation addressing new methods of antisepsis, if I recall correctly."

"Yes," said I tentatively, fishing for a memory to hook on to. I wasn't one to frequent such meetings, so the few I did attend stuck in my mind. "I believe I do recollect the conference—Dr. Halsted, rubber gloves, and all that."

The tall man offered a thin smile of corroboration. I suspect he had viewed the conference more intently than I.

I introduced my friend, and Playfair doffed his hat. His round head was remarkably bald.

Then he turned back to me. "Forgive my asking," he said, "but have you been summoned here to consult?"

"Do you mean as Mr. Frederic's doctor?"

"Indeed."

"No. Isn't that why *you* are here?"

"Yes and no," Playfair said with a quick smile. "As I understand the situation, I appear to be but one of many doctors who are to be called in, don't you know?"

"Curious," Holmes said.

Playfair furrowed his brow, an expression that seemed to be asking what *we* were doing there.

"Actually," I explained, "Mr. Holmes and I do have a vested interest in Mr. Frederic's well-being. We were requested, you see; and we've come to help in any way we can."

"Hmpf," Playfair grunted. "The more power to you then, gentlemen."

"Just what happened to your patient?" Holmes asked.

Playfair slowly shook his head. "The poor man's brain haemorrhaged. Mr. Frederic is paralyzed on his right side; his face is twisted all out of proportion. So powerful a man cut down by natural forces. A 'stroke,' people call it— from the sixteenth-century phrase, 'a stroke from God's hand.' It might as well be, don't you know?" He shook his head again. "Terrible."

41

I realized now that when Frederic had come to Baker Street those few weeks before, he must have been more gravely ill than I had suspected.

"No visitors for the next few days, mind you," Playfair instructed. "I've told him—and, to be certain, I told his wife—to curtail his vices. No smoking. No spirits. Plenty of milk. Frederic's a hard man to tame. Wants to do things his own way—fits right into his wife's manner of thinking actually. Mind over matter, don't you know?"

"Yes," I muttered. I could see that Holmes was growing impatient. We needed to move on.

But Playfair wasn't finished. "My wife's the same. Got a whiff of this Christian Science humbug. It's the reason we left London and moved out here to the countryside, don't you know?. Why, it's almost comical, the idea of a doctor's wife believing in magical remedies. It's like a vicar being married to an atheist. Too much to explain back in Harley Street."

Spiritual healing had become quite the rage recently. A growing number of people believed in the power of the mind to cure all physical ailments. As a physician, I would be the first to acknowledge the importance of a positive mental attitude, but never to the exclusion of sound medical practice.

Playfair checked his pocket watch. "Must be off," he said, replacing his bowler with a little tap. "Patients to see, don't you know?" He nodded at us, tugged at his short beard, and strode down the path to where the impatient horse was waiting.

Holmes shook his head as we watched the doctor snap his whip and rattle off down the road. "Christian Science," Holmes muttered. Then, raising his voice, he proclaimed, "You doctors are the true men of science, Watson. Never forget it. Despite all the latest fads, you must always remain wedded to logic and reason."

I smiled, but Holmes was already marching up to the dark-oak front door. He knocked, and no sooner had I joined him than the door was opened by an attractive young maid in a black uniform, her raven-hair rolled into a bun. Immediately behind her, I saw a straight-backed woman of grave demeanour whom I took to be Kate Lyon. She wore a dignified white shirtwaist and black skirt. In her arms nestled a small white cat.

"Thank you, Agatha," she said with a broad American accent. The maid curtsied and went off to her other chores.

"Miss Lyon," my friend said, "I am Sherlock Holmes. Your telegram requested my presence."

"That's '*Mrs. Frederic*'," she replied, "but thank you for coming so promptly. For some reason which I don't understand, Harold wanted you here."

"I am Dr. Watson, Mr. Holmes' associate," I said coldly. Unable to let go my disapproval of her alleged marital status, I would not pronounce her self-proclaimed title. "I just spoke with Dr. Playfair. He told us of Mr. Frederic's condition. When Mr. Frederic called on us a few weeks ago, I'm sorry to say that even then I detected some signs of his illness."

Kate Lyon nodded sombrely; and though struggling with the cat, which was just then trying to escape her grasp, she led us into the sitting room. I could sympathize with the animal. Miss Lyon presented no comforting figure. Her frame was thin; her dull black hair, tightly wound in ringlets; her dark beady eyes, shaded by thick, wire-rimmed glasses. Though refined, her broad accent didn't recommend itself either. She may have been the mother of three of Frederic's seven children; and she may—as others have charged—actually done some of Frederic's highly praised writing, but she was not his legal wife, and as a consequence I did not care for the woman.

Anticipating the response, Holmes looked grim as he dared to ask her, "Has anything happened recently that might have caused your husband's condition to advance so suddenly?"

Before she could answer, Miss Lyon had to surrender to the restless movements of the cat, which she now placed on the floor. Raising its tail high in victory, it leaned forward, extended its forepaws as cats do and stretched in what can only be described as utter satisfaction. Then it looked at Holmes and me, mewed softly, and padded off in search of more interesting distractions.

At the same time, Miss Lyon brushed off some stray cat hairs and smoothed down her skirt.

Holmes cleared his throat. "I repeat myself, Madam," he said forcefully. "Has anything occurred lately that might have triggered Mr. Frederic's stroke?"

Miss Lyon nodded. "How prescient of you to ask, Mr. Holmes. Something suspicious did occur last Friday, the morning of his—his seizure. A most odious man paid Harold a visit a short while before it happened"

Holmes eyes narrowed.

"Agatha opened the door; and although he asked for my husband, I attended almost immediately. Oh, he looked like some do-gooder—plump, clean-shaven, glasses, broad smile—except, of course, it all looked so false—too forced. In fact, it was the unctuous tone of his voice that revealed his true nature."

"His name?" Holmes asked, sensing the obvious.

"Why, I do believe he left his card," she said and rummaged through a stack of papers on a nearby sideboard. "Yes, here it is, just where I'd put it the other day."

She handed a visiting card to Holmes.

Clenching his fist, he passed the card along to me. Identical to the card Holmes had produced from his files at Baker Street, it read: *Charles Augustus Milverton.*

"He said he wanted to see 'Mr. Frederic'," Kate Lyon explained. "With Harold's work for the *New York Times*, you can just imagine the many strange types who come calling here. I'm not one to screen Harold's visitors, so I showed this Mr. Milverton into the study and told him to wait. Once Harold entered, it took only moments for voices to be raised, predominantly Harold's. The sounds were muffled until I heard Harold shout, 'Damn your soul!' Then Mr. Milverton left—but not without a smarmy grin in my direction."

"The blackguard," I couldn't keep myself from saying once again.

A furrow crossed Kate Lyon's brow. "There's another thing that caught my attention, Mr. Holmes. I only just remembered it."

Holmes leaned forward. "And what is that, Mrs. Frederic?"

"As the man was leaving, he engaged our maid in conversation."

"The maid, you say? The one you called 'Agatha'?"

"That's right. I don't know what they spoke of or for how long. My first concern was for Harold. Though I saw Mr. Milverton stop her, I was on my way to the study and thought nothing more of it—especially when I discovered that Harold's door was closed. I knocked but received no answer. Which was strange. I waited a moment and then knocked again. When he didn't respond a second time, I thought something must be wrong, and so I entered and discovered the room was empty. So I went searching and—oh, God—I found him lying on the floor of the bathroom. His lips were puckered; his complexion was red; his face was perspiring."

Throughout this report, Miss Lyon retained her composure. She breathed deeply and kept her hands clasped. It must have been quite horrifying for her to discover the man on the floor like that—apoplectic and unable to move. Despite my outraged sense of propriety, I could feel my initial hostility towards her thawing.

"Did your husband communicate with you in any way?" Holmes asked.

"He spoke *your* name, Mr. Holmes. 'Get Sherlock Holmes,' he said. That's why I sent you the telegram yesterday."

"Anything more?"

"Yes, though it took a great deal of difficulty. He whispered into my ear, 'Crane's letter. Desk.' Then he passed out. I immediately sent for Dr. Playfair; I'll be getting other doctors as well—as many as it takes. Not that I believe these medical men have much to offer my husband."

Medical men not having much to offer? Amanuensis to Harold Frederic of the *New York Times* or not, her ignorance was appalling!

I was about to respond, but Holmes grabbed my arm. "While it is noteworthy that we were summoned, Mrs. Frederic, I thought your husband left our meeting with the clear understanding that, if I was to make any progress on the matter he'd come to discuss with me, new evidence was required. You already have a doctor and intend to get more. What was his point in calling my name?"

"I don't know what any of this is about, Mr. Holmes, but I believe the letter from Stephen that Harold mentioned is only just recently arrived. Might it not be the 'new evidence' you're referring to? Harold didn't want me to read it; he said it was for *you*. I'm simply fulfilling his wishes."

Indicating that we should follow, she led us down a hallway. We passed the bedroom in which Harold Frederic—

sallow-cheeked, eyes shut, right side of his lip drooping—was stretched out. Next to the bed sat a heavy-set nurse, in a red-and-white pinstriped uniform. We looked in, and when she shook her head, Kate Lyon continued down the hallway to a wood-panelled study lined with books. A pine desk dominated the far wall, and, rolling open the curved top, she extracted from one of its many pigeonholes three folded, pale-yellow sheets, which she handed to Holmes.

My friend stared down at the papers while Kate Lyon arranged two cane-back chairs for our convenience

"Keep the letter when you've finished reading it, Mr. Holmes," she said. "Clearly, Harold wanted you to have it."

No sooner had she left the room than Holmes, holding the pages by their edges, began to scrutinize them one-at-a-time. The words "Gran Hotel Pasaje" were printed in Spanish at the top of the first one.

"Standard hotel stationery, medium weight," he scowled. "No clues here." Then we both sat down; and I, peering over his shoulder, read along with him the letter that Stephen Crane had most recently posted to Harold Frederic. In small, round letters leaning slightly to the left, Crane had written:

My dear Harold,

I'm still running that fever, but I may finally be done with the other problem that's been hounding me for so long, my sense of being watched.

On second thought, I should have written, "I fear I may be done with the problem." I insert the word "fear" because of the way in which I'm afraid the matter was resolved.

Some background: Since David and I have been staying here in Havana, I've suspected that we are being followed. Just the other night, we went out for dinner at a

small place called the Café Aguacate. We like to eat in the private rooms in the back where the Spanish officers aren't welcome. As we walked there, we thought we could hear footsteps behind us. But when we stopped, so did whoever was tailing us. Then, during dinner, I happened to look through the open shutters and could see somebody standing outside at the edge of the window frame and looking in from time to time.

Not that such behavior is all that unusual here. Havana is awash with spies—from America, from Spain, from Cuba. But this feels different. More personal. Sometimes when we return to the hotel, it feels as if our room's been invaded. We've never found any proof, but we share the same sense of invasion. When soldiers search, they don't care if they've been detected. In their mad hunts, they throw things all around. But on the occasions I'm talking about, we find things in place but slightly disturbed. Or so it seems. Papers on the desk turned at different angles. A drawer we left open that we later discover closed. I think we're being dogged by someone who works for that snake Milverton in London whom I already wrote you about.

Late the other night we heard a noise somewhere outside our window. David's not very tall, but he's fearless. He grabbed the baseball bat that I keep under the bed, one of those sweet Louisville Sluggers that Bud Hillerich makes. He went out and didn't come back for over half-an-hour. When he finally reappeared, he wasn't wearing his shirt, and he no longer had the bat. God only knows what happened.

He washed up thoroughly and, with a smile on his face, said he didn't think we had anything more to worry about. I had the good sense not to ask him what had just happened outside. I also didn't bother to remind him that, even if there's no one here in Havana left to report to

Milverton, that won't stop the man from draining me dry based on what he's already been told.

David's decisiveness—that's what I love about him. He's a man who can get things done. I just hope that as a result, we don't have any new problems to concern ourselves with.

This anxiety has been nagging enough to make me want to move. Charlie Thrall—he's a correspondent at the World, *for the time being—has been telling me about a lodging house here in Havana that other newspapermen have stayed at. He says it's run by a friendly old lady, who in another life could have been my grandma. Her name is Mary Horan, and she's originally from New York. Charlie describes her as big and bespectacled, a maternal type who bullies or nurses depending on what's required at the time. He says if you can tolerate her codfish salad, you shouldn't have any problems. Best of all, he tells me she charges much less than the Pasaje. With all the money I'm sending to Milverton, lower rent would mean a lot.*

According to Charlie, her little boarding house is quiet—unlike the Pasaje, which is four-stories tall and full of people. Mary Horan's place doesn't have an elevator, let alone electricity, but he says there's a quiet little patio containing an orange tree. Next to the tree is a set of winding stairs that lead up to the gallery and three sleeping rooms. Maybe I can get more rest there; my fever is driving me crazy. In the daytime, David could stay upstairs while I sit under the tree and write. If nothing comes into my head, at least I can enjoy the oranges.

I'm still working on my novel about the war in Greece, and soon enough I want to turn my attention to the book about David that I've been composing in my brain ever since I first met him back in New York. I'm thinking of calling it Flowers of Asphalt *after a book of French poems by*

Goudeau whose title I like: Fleurs de Bithume (although maybe it sounds better in French). Speaking of names, if we move, I'll start using my alias again. You can think of me once more as "Samuel Carleton." (I've kept my own initials to keep things simple.)

Thanks for looking after Cora, and please no word about any of this to her or to Kate. You know how those two hens like to cackle.

Burn this letter like the rest of them. With all that's going on out here, it's time for me to stay out of sight.

Adios.

S.C.

I had no idea who this man called David was, and I knew very little more about Crane himself. With two such men living together and Frederic sharing two households, Holmes and I seemed to have found ourselves in the midst of some kind of Bohemian fleshpot. Still, however repugnant I might regard these so-called relationships, I had to admit that even more distasteful was the horrible reach of Charles Milverton, who was feeding upon them with the aid of his minions. In no way did I condone taking matters into his own hands, as Crane's "companion" seemed to have done. But I could understand their desire to end being so shamelessly spied upon—even though, as Crane himself had rightly observed, the elimination of the spy in Havana didn't mean the end to paying off Milverton in London.

While it had been the unfortunate problems of Stephen Crane that prompted Frederic's visit to us a few weeks before, our sole purpose in setting out for Homefield that morning had little to do with Milverton. Our primary concern had been to provide moral support for the ailing Frederic. But with the unexpected appearance of Crane's correspondence, Holmes' interest in the Milverton connection reignited.

"It's time to return to Baker Street," Holmes said as he placed the folded yellow sheets inside his coat pocket. "Perhaps," he added cryptically, "there's something that can be done after all."

We headed for the door; but just then, taking my arm, Holmes added in a whisper, "I must speak with the maid called Agatha about her conversation with Milverton." Before I could reply, he was off to find the young woman.

A few minutes later, Holmes was back. "Nothing of note," he said softly, "if one believes her." Cocking an eyebrow, he added, "She told me that Milverton had simply asked directions for his return to London."

"Directions to London? That doesn't sound like the Charles Milverton we know."

Holmes offered a wry smile. "Ever the cynic, Watson."

It was Kate Lyon herself who opened the front door for our departure. We once again proffered our sympathies and, intending to proceed to our trap and driver, stepped out onto the porch. Just as we got through the doorway, however, we were stopped cold in our tracks. Neither Holmes nor I could have anticipated the vision that confronted us.

Standing on the porch and blocking our way was a curious-looking woman. Short and sturdy, she wore her golden hair plaited and coiled atop her head, a white orchid coquettishly angled at her left temple. With skin the texture of rich white cream, she stared confidently at us from the deepest of sea-green eyes, the thin lips of her small mouth slightly parted as if about to speak. Despite the informality of her clothing—open Greek sandals, a simple plaid skirt, and long-sleeved, white cotton tunic whose large buttons and bold stitching looked homemade—one could easily describe her as attractive.   Indeed, she was a handsome woman quite obviously prepared for pastoral living, although presumably not interested in dealing with it in the guise of an English gentlewoman.

"Mr. Holmes, Dr. Watson," Miss Lyon said at the doorsill, "may I present to you Mrs. Cora Crane."

Part II

Miss Cora

Chapter Four

In the desert
I saw a creature, naked, bestial,
Who, squatting upon the ground,
Held his heart in his hands,
And ate of it.
I said, "Is it good, friend?"
"It is bitter—bitter," he answered;
"But I like it
Because it is bitter,
And because it is my heart."
—Stephen Crane

Kate Lyon clutched both of her visitor's outstretched hands and pulled her close.

"I'm so sorry," Cora whispered.

The two women embraced; and while Kate wept on Mrs. Crane's shoulder, I was realizing that I had much to contemplate. Holmes and I had come to Croydon to attend the ailing Harold Frederic, yet the business involving the Cranes—personalities introduced to us by Frederic, after all—remained ever distracting.

Conflict roiled within me. Just as I felt trepidation about calling Kate Lyon "Mrs. Frederic, so too did I feel uncomfortable in referring to the visitor standing before us as "*Mrs.* Crane". At the same time, the behaviour of her husband, Captain Stewart, continued to irritate me. I favour the rules of marriage as much as the next man, and I could also understand how divorce could endanger the captain's social standing. Nonetheless, he wanted no more connection with his wife but would take no action to sever the legal bond between them. Not only was such an attitude unfair to Cora

Crane, it was also not the behaviour of an officer and a gentleman.

There was also Holmes' report that, whatever the legalities, Cora and Stephen were said to have married in Greece.

One can bend just so far, however—even if he is a modern thinker. I need not say that I have supported many of the demands voiced by the era's so-called New Woman. I am also no prude. My career in medicine had exposed me to knowledge about a panoply of human behaviours that would shock the uninitiated. But expected to recognize Mrs. Crane's previous profession—proprietrix of a disorderly house—as an acceptable form of feminine occupation? I daresay that at such a proposition I drew the line.

At the same time, I also couldn't forget that we'd come to Homefield to aid the stricken man lying in the house behind me. With his health paramount and the need for civility to be maintained, it would be heartless to hold Cora Crane accountable for her earlier wantonness, to condemn her for acts no longer characterizing her lifestyle. Those past indiscretions were part of a dark history, which I was sure she had left in America, where they belonged.

In the long run, it seemed far easier to accept Cora Crane's version of her history than take the side of the unfeeling Captain Stewart and regard her as immoral and unchaste. I resolved, therefore, to make every effort to treat Mrs. Crane—both ladies before me, in fact—with the same courtesies I reserve for any woman I meet in respectable social circles. With the mountain of grief resulting from Frederic's condition, I would be nothing if not polite.

I finished my ruminations just as Kate Lyon, giving her eyes a final wipe and indicating my friend, said to Cora, "This is Mr. Sherlock Holmes, the detective I told you about."

Cora fixed Holmes with a penetrating stare. "You mean," she asked in a cultured American accent, "the man Harold spoke to about Stevie?"

Kate nodded.

"Listen to me," Cora said, taking up both of Kate's hands again. "I'll send Adoni over to help your children get packed and ready. Then he will bring them back to Ravensbrook where we shall look after them. But I need to take Mr. Holmes and his friend here"— she extricated her right hand from Kate's and placed it on my arm where I felt a sort of electric shock exploding—"home with me. It'll be easier to talk with them at Ravensbrook."

"Yes, you're right," Kate nodded. "And I'm so grateful to you for putting up our children."

"That's what friends are for," Cora smiled.

Kate Lyon kissed her on the cheek, then dabbed at her eyes again and turned to us. "Gentlemen," said she before re-entering the house, "once more, I thank you for coming." With that, she closed the door behind her; and all seemed silent within.

Cora Crane now took centre-stage. "Mr. Holmes," she commanded, showing no inclination for approval of her plans, "tell your driver he's no longer needed. I'll arrange for your return to the train station when we've concluded our business."

Holmes arched his eyebrows, but did as he was instructed—compliance, I recognized, due more to his curiosity than to her overbearing tone.

Cora Crane then turned her green eyes on me. "And *you* are—?" she asked, making no move to remove her hand from my arm.

"Dr. Watson," I replied with as much determination as I could muster. "*John* Watson," I added for some inexplicable reason.

Mrs. Crane walked me down the flags to her dogcart while Holmes remunerated our driver, who'd been waiting patiently for passengers no longer in need of his service.

"Well, Dr. John Watson," said she when we reached the cart, "here's where I let go," and she slid her arm out from mine and proceeded to climb unabashedly up to the driver's position, settling herself on the small wooden plank that passed for a seat. As she did so, a long, golden strand of her hair worked its way out of the coil and came to rest on her shoulder. She brushed it back with one hand and picked up the reins with the other. I realized that the rest of her tresses were equally long and that she probably coiled them atop her head in order to give herself added height.

With no complaint from me, Holmes insisted that I climb aboard before he did. Three on the small perch made for a tight squeeze, and it was all I could do to prevent myself from pressing my hip into Mrs. Crane's. In light of the pall cast by Harold Frederic's affliction, this headstrong woman was causing an almost welcome distraction.

"Comfy, John?" she asked. "Mr. Holmes?"

I blushed, and Holmes nodded.

Cora responded with a wink. Then she barked "Gidd'up" at the horse; and with a flick of the reins, the cart proceeded to rattle down the rustic, tree-lined road.

"Poor Harold," Cora sighed beneath a canopy of branches thick enough to block the sun. "He helped Stevie and me find Ravensbrook, you know. That's why we live so close to each other. We're only seven miles away." She thought for a few moments, then added, "When Stevie and I first got out here, we stayed in a boarding house in Limpsfield Chart outside of Oxted. It's a tiny village with only one main street that's just a short walk from here. We like the area; actually, a number of writers live in the vicinity."

We jounced along in silence for the next few minutes, our reflections interrupted only by the rumble of the wheels, the clopping of the horse, and the trill of the odd sparrow. Each of us, I felt certain, must have been entertaining the same thought—what Harold Frederic and his fragility had to tell us about our own sense of mortality

Not surprisingly, it was Cora who spoke first. "I feel a bit shaky every time I drive this road," she said, twitching the reins to keep the horse at a steady pace. "Last year, Stevie and I rented a carriage to go to Homefield for Harold's birthday. But the goldarned thing overturned on the way—the horse had been harnessed badly. Stevie broke his nose. We were both covered in blood. The Frederics were kind enough to put us up for a week until we recovered. All things considered, I think we were lucky to escape with our lives."

"You were indeed," said I.

"Afterwards, Harold insisted that Stevie and I join them for a few weeks longer on the coast in Ireland. Harold's the generous sort."

"'Tis an ill wind that blows no good," I observed.

"Exactly, Doctor," she said, patting me on the leg. "I can see you're the type of man that has the right word for every occasion." She followed with a little squeeze of my thigh, and another electric shock coursed through me. How many other men had she handled in such a manner? I found myself wondering.

"R-Ravensbrook," I managed to say. Anything to put her off her game—whatever her game happened to be.

"Yes?" Cora asked. "Our home? What about it?"

"I—I've been wondering how—how it had come by its name."

"A good question, that one. The name actually derives from an old legend. The natives say that in the olden days, some Roman soldiers were marching around out here and ran out of water. Eventually, they saw some ravens; and the Romans, being clever fellows, waited until the birds needed to drink. Then they followed them and discovered the stream. Ever since, the stream's been called Ravensbrook; and since it runs all the way down to the house, somebody had the bright idea to name the house after the water."

"It's certainly beautiful here," I observed, the dogcart now paralleling the clear stream as it gently curved its way through a thicket of green fronds.

"Maybe under these trees," she said, "but there's the unavoidable fact that this very same stream runs beneath our house and causes all kinds of trouble—from dampening the walls to undermining the foundation. I shouldn't be surprised if one day it destroys the entire structure. In my opinion, that's the real reason the place is called Ravensbrook."

Cora Crane allowed herself a chuckle and then snapped the reins a few more times. Moments later she set her lips straight and appeared to be thinking. "Well done, John," she said at last. "I mean, asking about why the house is called Ravensbrook. You diverted my attention from the tragedies of the day. I appreciate that."

Offering such an escape had not been my intent— although it was kind of Cora to suggest it—appealing, in fact. I should imagine that it was this way she had of making a man feel good about himself that had attracted Stephen Crane when he'd first set eyes on her in the Hotel de Dream.

* * *

Villa Ravensbrook—the very name conjures a kind of romanticism. One thinks of knights, of damsels, of crenulated battlements. And now, thanks to Cora, of Roman soldiers.

In reality, however, Ravensbrook proved to be a small, suburban house of the red-brick-and-tile variety, stuck at the bottom of a steep chalky slope in the midst of the numerous other chalky slopes so typical of Kent and Surrey. No *bijou villa*, the structure itself was a simple enough square with a small outbuilding at the gate and a carriage drive leading into the grounds. The picturesque brook we had passed earlier did indeed bubble towards the building; but where it approached the house, its banks looked built-up like wastewater culverts. Indeed, a clammy dampness permeated the atmosphere—in the house, in the garden, in the valley.

"We moved here in June of last year," Cora said as we passed through the gate. "Stevie hates it."

She pulled the horse to a stop, and an immediate chorus of wild barking preceded the arrival of three energetic, dogs. "But he loves *these* guys," she said as the three bounded towards us. No sooner had we climbed down from the dogcart than she hugged them individually. "Sponge, Flannel, and Ruby," she announced, her eyes flashing.

"What kind are they?" I asked, stroking each one as it came to inspect first Holmes and then me.

Pointing to the black one, she said, "This guy's called Spongie." As she spoke, she bent down to scratch behind the animal's ears. "He's a cross between a retriever and an old English sheep dog." In a whisper, she added, "He's Stevie's favourite, but don't tell the others."

Why dog-lovers assume that, like themselves, all people believe that dogs understand human speech I'll never understand. Still, I found Cora's devotion charming. Holmes' tight lips suggested he was not amused.

"Flannel's a fox terrier," Cora resumed, "and Ruby's a Russian poodle."

At the sound of her name, Ruby jumped at Cora, trying to nuzzle Sponge out of the way.

"Ruby's not too smart," she said *sotto voce*, "but full of love."

When she finished her greetings, she brushed her hair back, and we pushed our way through the pack as best we could, the dogs trailing after us, leaping at Cora, still sniffing at Holmes and me.

Cora shooed the animals away and led us into the house. We followed her past deep armchairs and large oak tables, all of the furniture having that heavy, old-oaken feel. Traditional dress may not have mattered much to Cora, but it seemed obvious that she believed a fashionable home in the rustic English countryside should be accoutred with ponderous pieces created from solid wood.

Crane's study was another matter. The room clearly belonged to a writer. Stacked on the large oak desk were pages of manuscript—some printed, some handwritten on long, lined sheets of paper. I immediately recognized the round script leaning slightly to the left that we'd encountered in Crane's letter to Harold Frederic.

"The paper is legal cap," observed Holmes. "No doubt supplied by a barrister or solicitor."

"An excellent observation, Mr. Holmes. Stevie gets it from his brother William, a lawyer back in New York."

It was in this room, Cora informed us, that her husband had worked on such famous stories as "The Bride Comes to Yellow Sky" and "The Blue Hotel", works that over the years have come to be regarded—or so I am assured by literary experts—as amongst the greatest short fiction in the English language.

But Crane's den proved to be more than just a chamber of desktop foolscap and well-stocked bookshelves. It was also a miniature museum. As Cora explained, the room stood testimony to her husband's earlier travels in Mexico and the American Old West: pointy metal spurs rested on the desk; a brown-leather holster hung from a nail by the window; an Indian blanket striped in turquoise, green, and red covered the wall like a prized painting.

I pointed questioningly to a foot-long piece of dirty white tubing that hung beneath the blanket.

Cora lifted the strange object from its hook. "This, John," she smiled, "is the piece of life-belt Stevie was holding when he was almost drowned in the *Commodore* disaster."

Most people who have heard of Stephen Crane know that he wrote *The Red Badge of Courage*. Not nearly as many are aware of his narrow escape from death when he joined a crew of filibusterers hoping to deliver guns to the rebels in Cuba. I knew about Crane's ordeal because I had read his fictionalized account of it in the story he called "The Open Boat".

"You remember, Holmes," I reminded him. "It appeared last year in *Scribner's,* the American magazine."

Holmes nodded unenthusiastically. I knew he regarded all of this literary talk as time-consuming banter.

Yet I remembered the narrative quite clearly. From Crane's dramatic though fictionalized report, I'd learned how, on New Year's Eve, 1896, Crane, serving as both newspaper correspondent and able seaman, had joined a band of adventurers aboard the small steamboat *Commodore* to transport arms to rebels in Cuba. Not long after their departure, however, the boat foundered. Some of the men reached the mainland safely in lifeboats; but a handful, including Crane, who had helped commandeer the ship's ten-foot dinghy, ended up drifting aimlessly in the dark. Only after some thirty heroic hours at sea did Crane and all but one of the dinghy's occupants make it safely to shore. Their survival remained so doubtful that Cora had actually received word of Crane's death. With such a harrowing story as evidence, Harold Frederic seemed quite on target in calling Crane "a man's man."

"I was heartbroken at the initial news that Stevie had died," Cora said, clutching the piece of life belt to her chest. "We had only recently met, you see, and he had already become my guiding star. I was in Jacksonville and worried sick when I first heard of the *Commodore*'s sinking. But after what seemed like forever, I got word that Stevie's lifeboat had made it safely to Daytona. I was planning to rent a locomotive to bring him back to me—I had the money in those days—but I ended up going down there myself to get him. I found him sitting in a hotel. He looked terrible, and he was holding on to this very section of the life-belt. Now it's part of our collection of important memories."

Cora replaced her treasure on the wall.

"No matter what Stevie thinks of this place, you can see how much *I* love it here," she said proudly, her green eyes flashing. "But I have grander plans. I'm hoping that when he returns, we can move into a manor house. A man with his talent—not to mention his British heritage that dates back to the 1600's—deserves it.

"Our neighbour, the writer Edward Garnett, told us about a fourteenth-century estate that may be available. Currently, the place stands empty. It's called Brede Place, and it belongs to Moreton Frewen, the brother-in-law of my friend Jennie, Jennie Churchill—you know, Lady Randolph. Changes have been made over the years, of course; and I'm told it still needs more work done—a new roof, I think. Who knows? Maybe someday the two of you could visit us there."

"Quite so," Holmes said briskly, clearly tired of all this prattle.

Sensing his impatience, Cora seated herself behind the desk and motioned for us to take the two chairs opposite.

"At last," Holmes muttered.

Just as Mrs. Crane was about to speak, however, a young male servant clad in billowing white linen entered the room. He was a handsome, dark fellow with bright eyes, strong jaw, full moustache, and thick mane of coal-black hair combed straight back.

"Me—I bring tea," he said haltingly—and superfluously since he was carrying a salver with a white teapot and the fixings for a light tea.

"This is Adoni Ptolemy," said Cora. "We collected him and his twin brother in Greece last year; they're refugees. Stevie calls Adoni our 'butler in shirtsleeves'. We got his brother a job with our neighbour."

With great care, Adoni placed the tray at the edge of the desk between Cora and us. Then he touched at his forelock and exited the room.

"We travelled to Greece on account of Stevie. Ever since he'd finished *The Red Badge*, he was obsessed with witnessing actual combat. He wanted to see how real warfare compared with the fiction he'd created. The *Westminster Gazette* agreed to send him, so we went to see the Greeks fight the Turks."

Holmes sighed impatiently. Though I knew he was still wondering what all this had to do with him, the writer in me, found the tale quite engaging and Crane's concern most credible.

"What was his conclusion?" I asked.

"All in all, he thought he'd done a pretty good job. He reckoned his make-believe fighting stacked up pretty well against the real thing."

"Glad to hear it," said I, tongue firmly in cheek. The literary world could now rest easy with the news that Stephen Crane approved the authenticity of what many critics consider the most credible account of warfare in American fiction.

"You know," said Cora, "not to be stealing my Stevie's thunder, but he wasn't the only Crane sending accounts of the war back to New York. I was as well. Of course, I was writing under a *nom de guerre*—Imogene Carter—so you might not have heard of my contributions. Both of us were published by Mr. Hearst in the *Journal.*"

Is there no end to her talents? I wondered.

"It was on our way out of Greece that we picked up Adoni and his brother." Suddenly the green eyes turned sad. "We also found a puppy, a cute little guy. We named him Velestino in honour of the battle; but he died here at Ravensbrook just about a year ago. For eleven days, Stevie and I tried so hard to keep him alive. We nursed him on an ocean of pillows in my bedroom. We ended up burying him among the rhododendrons in the garden."

Earlier that day, Cora had shown great emotional strength in dealing with Frederic's stroke; now, talking about a departed dog, she was on the verge of tears.

All the while, the tea tray remained untouched. Holmes and I had eaten nothing since breakfast at Baker Street, and at first glance the tray seemed to contain the proper hallmarks of a traditional English tea—the steaming pot; the porcelain cups; a small pitcher of milk; a plate of biscuits, and small bowls of honey, butter, and jam. Yet on closer inspection, all seemed slightly off kilter. The white teapot proved to be filled with coffee; the cups were chipped; and rather than sweet British biscuits, the plate contained small, bread-like flat rolls without a hint of sugar—though Cora maintained that Americans nevertheless called these impostors "biscuits".

Cora caught me stealing glances at these very rolls and, taking my gaze as her invitation to serve, handed Holmes and me plates upon which she'd placed a pair of the so-called "biscuits."

"Mrs. Ruedy," she explained, offering us the honeypot, "was baking and thought we might enjoy these fresh from the oven."

As if on cue, the cook in question, a handsome, dark-haired woman with sharp-cut features, some thirty years of age, bustled into the room. Like Adoni, she too was dressed in white linen; but even with the flowing cloth, I could readily see she possessed the trim figure of a woman quite unlike the kind I generally associated with those who worked in kitchens. It was only later I would learn that in reality Mathilde Ruedy was Cora's companion from America—in point of fact, a former "employee" at the Hotel de Dream. She had accompanied the Cranes on their trip to Greece and in her present incarnation, apparently gifted in various aspects of feminine talent, now served as maid and cook for the household.

"Just came to see that everything was OK, Miss Cora," said she.

"Everything's fine," Cora replied and carefully poured coffee for Holmes and me.

My mouth full of biscuit, I conveyed my satisfaction to Mrs. Ruedy with a smile. The honey made the American rolls tasty, but I hesitated to look at Holmes who I'm sure was stifling his anger at being put off yet again.

"I was trained for serving tea from the best, you know," Cora explained. "My ex-father-in-law, Sir Donald Stewart, is a baronet."

"So Mr. Frederic informed us," said I between bites.

"The baronet is a gentleman," she observed. "I wish I could say the same about his younger son, my former husband. If only—"

Mrs. Ruedy interrupted. "I'm off to the kitchen now, Miss Cora," said she, dipping downward in what appeared to be an ill-managed curtsy.

"Mrs. Crane," an exasperated Sherlock Holmes announced as soon as we three were alone, "we have listened to your recent history; we have shared your food. Perhaps at long last you can explain what in the world we are doing here."

Still sampling a biscuit, Cora held up her forefinger as if to say, "A moment." In spite of Holmes' impatience, she winked at me. I must say that at the very least, she had lightened the mood following the solemnity we had experienced at Homefield.

I added milk to my coffee while Holmes, sitting bolt upright, continued to seethe.

Cora dabbed lightly at her lips with a napkin and then presented her case. "Mr. Holmes, I haven't seen my Stevie since he left here to join the U.S. Navy last April. For four months now he's been running around in the American South and in Cuba, and I want him to come home. Although I've seen his dispatches for Mr. Pulitzer and so I know he's alive, he hasn't sent much news my way. I don't have any idea what his plans are. While he did just cable me from Key West—that's in Florida—he didn't say anything about returning here. I don't know where he's staying. For that matter, I don't know if he's well, if he's got that goldarned Cuban flu, or even if—God forbid—he's been shot."

Sherlock Holmes had sampled the coffee while Cora Crane was speaking; now he replaced his cup on its saucer. "And just what would you have *me* do about all this, Mrs. Crane?" he asked.

"You don't understand, Mr. Holmes. While I miss Stevie beyond belief, I still remain a practical woman. To put it simply, without him, I have no money." As she listed her worries, she ran her fingers through her hair: "I live on credit and on the pittance I get from his publishers. I owe the butcher and the grocer. That's food on the table I'm talking about. Worse, some people—some shopkeepers—don't believe Stevie and I are even married. If they consider me an unattached single person and he doesn't return, I could be stuck with all the unpaid bills for the two of us. Mark my words, Mr. Holmes: it'll destroy me. I know your reputation. You've got to help me find him."

"I suggest you approach his publishers and bankers," replied Holmes. "What you've described is hardly the kind of work I do. I solve criminal matters, not money troubles. I'm a consulting detective--not a financial advisor." To me he said, "First, Harold Frederic, Watson; now, Mrs. Crane. These Americans seem to think that a consulting detective can remedy all their social problems."

Cora took a few deep breaths and tried a more gentle approach. "Now, now, Mr. Holmes," she said coquettishly, "I believe that you're much more than that. Didn't I hear that you have a brother who's very highly placed in the British government? I'm sure he could apply some pressure to find out something more about Stevie."

Holmes' eyes bulged at the audacious reference to his brother.

With her feminine approach so obviously scotched, Cora pulled open the top desk-drawer and removed a sheet of paper. In the process, I caught a glimpse of a cowboy-style six-shooter lying inside, probably the mate to the leather holster on the wall.

Waving the page above her head, she cried, "I have a list of names here of the people I propose to contact if I don't hear from Stevie by the end of the month." She offered the paper to Holmes, and I leaned over to read along with him.

Holmes smirked. "The name at the top, of course, I recognize." It belonged to his brother Mycroft. "Good luck reaching *him*."

Holmes moved his long, slender forefinger down the list. "John Hay, currently the American ambassador to the Court of St. James and rumoured to be appointed the next American Secretary of State. Paul Revere Reynolds?"

"Stevie's agent in the States."

"William Howe Crane? The brother?"

"'Yes," Cora nodded. "The lawyer who supplies Stevie with paper."

"William Heinemann?"

"His publisher in London."

"James Creelman?"

"Head of the *New York Journal* staff in London."

"Lucien Jerome?"

"The British Consul in Havana."

"I congratulate you, Mrs. Crane," said Holmes. "Besides the glaring omission, it's quite a catalogue."

"Omission?" she asked, eyes wide. "Who am I missing?"

It was not often Sherlock Holmes allowed himself a chortle, but he most certainly did snigger mischievously after he carefully announced, "Your President, Mr. William McKinley. It looks like you've included everyone else."

Biting her lower lip, she wagged her forefinger at him. "You're mocking me, Mr. Holmes."

"With all those names on that paper," Holmes said, his smile fading, "you certainly don't need *my* help."

The green eyes began to well up. I suspected it was a technique she had perfected in her many dealings with men. "But your brother, Mr. Holmes. Certainly you can reach *him* for me."

"My brother is heavily involved with matters of state, Mrs. Crane—no doubt helping to end the fighting in Cuba--the 'splendid little war', I believe your Ambassador called it. My brother will certainly *not* have time to seek out some missing pressman."

For a moment Mrs. Crane looked defeated. Just for a moment. She then placed her serviette on the tray and stood up. "Gentlemen, I believe I promised you a return to the railway station. Adoni will take you there. On his return trip, he will pick up the Frederics' children and bring them back here. I shall hire a governess, and the children shall stay at Ravensbrook during the horrible crisis at Homefield."

Suddenly, it appeared that Holmes and I no longer figured in Mrs. Crane's plans. She would shift her attention from her Stevie to the Frederics and their children. How she would pay for more mouths to feed and the additional accompanying staff I couldn't begin to imagine. It was yet another question about the woman better left unasked. In light of this new determination, Holmes and I prepared to depart, and I followed my friend as he stood and made his way toward the front door.

But just then, to my utter astonishment I felt a squeeze of my hand. Cora had grasped it and was holding me back. I turned towards her in wonderment, only to be further surprised by the closeness of her person. She was short enough so that I had to look down to gaze into her beckoning eyes, close enough so that I could feel her cool breath and inhale her flowery scent.

"John," she whispered into my ear, that wayward lock of golden hair falling softly against my chest, "I can tell that Mr. Holmes won't help, but I'm sure *you* could talk to his brother for me."

"Watson!" Holmes called from somewhere up ahead, I wasn't sure quite where. Indeed, I wasn't quite sure of anything save the woman's presence. She was pressing her entire body against me now; and in a soft, husky voice she said, "I know you can do this little task for me, John." And she squeezed my hand again.

Although I had been a widower for a few years, I was still totally unprepared to be thus accosted by a woman—unprepared, perhaps, but not completely ignorant. I understood that Cora Crane was using her feminine tricks to manoeuvre round Holmes, to wheedle me into providing what she asked without any help from my friend. And yet as certainly as I recognized all that, I also knew that I would do her bidding. Seductive women have that power over men— over *me*, at least—and let us not forget that Cora Crane was a professional.

Sherlock Holmes was standing by the open front door tapping his foot. Through the doorway I could see that Adoni was already seated in the dogcart. Holmes nodded curtly to Mrs. Crane, and I offered a small wave, and then we were striding down the path towards our transportation. Holmes said nothing to me. I was already feeling the fool in anticipation of what I was planning to do. There seemed no sense in compounding my foolishness by presuming Holmes unaware of what had just transpired between me and the ever-persuasive Cora Crane.

Chapter Five

A man said to the universe:
"Sir, I exist!"
"However," replied the universe,
"The fact has not created in me
A sense of obligation."
–Stephen Crane

I telegrammed Mycroft Holmes after our return from Ravensbrook, and he agreed to see me three days later in the Diogenes Club at five o'clock. On one level, my plan was most practical. I was hopeful that any details Mycroft furnished regarding the whereabouts of Stephen Crane would serve to settle Cora's concerns. Such information might also shed additional light on Milverton's involvement with the writer. And yet in the name of honesty, I must also confess to thinking that a meeting with Mycroft would keep the enticing world of Cora Crane still spinning before me. There was something about the woman that I didn't want to let go.

For the time being, however, I had to put Cora Crane out of mind. Some pressing professional matters related to my former medical practice had arisen which I needed to address. Faithful readers will recall that, following the death of my dear wife Mary, I decided to sell my practice in Kensington in order to make possible my move back to Baker Street. (It took a few years for me to learn that Dr. Verner, the physician who purchased my practice, was actually a distant relative of Sherlock Holmes and that, in order to facilitate my return to our old quarters, Holmes had obligingly provided Verner with the funds to meet my price.)

For some small time now, Verner and I had been consulting with each other. Not only did our meetings provide him the opportunity to ask questions about my former patients, but on those occasions when Verner might go on holiday or attend the odd medical conference, they also allowed me the chance to resume my surgery.

Prior to the weekend's tragedy at Homefield, I had told Verner I would be happy to commandeer his surgery that Monday when he was hoping to visit Brighton with his wife. We had also agreed to schedule our usual consultation for the day after I'd seen his patients.

For the purpose of this narrative, I mention this distraction only to explain my presence in the early afternoon at Potts' Medical Supply Shop near Harley Street on the same Wednesday as my visit to Mycroft. On Monday I had attended Verner's surgery, and the next day I had discussed my findings with him. During the course of our Tuesday chat, he happened to tell me that he was in need of a new mercury thermometer. Since I hoped to replace my dilapidated binaural stethoscope, I suggested to him that I might pick up the equipment in question for the both of us the following day. If I attended to business in the early afternoon, I knew I'd have plenty of time to complete my business at Potts' before my afternoon trip to the Diogenes.

My arrival in the shop that warm summer's day was announced by the metallic jingle of a little bell attached atop the inside of the entry. In his white smock, Mr. Potts, a short, bald man squinting through round glasses, assisted me with alacrity; and once my transactions were completed, I opened the door to take my leave. The little bell jingled again, but I didn't get far, for after a single step, I quite literally bumped into Dr. Playfair, who'd been about to enter.

"Sorry," we both said before actually recognising each other.

We were standing on the hot pavement outside the shop amidst jostling pedestrians, shouting carriage drivers, and clattering hooves. Mindful of my appointment with Mycroft and longing for a meal before hand at my club, I didn't fancy exchanging long-winded pleasantries in the summer sun with the gregarious Dr. Playfair.

Yet he immediately commanded my attention when he asked, "Have you heard the latest from the Frederic household, Watson? As a medical man, you might be interested."

I caught my breath. "I am indeed."

"One would assume," said Playfair, "that so prominent a patient would receive the best medical care available. Wouldn't you agree?"

"Of course. I should imagine any number of doctors— in addition to yourself, of course—would be called in to attend the man. You said much the same when Holmes and I saw you at Homefield."

Shading my eyes from the sun allowed me to see his wry grin.

"Yes—a *few*," he said pulling at his beard. "But Mrs. Frederic has called in enough medical men to staff a hospital, don't you know? In addition to myself, there's Dr. Boyd—an American, Dr. Brown from the neighbourhood, and Dr. Murray from Charing Cross Hospital. What's more, I'm told she's about to add a specialist to the collection."

"Sounds promising," I observed. "Calling in a specialist is a capital idea."

"Indeed, my good man, except for the fact that, despite all those doctors in attendance, Mrs. Frederic herself has come to prefer the services of a Christian Science healer, a woman called Athalie Mills—Mrs. Athalie Goodman Mills, don't you know? In point of fact, just yesterday, Mr. Frederic himself sent this Mills woman a telegram that read "No

Doctors," and Mrs. Frederic has actually invited the woman to stay at Homefield."

"No doctors?" I exclaimed. "Why, they're playing with the man's life!"

"To be sure. With all those people running about in addition to the doctors, it's quite a circus they have there. Mrs. Mills will just add one more to the crowd."

"Who are the others?"

Dr. Playfair grinned again. "Well, there's Frederic himself, of course. And Mrs. Frederic. And Ruth, his older daughter from his first marriage has been helping. There's Mr. Frederic's assistant, John Scott-Stokes—he's cousin to the Duke of Norfolk. A number of celebrated writers have also made their appearances: H.G. Wells, Henry James, Joseph Conrad. Oh, I tell you, it's quite the literary salon. And now Mrs. Mills joins the menagerie. How will the man get any rest? If, indeed, rest is even prescribed by his new faith healer."

I could only shake my head.

"To make matters worse, there's a parlour maid there—I believe she's called Agatha."

"I remember her," said I, recalling the handsome features of the young woman.

"Apparently, she too is a faithful adherent of Christian Science. Said it's all the rage in America. She's egging Mrs. Frederic on. I warned Mrs. Frederic that I for one wouldn't be coming back if she persisted in maintaining such fanciful care for her husband. Yet the other doctors continue to remain on her ledger. 'One can never be too safe,' she told me. 'Too safe'! As you and I both know, Watson, we medical men advise moderation for someone in Frederic's condition, am I not correct?"

I nodded my agreement.

"Well, with the approval of his *new* healer, the Christian Science lady, Mr. Frederic plans on sticking with beer, whiskey, and cigars, don't you know?"

"Alcohol and cigars," I cried. "You can't be serious."

Playfair poked bony forefinger in my face. "You mark my words, Watson," said he. "Those two women are going to kill that man before they're through with him, and there are some—like me—that will call it 'murther'."

His archaic pronunciation of the word made it resonate all the more, especially since he punctuated his charge with a dramatic bow of his head. He turned to enter the shop; but before he did so, I caught him by the arm.

"Do keep me informed, Playfair," I said. "Holmes and I share rooms at 221B Baker Street."

The doctor nodded and opened the door. On the heels of his ominous prediction of Frederic's fate, the ringing of the entry bell sounded more macabre than welcoming.

* * *

Of the many famous clubs that stand in Pall Mall—the Athenaeum, the Guards', the Carlton, to name a few—none is more curious than the Diogenes. Although it was named for the Greek philosopher who held socializing in disdain, I have always thought it might just as easily be called the Temple of Irony. For what could be more ironic than a gathering place for respectable gentleman who prefer to remain solitary? As I'm certain my readers are aware, the club's cardinal rule prohibits public discourse within the confines of the building (excluding the Strangers' Room where limited conversations are allowed). On a member's third infraction of this dictate, the offending party may be asked to relinquish his association with the group.

Mycroft Holmes, one of the club's founder-members, lived across the road; but he appeared within the Diogenes only between the evening hours of 4:45 and 7:40—thus, his scheduled meeting with me at five.

Although I had been to that peculiar institution on a few occasions with Mycroft's brother, I never could avoid the dread that always accompanied me. From my ever too-loud articulation of my name at the door—well outside the confines of the entry hall, I might add—to the thunderous footfalls of my tiptoeing on the checkerboard-tile floor, I constantly feared upsetting the treasured silence demanded by the club's membership.

Yet after successfully reaching the Strangers' Room that Wednesday afternoon, I found little relief in the impassive demeanour of Mycroft Holmes. A very large man to whom physical movement seemed anathema, he was seated in a deep brown-leather armchair near the bow window that overlooked Pall Mall. Besides a glance and nod in my direction, he made no other effort to welcome me save the flick of his wrist in the direction of a nearby chair, which I took as an invitation to sit down.

"Peculiar, Watson," he said placidly.

"Sorry?"

"Your being here without Sherlock. I trust he's in no distress. I usually learn about his activities immediately, but nothing of consequence has crossed my desk. Nothing, that is, beyond the already-solved problems of the dancing men, the Coptic Christians, and those murders in Lewisham involving the colourman."

However accurate Mycroft's list of our current cases, I noted that he had not included Milverton's name. Whatever the cause of the omission, I saw no point in referring to the rogue and risk clouding what I hoped Mycroft would regard as a simple request. Locating a famous writer like Stephen

Crane should be child's play to a veteran diplomat like the man before me.

"No, sir," I answered him, "Your brother is fine. Actually, today I have come by myself on behalf of a lady."

Mycroft allowed himself a stifled laugh. "No wonder then that Sherlock is not here."

I proceeded to inform Mycroft about the missing Stephen Crane, who'd gone off to record the conflict in Cuba and whose wife had heard next to nothing about him ever since. "We—that is, she—was hoping that, with your connections in government, you might be able to find someone in Washington who could discover what's become of her husband."

Mycroft's eyebrows rose at the word "husband." He looked as if he was going to say something about it, weighed the matter, and concluded that it wasn't worth the effort.

Instead, he asked, "Crane is still in Cuba?" though his flat inflection made it sound more like a statement than a question.

"Yes, sir. Probably in Havana, but his wife knows nothing specific about where."

"Quite attractive is she then, Doctor? I know she's turned countless heads—Captain Donald Stewart's for one."

I could feel my cheeks flushing. "Some have found her so," I agreed, hoping that my embarrassment was not too obvious.

"I'll cable Russell in Washington."

"Russell?"

"Russell Alger, the American Secretary of War. He'll contact General Wade in Havana. Wade's involved with evacuating the Spanish troops at la Machina wharf now that the Protocols have been signed. The general should be able to track your man down."

"Thank you, sir."

"Tell this woman to wait a few days and then have her write to Alger and Wade herself; the cables I send will make it easier for her."

"I'll be sure to tell her."

"Good," said Mycroft with an air of finality, obviously trusting that the single word sufficed to close our conversation. For following its utterance, the large man rose with surprisingly little effort, nodded and exited, leaving me on my own to contemplate my silent retreat through the silent halls.

* * *

I had intended to present Cora Crane with Mycroft's hopeful news on my own. I certainly hadn't planned on Holmes' accompanying me to Ravensbrook for the occasion. As yet, I hadn't even told him of my visit to his brother. To my request for a meeting with her, however, Cora responded to the two of us with a written invitation of her own. Despite all the turmoil involving Milverton and her missing husband, she wanted us both to see Brede Place, the manor house in East Sussex that she'd already told us she was intending to let for "Stevie". Her note proposed the visit for two days hence—Friday, the nineteenth of August, which just so happened to be Harold Frederic's forty-second birthday. Would it not be thrilling, she asked, for Holmes and me to join her and Kate at Brede in a celebratory picnic for the poor man—assuming, of course, he was well enough to partake in the festivities?

As far as I was concerned, Harold Frederic shouldn't be permitted to attend any such gatherings. He should be confined to bed and granted as much time to recuperate as necessary. But then I wasn't one of the many attending physicians, and apparently even their advice was being shunted aside in favour of the faith healer's. The invitation came from Cora, however; and Frederic himself might not even be present.

No sooner had I informed Holmes of Cora's proposal than I could only marvel at how foolish I'd been to believe he wouldn't learn of my meeting with his brother.

"Quite a production planned by Mrs. Crane, Watson, just to learn what Mycroft had to tell you."

"But Holmes, how did you—?"

"My good fellow," said he, "the next time you choose not to let me know you're visiting someone, don't leave the telegram confirming your appointment on our sitting room table."

I must have wanted Holmes to find out. That could be the only explanation for such a brainless oversight. Hoping my exchange with Mycroft would be forgot—not to mention my desire to help Cora Crane—and seeking to cover my embarrassment over the revealing telegram, I changed the topic. I asked my friend's opinion regarding Mr. Frederic's anticipated appearance at the birthday celebration.

"It's difficult to say, Watson. If what Dr. Playfair reported is accurate—that Mrs. Frederic has been letting her husband drink whiskey and smoke cigars—then taking him on carriage rides seems the next logical step. As I understand the matter, if Mrs. Mills, the Christian Scientist in attendance, says he can travel, then he will."

"I'm not his physician, but—"

"To hear Playfair tell it," Holmes offered with a quick smile, "neither is anyone else. But if Frederic does show up, there might be more information to gain about Milverton. I suggest you inform your friend Mrs. Crane that we shall both attend."

I did as Holmes suggested, and Cora immediately telegraphed in response that she hoped to meet us in London so that we three could journey by railway together to Hastings, the most convenient station for Brede Place. She intended to spend the night at her favourite London hostelry, the new Queen Anne's Mansions near St. James Park in Petty France, Westminster.

"Its height has made the Mansions the talk of the town," I observed. "Some of its wings climb well over ten storeys,"

"Its notoriety," said Holmes in a voice edged with sarcasm, "is doubtless the source of its appeal to Mrs. Crane."

Chapter Six

Once I saw mountains angry,
And ranged in battle-front.
Against them stood a little man;
Aye, he was no bigger than my finger.
I laughed, and spoke to one near me,
"Will he prevail?"
"Surely," replied this other;
"His grandfathers beat them many times."
Then did I see much virtue in grandfathers, —
At least, for the little man
Who stood against the mountains.
--Stephen Crane

The grey overcast that greeted us Friday morning came as no surprise. Anyone who's ever spent a summer in London can testify that neither July nor August guarantees warm weather. All we could do was hope for the best. To that end, Cora had dressed in a summery pale-blue cotton dress buttoned to the throat and a large white hat encircled by a wide brim. In deference to the mercurial weather, a burgundy cape adorned her shoulders; but besides my bowler and Holmes' deerstalker, neither of us had brought along so much as an umbrella or overcoat to protect us from the elements. One hopes to be positive on such occasions, and yet I couldn't escape the feeling of gloom cast upon our luncheon plans by the threatening skies.

A hotel porter in plush, gold-braided livery escorted Cora to our four-wheeler. She had hardly settled in next to Holmes before she began questioning me of my meeting at the Diogenes Club. Imagine the relief I felt, the good fortune I sensed, in having already discussed the matter with Holmes.

Had I kept my visit with Mycroft secret only to have it blurted it out by Cora in front of my friend, I think the long-standing sense of trust between Holmes and me might have been forever altered.

"Mr. Mycroft Holmes," I told her, "has promised to communicate with the American Secretary of War, Russell Alger. He'll ask Alger to cable General Wade in Havana regarding the whereabouts of Stephen Crane."

Sitting across from me, Cora grabbed both my hands and leaned forward to plant a kiss on my cheek. A blush painted my face, and I perceived Holmes' stoic expression as he gazed out the window at the passing countryside.

Unable to contain my embarrassment, I tried to sound professional. "Furthermore," I said as formally as I could, "Mr. Mycroft Holmes encourages you to follow *his* cables to those gentlemen with messages of your own in a few days' time."

"Next week," Cora said, settling back in her seat. "Next week I shall send a telegram to the Secretary and to the General. I promise. A double-barrelled approach from both Alger and me should shake some information loose."

"The thoughts of Mycroft Holmes exactly," I reassured her.

An uneventful railway journey of some two hours allowed Cora plenty of time to inform us of her plans for the day. She said that despite the leaden skies, Adoni Ptolemy was going to meet us at Brede Place with a picnic lunch from Ravensbrook. Harold and Kate Frederic were still hoping to attend. I was particularly excited to learn that the writer Joseph Conrad and his wife Jessie were travelling in Kent not far from Brede and had agreed to join us.

"They want another look at The Pent," said Cora. "It's this picturesque farmhouse in Romney Marsh they're planning to sublet. Another writer, Ford Madox Hueffer, is currently living there."

According to Cora, Hueffer, (who, following the Great War, would assume the surname of Ford to sound less German), had met Conrad at Ravensbrook the previous February. Crane, Conrad, Hueffer, Garnett—it was as if all these writers were part of an extended family.

For most of Cora's chattering, Holmes had sat with his eyes closed, but he opened them upon hearing Conrad's name. "I should like to see Conrad again," said he. "Indeed, I should have met with him on my own before now."

Whatever Holmes might have wanted to communicate to Joseph Conrad remained unspoken; for once Cora began prattling on about the fuss Adoni had made over the Conrads' little boy, Holmes closed his eyes again.

In Hastings, we hired a four-wheeled trap to take us the six miles from the train station to Brede Place. Perhaps it was the increasing gloom of the day; but the deeper we plunged inside the hundred-acre park that enclosed the manor house, the more quickly the bucolic countryside with its grazing sheep, wide pastures, and swaying hop-fields metamorphosed into an isolated, overgrown, and menacing landscape. Not far beyond, the dark River Brede, lined as it was by impassive wooden dykes, coursed coldly across the valley.

The uninviting terrain didn't bother Cora. No matter the dark skies or the curtain of pines, once we'd entered the park, she scanned the surroundings for a glimpse of the medieval manor house. The hopes she instilled in that fairy castle made it a certainty that Brede Place was going to suit her Stevie.

"There's an ancient room above the entry hall," she said. "I'm going to turn it into a study for Stevie. Can you think of a more inspiring atmosphere in which to write?"

"I take it that *you* can't," I observed. "Though I must confess that I don't associate a British manor house with a chronicler of wars in the American south and Cuba."

Cora shifted her gaze from the countryside to me. "Oh, Doctor Watson, when Stevie comes back, he will be a new man. I'm going to bestow upon him a title befitting his new home. I shall call him 'the Baron of Brede Place'."

Whatever thoughts I might have had regarding this reincarnation, they were immediately interrupted by Cora.

"There it is!" she shouted, jumping up from the seat. "That's Brede Place!" She was pointing in the direction of a large thicket of boxwood hedges and Scots pines; and, indeed, we could discern five stately chimneys rising from behind their shadows.

Even with the grey background of dark, rolling clouds, the stone house now emerging in the distance looked impressive. In another life, it might have perfectly suited Lady Cora Stewart. But once we got within the confines of the ancient, gnarled hedgerow surrounding the place, the more the adjective "rundown" seemed a better descriptor. Built of sandstone ashlar, the original building, the gaunt central block consisting of two storeys and an attic, was connected to two newer projections of red brick. A lesser outcrop, the chapel, contained square-headed windows with cinquefoil-headed lights. There were dormers in the gables, and I counted a number of dark, leaded windows in Caen-stonework casings in the front. The closer we got, however, the more clearly I could discern that rather than leaded, most of the panes were simply broken, and what I was seeing was not the remnants of ancient, leaded glass but rather the black innards of the house itself.

The outside walls were blanketed with a kind of creeping ivy, which seemed to erupt from the tangles of clutching weeds at its base. Cora pointed out a few white owls nesting high in the thick vines; and higher still one could see the snarling gargoyles that at one time must have looked vicious, but now looked cowed and defanged. Like so much of the rest of the house, they'd been worn down by years of fighting a losing battle with the elements.

"I should imagine," observed Holmes drily, "that overseeing such a place will be quite a challenge."

"The heating, for one, " I murmured.

Cora, who'd heard me, shook her head "Naw," she said, gesturing across the dead lawns. "There's lots of trees around for firewood. And, do you know, the more we cut down, the more open space there'll be for Stevie to practice his target shooting. He likes to fire away after lunch with his big Mexican pistol. He's actually an excellent shot. I'm not as accurate, but I join him when I can."

A pair of gunfighters. How distinctly American!

"What about the amenities?" I wanted to know.

"'Amenities'?" she repeated. "Well, there's no electricity, if that's what you mean. And the plumbing's virtually non-existent."

"So how will you manage? What will your guests do?"

"I really *have* given it some thought, John. The women can use thunder jugs, and the men can fend for themselves outside."

Not an image I fancied recreating, especially in cold weather.

My distaste must have been apparent, for it was then that Cora described the main attraction of the decayed and rambling manor house: "Actually, when all is said and done, Brede Place will cost less to rent than Ravensbrook."

"Good show," said I, finally comprehending what I regarded as the primary motive for the move.

No sooner had we begun to rattle our way up the drive than an elderly man emerged from an outlying brick building.

Wrapped in a long black ulster, he wore a black scarf at his neck and a wide-brimmed black hat with a rounded crown atop his head. A great expanse of white beard fanned out well below his chin. He leaned against the small building for support.

Cora waved a gloved hand in his direction. "Mr. Mack!" she shouted. Lowering her voice, she explained, "He's the caretaker as well as the gardener and coachman."

"All that at his age?" I asked.

"Actually, he's not alone. When the Frewens rented Brede Place to me, they said that in addition to Mack, a cook and a serving man come along as part of the deal."

"Quite a staff," I said.

"And that doesn't include the ghost," she said proudly as we pulled up in front of the house. "Or the bats."

There was no time to contemplate the gothic qualities of the manor, however; for no sooner had we climbed out of the trap than Adoni and the carriage from Ravensbrook rumbled up behind us. We were paying our driver to wait for us just as Adoni pulled his horses to a stop. Immediately thereafter, a black dog leaped out of the carriage, loud barks and mad dashes announcing the arrival of Sponge. The only dog to make the trip, Crane's favourite obviously warranted special privileges. Cora accommodated the creature by hugging and kissing him, while Adoni produced a large wicker hamper filled with the cold beef sandwiches and apples he and Mathilde Ruedy had prepared back at Ravensbrook.

The sky continued to darken, and the Cranes' "butler in shirtsleeves" quickly spread a blue blanket on a flat section of sparse prickly lawn and laid out place-settings for each of us.

"We'll tour the house after we've eaten," said Cora, glancing nervously in the direction of the black clouds rolling in from the sea. "If the weather holds. It'll be no pleasure to see in the rain."

Everyone moved with haste. As soon as we had arranged ourselves on the blanket, Cora opened the wicker basket and produced a bottle of champagne.

"If it weren't so goldarned cold," she laughed, "we might re-enact that painting by Manet, *Le Déjeuner sur l'Herbe.*"

"My dear Mrs. Crane," Holmes replied with a mischievous twinkle, "I believe *you* would be the only one required to make any adjustments."

Shocked as I was to think Holmes familiar with the scandalous depiction of a nude woman picnicking with two men, I focused instead on the flutes that Adoni was handing the three of us. He proceeded to uncork the bottle and fill them with champagne. At the moment we were about to drink, however, another carriage rolled up the drive.

I hoped it might be the Conrads; but once the horses were reined in and the four-wheeler came to a stop, the door opened, and out climbed Agatha, the Frederics' dark-haired maid still dressed in black. Carrying a furled umbrella in one hand, she turned and helped Kate Lyon out with the other.

Obviously, someone in charge at Homefield had deemed Harold Frederic, now wrapped in a great overcoat, well enough to travel. The two women proceeded to ease the burly frame out of the carriage into which he'd been wedged and onto *terra firma* upon which he tentatively stood. Had they let go of them, I am certain he would have tumbled to the ground; but they guided him in our direction, his right foot dragging behind.

The resourceful Adoni found a dilapidated wood bench, which he carried over to our gathering; and the women slowly eased their human burden onto it. A low moan accompanied Frederic's seating, and I couldn't tell whether it was a protest from the ancient bench or an expression of pain from the afflicted man himself. In either case, the right side of Frederic's face appeared immobile, and his right arm hung useless by his side.

"Happy Birthday!" Cora crowed incongruously, raising her glass in Frederic's direction, and taking a sip.

Kate Lyon joined us in toasting the poor man; and Harold Frederic—breathing heavily, eyes half-closed—nodded slowly in response. Whether or not he ever recognized our celebratory gesture I'm certain no one ever discovered.

The postponement of lunch seemed to be the order of the day. First, it had been the arrival of the Frederics that interrupted us. Then, just as we were about to begin for a second time, another carriage came rolling up the drive. Once it halted, the coachman in top hat and overcoat climbed down from his perch and opened the door. From out of its cabin, stepped a short, round-shouldered gentleman wearing a black bowler and supporting himself with an ebony walking stick. He was dressed in a formal black suit and waistcoat, a silk black tie meticulously set just beneath a tall, white celluloid collar. His dark face sported a sharply-pointed goatee and large moustache whose ends turned up slightly. Although his physical rigidity gave him a military air, his lined brow and deep-set eyes suggested a man who seemed to find no easy explanations for a world that he must have found troubling.

A much younger woman of sturdy build followed. She was holding a baby that had been tightly swaddled in blanketing to fend off the winds.

Cora popped up immediately and escorted the trio to our group. It was obvious that the man's stick was more than just a fashionable accessory, for he noticeably limped as he made his way over to us.

"May I present to you," Cora announced, "Mr. Joseph Conrad, his wife Jessie, and their son Borys."

We smiled and bravely hoisted our glasses once more. Above, the rainclouds threatened.

"Mr. Conrad is a writer," Cora needlessly reminded us.

"Conrad," said Sherlock Holmes, getting to his feet, "it is good to see you again. When last we met, the singular outrage at Greenwich was our topic of discussion."

A broad grin formed beneath the wings of Conrad's moustache. "Of course, Holmes," said he in a quiet voice. "That discussion I still have cause to remember—for the book I've been thinking of writing. The idea remains in my mind."

(At this point, I feel compelled to offer a word of explanation. Although Joseph Conrad would go on to write many works of great literary merit in English, I always found it difficult to decipher his pronunciation. Because of his late acquisition of our tongue, the writer's spoken words were marked by a thick French accent coated in guttural Polish, two languages he had learned as a child. When he was an adult, Conrad had apparently taught himself English through reading. It was only thanks to diligent oral practice during his many years in the British merchant navy that he cultivated dexterity with vocalized English.

(Whatever his linguistic strengths, Conrad could never rid himself of his accent. Most of his *w*'s sounded like *v*'s, and he had the tendency to pronounce the final *e*'s in words like "these" and "those." His self-awareness of such problems—one might even say his embarrassment by them—resulted in the development of a sort of softness or weakness in his voice, and in various discussions he would often give up on English altogether, expressing himself in French instead. I report all this to you, dear reader, so you may understand that, while I have endeavoured to record Conrad's uttered words as accurately as I can, the task required great personal effort on my part, and I fear I may not always have fully reflected his sentiments.)

As Conrad approached our group, I too stood; and Holmes, after briefly introducing me, motioned in the direction of the gravel path leading up to the house. "If it is not too much trouble, Conrad, perhaps we might have an intimate word beyond the ears of eavesdroppers? It is about that very book you mentioned which I would like to speak with you."

The writer raised his thick eyebrows. "Of course," he said. Pointing his stick in the direction Holmes had indicated, he nodded questioningly to his wife.

"We'll be fine," Jessie Conrad called out to him. "Go." It was the voice; I am pleased to say, of a native English woman.

His gait stiff, Conrad ventured forward; and Holmes and I followed. In a line, we made our way towards the front entrance of the empty house some distance from the picnickers. Although there were but a few steps to climb, Conrad winced as he negotiated each one.

"Gout," he said. "Some days are worse than others."

Soon we were standing in the shadow of a Gothic stone archway before the entrance to Brede Place. The outer door was of massive oak riddled with iron studs and flanked by fluted stone columns. Above us hung an ancient portcullis held together by rust-riven metal joints. As we looked about, I wondered whether this was the moment in which Holmes was going to tell Conrad about Milverton's implied threat.

"You say you recall our earlier discussion about Greenwich?" Holmes asked the writer.

"Yes. We spoke about the Observatory bombing and the feasibility of my composing a novel that dealt with it. I had hoped that you would have something new to tell me about the event; but, alas, you did not."

Holmes nodded. "And are you still planning to write such a work?"

Conrad smiled. He had a way of tilting his head back so the sharp point of his beard seemed ready to spear whomever he was addressing. "Not immediately. No. I am working on other things. Right now I'm writing about a young sailor who loses his moral courage when he fears his ship is about to sink. And I'm planning to begin a new story about a civilized man who becomes lost in the heart of the jungle and turns into a kind of savage."

Obviously, a former sailor like Conrad would never run short of tales.

Holmes offered a quick smile. "You're always probing," he said, "but all the same I'm glad to hear you've dropped the Greenwich story."

"Not 'dropped'," Conrad corrected. "Just postponed. A friend who chooses to remain anonymous supplied me with details last February. He and I talked about the politics of the affair; but even so, I haven't given the plot much thought. At least, not recently. I claim no knowledge of anarchists—if, indeed, anarchists are the responsible party."

(It was only years later that Ford Madox Ford, the writer whose farmhouse Conrad hoped to sublet, would identify himself as the "friend" responsible for kindling Conrad's interest in the Bomb Outrage. The two authors had speculated about the event the first time they'd met while visiting the Cranes at Ravensbrook.)

Holmes' mien seemed to have taken on the darkness of the skies. He looked more sombre than usual. He made only veiled reference to our meeting with Milverton, but he conveyed the implied danger to Conrad nonetheless.

"Last month," Holmes said, "I gained information regarding what might have been the actual cause of the Greenwich explosion; and if I'm correct, the person behind it would stop at nothing to prevent someone—especially a talented writer like yourself—from reawakening public interest in the matter. Such an effort on your part could put your life in jeopardy."

A roll of thunder echoed from the direction of the sea. Behind us, the group were hastily finishing their meals.

"It is true, Mr. Holmes," Joseph Conrad said, "that when I first heard about the event, I was specifically interested in the nature of the explosion. Or rather, who had caused it. Originally, I even thought I might try my hand at writing a crime story about the deed and, following my own investigation, reveal in my novel the true perpetrator. A crime story is, after all, the perfect vehicle for depicting the most orderly of chronologies. And yet, the police managed to smother the details of the actual affair so nicely—and so predictably—that I concluded there were not enough reliable facts upon which to construct the kind of logical plot I hoped to devise."

Turning, he addressed his next comment to me. "As the recorder of Mr. Holmes' cases, Dr. Watson, I'm sure you know what I mean. In fact, I blame my intentions on *your* successes in reporting true crime."

I'm afraid I blushed in response.

"Yet I had to remind myself that unlike you, Doctor, I do not write history. I find that in fiction I can delve deeper than history can. It is ironic, is it not? Fiction produces the greater truth. If I do complete a novel about the Greenwich plot, I shall present the account as purely imaginative."

Holmes smiled in appreciation of the irony. I remained content to bask in the glow of the author's compliments.

"Besides," Conrad said with what one could almost describe as a twinkle in his eye, "I have always been much more interested in writing about what goes on *beneath* the surface. What interests me is not the political spectacle, but rather the personal drama. As I say, I know little about anarchists. But what I do know informs me that, like the rest of us, their lives are full of malice and pettiness. Indeed, should I ever write such a novel, I wouldn't bother to use the names of the actual people involved. To me, the names wouldn't matter. *Au contraire.* I would do nothing less than envision all the characters in the drama as *imbéciles.*"

Allowing himself a chuckle, Conrad pulled at his beard. "You see, gentlemen," he said, "I am more interested in depicting emotional *reactions* to events than their specific *causes*. It is the twisted psychology of human nature that intrigues me—and the hypocritical moralizing that people invent to explain it all. No, in my mind, the identities of the actual perpetrators of the bomb outrage will remain an impenetrable mystery. That, I have slowly come to realize, is the way I prefer it—at least, from an artistic perspective."

"Very good thinking indeed, Mr. Conrad," said I. Only after the words were out did I realize the fatuousness of giving my encouragement to an author of Conrad's status.

"It is ambiguity, gentlemen," Conrad said with a smile, "that allows me to invent my own journeys into the darkness of people's souls. A *factual* account would have to deal with the political certainties found in the *real* world, while I am more interested in the murky secrets people hide within themselves. It should please you to know, Holmes, if I ever do write a novel about the affair at Greenwich, that in order to cloud the issue even more, I'll not only alter names but I'll even change the date of the explosion. Truly, the reality of the actual occurrence is of no consequence to me."

"Excellent," Sherlock Holmes observed.

At the time of this—our first--meeting, I had read none of Conrad's works, yet it was obvious to me that the man maintained a dark perspective on the world. It was not *my* perspective; but as a fellow-writer, I could certainly appreciate the consistency in his outlook.

"Do you know, gentlemen," Conrad said with a wry smile, "that after all was said and done at Greenwich—the anarchist diatribes, the police condemnations, the threats of changing the world—the stone wall of the observatory where the device exploded never showed as much as the faintest crack?"

Just then, as if to punctuate Conrad's final point, the long expected rain finally began to pelt the countryside. Amidst shrieks and cries, the diners behind us rose quickly, attempting to cover themselves.

"Get Mr. Frederic inside the house!" Agatha implored.

"No!" Cora countered, checking the dark sky. "It won't be any drier in there—especially not against what's coming. There are holes in the roof, doors that don't close, and upstairs-rooms that don't have any floors. With the baby and Mr. Frederic's condition, it'll be safer for everybody to return home."

"But we haven't seen the inside yet," Mrs. Conrad protested.

"I know, Jess," said Cora, gazing up once more at the angry heavens. "But there'll be plenty of next-times."

The rain thundered down as we retraced our steps like a stage play produced in reverse: With a frowning Mr. Mack shaking his head in the wings and the glistening horses stomping on the wet grounds, the Conrads carried their baby back into their carriage while Kate Lyon and Agatha bundled Harold Frederic inside theirs. At the same time, Cora helped Adoni collect the food, the drink, and the soggy blanket. She would return with him to Ravensbrook. It fell to Holmes and me, followed by a now wet and aptly named Sponge, to carry the wicker basket through the slippery mud to Cora's awaiting carriage.

With the interior of Brede Place left unseen, Holmes and I climbed into our open trap. With only the hats upon our heads to protect us from the summer downpour, we hoped for a quick return to the train station in Hastings. From there, in the luxury of a dry railway compartment, we would wend our way back to London.

Chapter Seven

I saw a man pursuing the horizon;
Round and round they sped.
I was disturbed at this;
I accosted the man.
"It is futile," I said,
You can never—"
"You lie," he cried,
And ran on.
--Stephen Crane

From the start of September, the intertwined narratives of the summer of '98 maintained their contrapuntal progress like a well-played fugue. Harold Frederic continued to decline; Cora Crane continued to seek her husband *manqué*, and Charles Augustus Milverton—it seemed safe to say—continued to extort money from his numerous victims.

In the middle of the month, Dr. Playfair sent a letter to inform Holmes and me of the drama surrounding Frederic's deteriorating condition.

"Mrs. Athalie Mills, the faith-healer," I read aloud to Holmes, *"continues to monitor the patient. Because she claims her proximity is not required to improve his condition, however, she no longer puts in her daily appearances. Thanks to what she calls the "absent treatment", she asserts that, like others of her ilk, she can project her curative will from her home just as effectively as she can from Frederic's bedside. "What need is there for me to be here?" she asks poor Mrs. Frederic. And yet strange to say, gentlemen—the 'absent treatment' seems absent itself whenever it is time for Mrs.*

Mills to be paid her weekly salary. For that august transaction, she arrives at Homefield in person.

"In all fairness to the medical staff, I must remind you (as one who has attended Harold Frederic myself) that the man is a most mercurial patient. If his doctors annoy him with too many rules and regulations, he turns to the Christian Scientist to minister to him (with the encouragement of the maid Agatha); when Mrs. Mills becomes too stringent in her admonitions, he reverts to the suggestions of his doctors. And yet no matter how contradictory the instructions or how varying his ailments, Frederic continues to work. Every week he still manages to cable his columns back to New York—albeit with a great deal of help from his assistant, Jack Stokes."

Dr. Playfair closed his letter with the usual flourishes, but it was to his final comment regarding Jack Stokes that Holmes referred. "I should imagine," said Holmes, "that Frederic's writings were being completed with a great deal more involvement on Stokes' part than the word *'help'* implies."

Holmes and I also received periodic messages from Cora Crane regarding the search for her husband. Consistency was not Cora's strong suit; and though she had written to many of his friends and associates, she confessed that in her on-going hunt, she had for some reason not yet communicated with Secretary Alger or General Wade—the very authorities Mycroft had had indicated would be most effective in locating the man. As we'd heard from Cora before, such letters would be forthcoming.

In the meantime, no one could offer anything new regarding the whereabouts of Crane himself. Thanks to the letter that Kate Lyon had given us, Holmes concluded that Crane must have still been living in Mary Horan's boarding house in Havana. But since we couldn't be certain, we didn't convey this information to Cora. As a consequence of receiving no news, the poor woman grew quite adept at inventing explanations and believing what others had simply surmised.

Foremost among such theories was Cora's concern that her Stevie had found another woman. No less a world traveller than the sophisticated Joseph Conrad had confessed to Cora that he feared such might be the case. A related theory had Crane returning to Washington and taking up with a former lady friend. Lily Brandon Munroe, the handsome woman in question, was still living in the American capital and, by most accounts, embroiled in an unhappy marriage. Questions of Crane's health plagued Cora as well. Might he be suffering from malaria or typhoid or Spanish flu or even— God forbid—syphilis? Had he grown addicted to some sort of drug? Had he become a "morphine eater"?

Nor were such concerns about her Stevie the only source of Cora's torment. Money remained a major issue. Conrad, upon whom she'd come to depend, had told her that magazine publisher William Blackwood had begun wondering aloud about ever seeing the money Crane owed him. With Conrad's future work as security, it had been Blackwood, who in April, had financed Crane's trip to Cuba. Moreover, when Cora had written to Paul Reynolds, Crane's agent in New York, about the money the writer must certainly have been paid for the nineteen dispatches her Stevie had sent to Pulitzer, Reynolds did not reply.

Also unknown to Cora was the incriminating knowledge Holmes and I possessed—that Milverton's threats of blackmail must still have been hanging over Crane's head. One was forced to assume that Reynolds hadn't sent Cora the money from Pulitzer because the agent had forwarded it directly to Crane to pay off Milverton rather than to relieve the writer's impoverished wife.

* * *

Holmes and I remained observers of these various narratives until the mid-morning of Thursday, the twenty-second of September. On that date Mrs. Hudson ushered a frantic Cora Crane into our sitting room, and our roles as spectators began to change.

I had just finished perusing *The Times*, and Holmes was editing his files.

"Mrs. Cora Crane," we heard our landlady announce, and both of us rose to greet her.

Even Mrs. Hudson, who was inured to the strangest of characters calling on Holmes, looked askance at Cora's dishevelled appearance. I know I did. Her golden hair was wild; and her shapeless blue smock, wrinkled plaid skirt and American-style cowboy boots suggested that she'd made no attempt to render her clothing suitable for a trip to town.

No sooner had Mrs. Hudson closed the door than Cora plunged her hand into the leather Gladstone she was carrying, fumbled about, and produced a wrinkled newspaper cutting.

"Here!" she said, pushing the small piece of paper at Holmes. "It was sent to me by a writer in Havana."

Holmes perused the short text, arched an eyebrow, and passed the article to me.

Headlined "Cuban Gossip," the story from the Florida *Times-Union,* had been written in Havana some two weeks earlier, bearing the date of 7 September. "Stephen Crane Missing" the title read. The story alleged that once the peace was agreed to, the author, having recently left Cuba, had disguised himself as a tobacco buyer in order to re-enter Havana, and then simply disappeared.

"I'm in great distress, Mr. Holmes," Cora said, pulling at various strands of her hair. "In fact, I'm going crazy! I didn't know Stevie had ever left Cuba—let alone returned and disappeared. Right now I'm thinking of trying to raise enough money to go out there and find him myself. I want to hear from his own lips exactly what he's planning to do. Is he going to come back to me? Is he going to leave me? Is he actually counting on *me* to pay *his* bills? You know, if he won't even say whether he's returning to Ravensbrook, I'll just give up the goldarned place."

"Pray, sit down, Mrs. Crane," Holmes said calmly as he guided her to the settee. "As I'm sure you're well aware, simply because a story appears in print doesn't mean it's true."

Catching my eye, he nodded in the direction of the crystal brandy decanter. I poured each of us a glass while he returned the newspaper cutting to her and settled into his armchair.

Cora Crane took a long pull. Holmes proceeded more judiciously while I seated myself and sampled the brandy as well.

Soon Cora was breathing more deeply and regaining control. "I have no idea what Stevie is up to," she said at last, "I mean, if he really *is* in Cuba like the paper says. I've heard that the Spanish are still rounding up news correspondents despite the peace treaty, and who knows what will happen to them? I need money, Mr. Holmes. I've already told you that, if our creditors think Stevie and I aren't legally married and he doesn't come back to me, I can be stuck for *all* of it. I shudder to think what'd happen then. If only Donnie would give me that divorce . . . ."

"Speaking of the money, Mrs. Crane," Holmes cut in, "I think it's time that we offer you more information than we've previously shared."

Cora's green eyes widened; and she laid her free hand on her chest.

I surmised that Holmes was about to acquaint her with the Milverton story. As nervous as she appeared, I wondered if he was making the right decision. Then again, if any woman could tolerate hearing such news, I assumed it would have to be an independent spirit like the woman drinking the brandy before us.

Cora Crane peered suspiciously at one of us, then the other, and then back again. Undaunted, she finished her drink and held out the glass for more.

I obliged her while Holmes filled his long-stemmed cherry-wood pipe with shag.

"I shall first give you some new facts," he said to her as he lit up, "and then I propose to offer some practical advice not only to get you results, but also, I confess, to keep you occupied. You will go mad if you continue to focus on your problems instead of your solutions."

"Go on," she said, still wary.

Holmes exhaled a cloud of smoke. Then he proceeded to summarize for Cora Crane the letter from her husband to Harold Frederic, the letter Kate Lyon had given us at Homefield. In such a manner, Cora first learned not only of Milverton's blackmail scheme, but also of Crane's secret relationship with another man. Her green eyes grew wide again as Holmes described Crane's plans for writing *Flowers of Asphalt,* the novel about his companion called David.

"Let me emphasize," Holmes stated in the clearest of terms, "that the exact nature of the connection between this man and your husband is never described in the letter we read."

At first, I feared Cora might faint upon hearing the sort of decadent book it would be—no doubt full of inverts, Uranians, homosexuals, transvestites, and who knew what else? But she quickly regained her composure, dismissing with the wave of her hand the news about Crane's relationship, returning instead to her concerns about paying the creditors.

"What does this book have to do with my finances?" she demanded. 'You said you were going to tell me about the money."

"Whatever the exact connection between the two men," Holmes said, "Crane has attempted to keep the friendship hidden. To such an end, he has paid a substantial amount of money to a notorious blackmailer here in London, one Charles Augustus Milverton, who has threatened to make public the clandestine relationship."

Cora knit her usually unlined brow as the economic implications of Crane's activities began to dawn on her.

"I daresay," continued Holmes, "that a major cause of the lack of funds during your husband's time in Cuba has been this diversion of his literary advances."

Cora set her teeth. "Do you mean to say that Stevie has been sending this goldarned Milverton all of the money he should have been sending to *me*?"

Holmes emitted another cloud of smoke before answering. "Such appears to be the case. Instead of forwarding his earnings to you, your husband has been paying off the rogue who has threatened to make public what some might consider an inappropriate association."

Cora took another sip of her brandy. And then another. She narrowed her eyes as if she could already envision the vengeance she planned to mete out.

Holmes saw it as well. "Now, Mrs. Crane," he cautioned, "I must emphasize again that we don't know the entire story. We're drawing conclusions from only a single letter and whatever else Harold Frederic could recall."

"Harold," she spat out. "He didn't tell me anything about this—nor did my 'good friend' Kate. And *I'm* caring for their children at Ravensbrook this very minute—all of them!—Helen, Héloïse, Barry. Well, Adoni and Mathilde—and Mrs. Burke, the governess—are."

I had feared that the news of her husband's reputedly decadent lifestyle would devastate Cora Crane. Yet much to my astonishment, it was Holmes' revelation of the blackmailing scheme and the consequent money it had cost her that seemed of more concern to Cora than any unnatural behaviours of her Stevie.

"Appreciate the fact, Mrs. Crane," Holmes reminded her, "that Harold Frederic was attempting to be faithful to your husband. And we really don't know how much, if anything, Kate Lyon knew about any of this. For that matter, she too may have been honouring Crane's request to keep you from discovering this part of his life."

"Oh bugger!" said Cora. "They should all know me well enough by now. *You* know about my past, gentlemen. I encountered all kinds of men at the Hotel de Dream back in Jacksonville—strong, weak, shy, violent, fearful—all kinds! Romantics. Inverts too. Nothing my Stevie could be up to would ever get me to leave him. And even if what he did shocked me a little, it certainly wouldn't shock me enough to give away all our money the way *he* did—just to make somebody shut up about it."

"Quite open-minded of you, really," I said with genuine respect. To some degree, I envied her freedom, her ability to embrace all types of human behaviour. I knew I couldn't—nor was I sure I wanted to.

As if reading my mind, Holmes asked no one in particular, "Was it not the *philosophe* Montaigne who observed, 'We call barbarous anything that is contrary to our own practices'? Mrs. Crane calls for tolerance, Watson. Mrs. Crane is worth heeding."

Holmes' praise evoked a slight smile from Cora. It was the first glimpse of optimism she'd revealed during her visit.

"I keep a journal, gentlemen," Cora announced. "Here's what I wrote not too long ago." She reached into the Gladstone and, withdrawing a small red notebook, flipped through it until she found the passage she was looking for. Smoothing down the pages, she proceeded to read: "'Oh, happy is the human being who has never yet had occasion to cry: I cannot bear it! But we bear things.'"

Cora Crane was quite the woman. Whatever Stephen had got himself into, who could not respect her resilient nature?

"I love my Stevie, Mr. Holmes," said she, "but that money he's been throwing away still bothers me. What can we do about this rat Milverton?"

"So far, very little. He keeps himself above the law—or, at least, beyond it. We must bide our time until one of his victims speaks out."

"Or shoots him!" she declared with a glint in her eye. "I'm a pretty good shot, you know." Pointing her right forefinger at me as if it were a gun, she pretended to fire. Then she pursed her lips, still moist from the brandy, and blew the imaginary smoke in my direction.

"Now, now, Mrs. Crane," I cautioned, "you're not in America anymore."

"No," she said with a rueful smile, "I guess not."

There is something to be said about American women. The fight in Cora's nature put me in mind of another young lady from one of Holmes' cases, Miss Hatty Doran of San Francisco. In calling her "a tomboy, with a strong nature, wild and free, unfettered by any sort of tradition," the unhappy but noble bachelor, Lord St. Simon, might just as easily have been describing Cora Crane.

While I pondered cowgirls and frontier justice, Sherlock Holmes tamped the shag in his pipe, inhaled, and proceeded to blow out a belt of blue smoke.

As if to calm herself, Cora turned away from the cloud. Perhaps she was seeking new strength. By the time she faced my friend again, she had refocused her argument. "You said something earlier about giving me advice, Mr. Holmes. Just what do you recommend a lady should do with a missing invert of a husband and no money to pay off the creditors?"

"I take it that you have still not got round to writing Mr. Hay or Secretary Alger."

Cora looked down, the sad little girl. "No," she admitted shamefacedly. "But there's been so much to do with the Frederics' children and all."

"No excuse needed," Holmes said with greater tolerance than he usually displayed. Indeed, he might have been speaking to a school child. "But let's compose the letter to Hay right now, shall we?"

Wide-eyed, Cora nodded eagerly.

Holmes settled her at his desk and placed a sheet of paper on front of her.

"Write what I tell you," he commanded, handing her a pen. "You can make adjustments to suit the other recipients."

With Cora scribbling along as fast as she could, Holmes slowly dictated the following: "Dear Sir: Knowing you to be a personal friend of my husband, Stephen Crane—I appeal to you to use your influence to find him. News has reached me that he is missing from Havana. He went there for the New York *Journal,* as you doubtless know, and was watched, I understand, by the Spanish police. He was stopping quietly at Hotel Pasaje—and disappeared about 8 September. I am beset with grief and anxiety. I hope you will

Daniel D. Victor

personally ask the President to instruct the American Commission to demand Mr. Crane from the Havana police."

The scratch of Cora's pen dominated our otherwise silent room as in her small, tight handwriting she finished up all that Holmes had recited.

"Feel free to change anything with which you're uncomfortable," Holmes said, "but now that you have the pattern, you can write similar letters to Secretary of War Alger and General Wade. And it wouldn't be a bad idea to follow each of your own letters with a cable."

"Mycroft said the same," I put in.

"Oh, I will Mr. Holmes," promised Cora. "And I'll write to Stevie's agent in America again. I'm going to tell him I'm distressed and in great need of money. Then I'll write to Stevie's brother William, the lawyer. That should be something—he doesn't even know Stevie's married!"

"Good for you!" I beamed.

"You've lit a fire under me now, Mr. Holmes. I'm glad I came." She sprang up, popped the letter into her Gladstone and made for the door. Then she ran back to both of us, hugged us individually, and—just like that—ran down the seventeen stairs to the street.

Sherlock Holmes stood as rigid following Cora's assault as he had during it. But then, as if to collect himself, he strode to the window, drew back the curtain, and stared out at Baker Street.

"Mrs. Crane's hailing a hansom," he noted. "For Victoria, no doubt."

"Honestly, Holmes," said I, "with a wife as charming as Cora, how could her husband get himself into so compromising a situation that Milverton could gain a foothold?"

Holmes continued staring out the window as he spoke. One must be careful when making such judgements," said he with careful deliberation. "When Harold Frederic visited us in July, old fellow, I believe that he said much the same about Mrs. Crane as you—except that what you termed 'charming', he called 'wild'. Who amongst us could not be compromised if all one's secret actions—let alone one's secret thoughts—were made available to the blackmailer whose very lifeblood thrives on his victim's desire for concealment? Ah, Watson, is it not our own secret *penchants*, our own addictions, that do us in? In our righteousness, we condemn extortion; but if we were honest, should we not recognize in our contempt for the blackmailer the simple act of preserving our own secret selves?"

Holmes let the curtain drop.

I couldn't argue with him, especially not with memories of my own behaviour floating through my brain. My late wife Mary, for instance—I never made her privy to the two pounds per week from my wound pension that I used to spend on the horses. If an ordinary person like me sought to conceal his foibles from his wife to avoid ill will, to what extent might others with far greater indiscretions go to preserve the sanctity of their own surreptitious lives?

Holmes had a way of putting matters into perspective. One could do worse than follow the implications of his wisdom.

* * *

A warm September transformed into a chilly October, and the game of musical chairs played by the doctors and healers of Harold Frederic became more urgent. Such was the news delivered by Dr. Playfair.

On a cold Thursday morning during the first week of October, I was sitting alone with my copy of *The Times*, a fire burning in the grate, when Mrs. Hudson brought up the doctor's card. I knew that Holmes, who was off buying more of his infernal shag, would miss receiving a first-hand report from Homefield, but I could do no less than welcome our visitor and invite him to give me the most recent information.

"Hope you don't mind my dropping in like this, Watson," said he, "but since I was here in London, I thought I might deliver the latest news of Mr. Frederic in person."

My offer of tea dismissed any worries he had of disturbing me. He turned down the repast, however, explaining that he had patients waiting for him in Croydon.

"And yet," he said, "I wanted to share with you my growing concern. You see, I attended Mr. Frederic yesterday; and frankly I was shocked by his deterioration. Not *surprised*, mind you, but shocked. Mr. Frederic continues to play his doctors against his faith healer. One of them was so put off by Frederic's denial of the gravity of his condition that, to prove how afflicted Frederic really is, the doctor told the male nurse to let Frederic get out of bed on his own and fall to the floor. Which is precisely what happened. What's more, he's getting worse. Mrs. Frederic told me that next week she's calling back the London specialist, Ludwig Freyberger."

"Freyberger," I repeated. "I've heard the name."

"Physician to Friedrich Engels, don't you know?"

"The man who collaborated with Karl Marx."

"Exactly. What's more, from what I've been told, Freyberger said that he'd return to Homefield only if special terms were agreed to in advance."

"'Special terms'?"

"Freyberger wants proof in writing that he will not be held responsible for Frederic's death."

"Which, I presume, runs afoul of Mrs. Mills."

"Precisely. Frederic tolerates her because she lets him smoke and drink. And the sad fact is that from my own observations—and I believe Freyberger has said much the same—the poor man could actually be recuperating this very moment if he followed his doctors' recommendations instead of Mrs. Mills'. Mind you, he'll never be back to full strength. But as weak as he's been, he's still writing—though probably with the help of his secretary."

"I shouldn't wonder that at this point Mr. Stokes is doing *all* of the writing."

Playfair nodded. "One last detail you might find interesting. Do you remember that parlour maid out at Homefield, the cute young thing who was always encouraging Mr. Frederic to throw out the doctors and listen to Mrs. Mills?"

"Agatha," I said, recalling the attractive young woman quite clearly.

"Well, apparently, one of the doctors had enough of all that encouragement. And he probably wanted to spare Dr. Freyberger having to hear it as well. He told Mrs. Frederic that if the maid were not let go, then *he* would leave. So two days ago, Mrs. Frederic sacked the girl—without any explanation, don't you know? Stranger still, there seemed no resistance on the maid's part; she simply gathered her belongings and left. No need to worry about her, however. It seems that she immediately got a new position in some grand house in Hampstead."

With that final titbit, a complacent Dr. Playfair could now devote his full attention to the fireplace. Retreating to the bearskin hearthrug, he stood with his back to the flames and soaked up the heat.

Only when he felt sufficiently warm did he extend his hand and prepare to depart. I thanked him for the news, but I must confess that he left me much to ponder concerning the ever-bleaker prognosis for Harold Frederic. The re-appearance of the specialist Freyberger offered some degree of hope; and yet, in the end, there seemed little that anyone else could do to save the man.

From Frederic's "legal" family—his wife Grace and their four children—neither Sherlock Holmes nor I heard anything at all.

Chapter Eight

A learned man came to me once.
He said, "I know the way—come."
And I was overjoyed at this.
Together we hastened.
Soon, too soon, were we
Where my eyes were useless,
And I knew not the ways of my feet.
I clung to the hand of my friend;
But at last he cried: "I am lost."
                    –Stephen Crane

Harold Frederic, noted American pressman and novelist, died at 12:30 Wednesday morning, 19 October 1898.

During that same week, Cora Crane was writing for money to Paul Reynolds, her husband's literary agent in America; and the Frederics' parlour maid, Agatha Rimes, was getting adjusted to working for her new employer in Hampstead.

While the news of Frederic's death was unsettling, it came as no shock to Holmes or me. With the irresponsible care Frederic had received, what other outcome could one expect? Yet Holmes could still not forgive himself for providing Frederic's name to Milverton at our meeting in Hampstead the previous July. Without such information, the blackmailer—the man whom both of us considered the catalyst for Frederic's seizure—would never have known of the writer's connection to Stephen Crane. To be sure, Frederic himself had threatened to confront Milverton on his own, but in the end he had not. More's the pity. Had he done so, the catastrophic results would doubtlessly have been the same; but at least the decision would have been Frederic's alone, and my friend would have been able to avoid berating himself.

Nor did we expect the controversy attaching itself to Frederic's care to end any time soon. The Coroner's Inquest was scheduled to take place two days later, and Holmes fully expected charges to result from the proceedings.

"You can't be serious, Holmes," said I. "Kate Lyon may be accused of making questionable decisions, but you don't really expect criminal complaints to arise from Frederic's death?"

"Yes, I do, Watson. It's always difficult to predict how a jury will turn, but there should be some reckoning for the incompetent care given to the man."

"Ignorance, surely, but criminal behaviour?"

"As usual, Watson, it depends on how the details are presented. Even the most hard-boiled of facts are subject to interpretation—which is why I have no intention of attending the inquest."

"Something new might turn up," I suggested.

"I know all I need to know about the travesty," he said with finality. "My appearance will add nothing to the proceedings."

I could not be dissuaded from going, however; medical science itself would be on trial.

* * *

Friday morning dawned grey and damp, a gentle but persistent cold drizzle washing all outdoors. Wrapped tightly in my overcoat and armed with an umbrella, I caught the early-morning train to Kenley. The inquest for the Croydon District of Surrey was being held in a spacious room of the

Kenley town hall. Arriving a half-hour before the proceedings were to begin, I was fortunate to find a seat. The death of a prominent figure generally draws large numbers of curious spectators. In Harold Frederic's case, so august and prolific a man of letters had he been that in addition to the public, not only were countless representatives of newspapers and magazines in England and America anticipated, but also a significant number of distinguished figures from the world of *belles lettres.*

The central issue for all concerned was how much a factor in Frederic's death had been Kate Lyon's faith in Christian Science, an issue—as I had occasion to mention earlier—not solely limited to the Frederic affair. A good part of the interest surrounding Frederic's demise had been stimulated by news of other recent deaths related to faith-healing, deaths dredged up by various periodicals, deaths reported by some of the same pressmen who'd now come to expand upon the demise of their former colleague. If left to the press, the inquest concerning the end of Harold Frederic would ultimately question the very foundation of Christian Science. At the very least, such debates sold newspapers.

Amongst the crowd already seated were familiar faces. In the front row, I noted a scowling Kate Lyon in a dark wool coat. Presumably, the defiant-looking woman sitting next to her and wrapped in expensive furs was Athalie Mills. I exchanged glances with Cora Crane, who'd come to offer moral support to Kate Lyon; and I nodded at Dr. Playfair, who sat amongst his bearded medical brothers, any number of whom might be called upon to give evidence. I also recognized the raven curls of Agatha Rimes, the Frederics' former maid. Occupying a chair at the rear, she glanced nervously round the hall.

The enquiry officially began when the coroner, a dark-suited man called W.P. Morrison, took his seat behind the oak table at the front of the room. Stroking his Van Dyke, he read aloud the statement of Ruth Frederic, Harold's adult daughter from the "legal" family, who had actually gone to Homefield to help care for the stricken man. She identified the body in question as that of her father Harold Frederic, the late London correspondent of *The New York Times*.

From then on, a parade of witnesses spoke in defence of Frederic's faith in the power of positive thought. Knowing I would be reporting all this to Holmes, I attempted to pay close attention to the testimony—closer attention, it turned out, than the repetitive nonsense deserved. Hour after tedious hour, friends and acquaintances, including Mrs. Mills, explained how personal optimism influenced Frederic's belief in improving one's condition on earth.

Inwardly, I had to laugh. With the proof, as they say, in the pudding, given the man's dramatic death, the countless anecdotes supporting Frederic's spiritual treatment seemed quite feeble indeed. Nonetheless, such benighted testimony went on for four days.

To his credit, the coroner cautioned the jury not to forget a life 'thrown away merely for the want of proper medical care'. Nonetheless, given the massive testimony supporting the tenets of Christian Science, I fully expected a lengthy debate followed by a verdict exonerating the two women. In short, I assumed that no one would be held responsible for the death of Harold Frederic.

In retrospect, I should have been more wary. Holmes had warned how difficult it is to predict which way a jury will turn. Not only did this group re-enter the hall after only thirty-five minutes of deliberation, but they also confounded my thinking. There was no support of faith-healing. On the contrary, Kate Lyon and Athalie Mills were charged with manslaughter. Loud gasps of shock accompanied the ruling, but these were almost immediately undermined by a sprinkle of spirited applause. The two women stood open-mouthed as a police inspector directed four uniformed officers to arrest them.

"Don't worry about your kids, Kate!" Cora Crane shouted as the stupefied ladies were marched out of the chamber.

It all had transpired so shockingly fast that many of the spectator sat lingering in the hall. Blank faces and dazed expressions were the rule, and it took a half-hour for some people to realize that the legal theatrics had ended and that there was nothing left to do but don their macs, ready their umbrellas, and make their ways to the exit. In just such a fashion, I too was preparing to leave when I suddenly discovered that for me, at least, the drama had not yet run its course.

Within the dispersing crowd, I caught a glimpse of Agatha Rimes in deep conversation with a mysterious figure. Too far away to be overheard, she was speaking confidentially to a short, plump gentleman wearing a shaggy astrakhan coat— a coat much too fine for the companion of a simple parlour maid. His back was turned to me, and yet there was something familiar about his appearance. What the two were conversing about I could only guess, but certainly something was afoot. When he turned my way, I was convinced of it.

The image of the man and Agatha huddling together stuck with me during the chilling journey back to Baker Street. The cold weather had persisted throughout the inquest; and as soon as I returned to our rooms, I immediately took up a position upon the hearthrug in front of the grate.

Attired in his comfortable dressing gown, Sherlock Holmes occupied his favourite armchair, long legs stretched out before him in the direction of the fire. However blasé he appeared, I knew he eagerly awaited my announcement of the verdict.

Before engaging in conversation, however, I wanted to warm up. Besides, recalling how cryptically Holmes so often explained his own thought processes, I confess that I secretly enjoyed delaying the news—especially the meeting between Agatha Rimes and the man in the astrakhan coat. The delay seemed to fill me with power.

Holmes fiddled his long fingers, fingers he generally kept steepled and still.

Only after I felt suitably heated did I finally reveal to him the judgement of the inquest.

My friend raised his eyebrows. "Manslaughter," he mused, now rubbing his hands together in the most delicious manner. "So the jury showed some spine after all." He reached for the brandy decanter and poured us both a glass.

"To British justice!" he proclaimed, and we both drank.

Cradling the rounded glass in his upturned palm, Holmes returned to his armchair.

"It was a remarkably swift decision," said I, "especially in light of the countless hours of testimony in support of faith-healing. The faith-healer herself got the chance to speak."

"Tell me what she had to say; you can forget about the others."

"Mrs. Mills attempted to defend herself, of course. She presented the argument that, even though Mr. Frederic thought himself to be ill, she trusted that she could influence him to believe in himself and in God and that, as a result, he could improve his condition without recourse to medical doctors."

"And she came to this conclusion *after* examining Mr. Frederic?"

"But she didn't examine him."

Holmes snorted in derision. "I didn't expect that she had, Watson. And yet without an examination, she still adhered to the faith-healer's creed that, if their patients maintain enough trust in themselves and God, they actually can defeat death."

"Yes, she as much as said that Death is merely a belief."

"'Hah!" Holmes ejaculated.

I made no reply. For not a small time I'd been working my legs to increase the circulation.

"Oh, do sit down, Watson," said Holmes, pointing at my chair, "and allow the elixir to warm you up."

With a shrug, I exchanged hearth for chair. "By the way, Holmes," said I, reaching for the wool afghan, "I was pleased to note that, throughout the proceedings, the so-called 'Mrs. Frederic' was actually referred to as 'Kate Lyon'."

"A legal necessity, I'm afraid."

"A moral truth totally consistent with my own point of view," I countered, though not feeling all that victorious. "Do you know, Holmes," I found myself admitting, "that the more Miss Lyon revealed of her steadfastness, the more respect I developed for the lady—however much I might disagree with her views."

"I'm not surprised. She seemed a forthright person when we met her at Homefield."

"Indeed. At the inquest, she stood firm in the face of the damaging testimony of Doctors Freyberger, Boyd, Brown, Murray, and Playfair. They all corroborated Miss Lyon's vacillation between the benefits of medical science and the power of spiritual healing, not to mention her coping with the mood shifts of Harold Frederic. She stood firm even when all the doctors agreed that Mr. Frederic's life could have been spared and his mobility greatly improved had their advice been followed rather than that of Mrs. Mills. Miss Lyon did confess a reluctant dependence on the various doctors she'd called in, but throughout the inquest she maintained her committed devotion to Mrs. Mills in particular and to the Christian Science faith in general."

"And after the ruling?"

"She and Mrs. Mills were arrested by Inspector Cameron."

"Good fellow, Cameron. No nonsense."

"The proceedings ended when the police took the women away."

"An excellent account, Watson," Holmes clapped. "Well done. Save for the unfortunate death of Harold Frederic, I suppose one can find sardonic humour in the outrageous ideas expressed in this tawdry story." He sampled some more of the brandy and then asked: "Any other news of note?"

At last—my opportunity to present the most tantalizing detail. "One last bit remains," said I, holding up my glass as if in appreciation of the brandy rather than for the information I was about to reveal. "It's more than a bit, actually, but I was saving for last what I imagine will intrigue you the most."

"You have my full attention, Watson," Holmes said as he placed his glass on the side table, the briefest of smiles passing his lips.

"You'll remember that I mentioned to you that the Frederics' former maid was in attendance."

"Agatha Rimes," Holmes nodded, "who found new employment in Hampstead."

"Well, Holmes," said I slowly, enjoying the suspense I hoped I was creating, "I believe I can tell you the identity of her new employer."

Sherlock Holmes leaned forward, grey eyes aglow.

"Imagine my astonishment at the inquest when I observed Agatha Rimes exiting before me on the arm of a short, stout man in an expensive astrakhan coat."

"I have my suspicions. And yet I invite you, my dear Watson, to reveal the name of this gentleman of mystery to whom the distinctive overcoat belonged."

"At first, I couldn't see the man's face. Then, for whatever the reason, he turned round."

"And?"

"It was none other than Charles Augustus Milverton."

"Milverton!" Holmes exclaimed, "Just as I'd expected. Bravo, Watson!" he said, clapping his hands again. His appreciation was all the reward I needed to convince me of the importance of my revelation.

* * *

Many years have passed since I first described Holmes' pursuit of Agatha Rimes, but even today I haven't overcome my distaste for his ungentlemanly behaviour. The report I'd delivered connecting the young woman to Charles Milverton had set Holmes in motion, and he began ingratiating himself into her life between the end of the inquest and the start of the trial—that is, during the first week of November 1898 (not in early January of the next year as I had falsely reported in the original narrative).

Although Holmes couldn't state with certainty what he hoped to learn from the attractive parlour maid, he remained convinced that whatever he could glean from her regarding the inner-workings of Appledore Towers would one day prove most valuable.

To initiate his caddish duplicity, Holmes assumed the guise of an accomplished plumber called Escott. Dressed in the rough clothing of a working man, he secured a goatee with spirit gum, applied dark make-up for a swarthy look, popped a clay pipe between his lips, and—for good measure—assumed a swagger to represent Escott's supposed business successes.

In the beginning, all seemed well and good to me; disguises are part of the detective's tools. He gained her attention one afternoon when she left the house and he asked if there were any water taps or pipes inside that needed attention. It didn't matter that she had no answer because the innocent question offered Holmes his *entré*.

As far as I was concerned, however, he travelled a good measure beyond the limits of fair play when, posing as Escott, he actually began courting the maid. Even now, though I realize how badly he needed to gain a working knowledge of the ways of Appledore Towers, I am convinced that there had to have been other means of acquiring such information besides toying with the affections of a young woman. Holmes' rationalization—that another suitor stood in the wings ready to pursue the raven-haired beauty as soon as Escott had left the scene—did little to assuage my sense of indignation.

* * *

"You cannot imagine, Watson, how much the woman likes to talk." So Sherlock Holmes greeted me in the late afternoon following his first social engagement with Agatha Rimes. He had taken her to tea.

"One can assume then," said I disapprovingly, "that she didn't see through your disguise. After all, she encountered you as your regular self at Homefield."

"No," said my friend with a proud grin. "I fooled her completely. She appreciated having someone with whom to converse—that is to say, someone willing to listen. She has much to relate: about her mum who lives in Salisbury, the other young man who fancies her, the clothing she hopes to buy, what she wants to do with her hair, and the holiday she longs for in Paris."

"I'm sure you were quite helpful in all those matters," said I sarcastically.

"As a matter of fact, I was. I told her to let her hair down, old fellow. It's quite attractive, you know." Motioning me to follow, he added, "I shall tell you more, Watson, but let's allow Mr. Escott to disappear for the present."

We climbed the stairs to his bedchamber so he could remove his disguise. "I had no choice but to encourage her," said he, removing his clay pipe from a pocket and placing it in the pipe rack on a mantel already full of smoking detritus. "After all, as they say in the theatre, an actor must always maintain his character. But I did point out that new clothing and fancy hair styles and trips to France cost a lot of money, which—as I had intended—led her to discuss her employment, first with the Frederics, then with Milverton."

"Did she tell you why she'd left the Frederics without so much as a peep of protest?"

"For money," he crowed, rubbing his thumb and forefinger together in the time-honoured tradition. "For Milverton's money. Why else?"

Stared at by the portraits of infamous criminals Holmes had mounted on his walls, I sat on the coverlet at the edge of the bed and watched the unfamiliar workman metamorphose into my old friend.

Holmes had seated himself beneath the mirror at his make-up table. Before him were a yellowed sponge, a boar-bristle hairbrush, a pair of white towels and a large pitcher and bowl. He tossed his brown wig to the side and began peeling the false whiskers from his chin.

"A little water clears us of Escott the plumber, eh, Watson?" said he, filling the bowl, then washing his face with the sponge.

Holmes blotted his cheeks with one of the towels, observed his handiwork in the glass, and spoke to my reflection. "Money, Watson," said he. "Money is the lifeblood that connects Milverton to his agents round the world."

"All the way to Crane in Cuba," said I to his own mirror image.

"Just so. 'Money talks,' is the operative expression. It gets people to do things they might ordinarily not do, and Milverton is a master at ferreting them out. He once paid a footman seven hundred pounds for a written note of two lines that would incriminate the servant's master. Seven hundred pounds, Watson! Think of it!"

He let me digest the sum while he employed the second towel to wipe away whatever spirit gum, make-up, or grime still remained. Then he fixed me in the mirror again.

"When Milverton first met Aggie at Fredric's home in Croydon—have I told you she likes me to call her 'Aggie'?—he immediately recognized another pawn that money could manipulate. Her expressive eyes flashed with pride when she told me how he'd pulled her aside that day at Homefield. He asked her if she wanted to make an extra pound or two by keeping him informed as to what was going on in the Frederic household. He offered her more if she could filch any personal documents."

"Like those letters sent by Crane, I should imagine."

"Precisely."

"Aggie never saw any letters," said Holmes, now easing the brush from front to back through his dark hair. "But that didn't stop her reports to Milverton about Frederic's deteriorating condition. And once Milverton learned that Frederic was so amenable to faith-healing, he paid Aggie more money to encourage Kate Lyon's aversion to doctors. In fact, it was Aggie who left Mrs. Mills' card for Kate Lyon to find."

"But why?"

"Harold Frederic committed the grievous error of challenging Charles Milverton. That was enough. Milverton has always sought to make life as miserable as possible for anyone who stands in his way. His success depends on people fearing his cold-hearted reputation. The more stories he can produce about the 'ill-luck' that befalls those who cross him, the less likely it is that any prospective victim will attempt to call his bluff."

"Like Sir Nigel Chandless and the Greenwich bombing."

"Exactly, Watson. Milverton brought up the Greenwich affair to let us know the consequences of crossing him, and he must have hoped that we'd convey those threats to Crane and Frederic as well."

It all made sense in a twisted sort of way. "And your immediate future with Miss Rimes?" I couldn't keep from asking Holmes' reflection in the mirror.

"She intends to testify at the trial and will gain even more money. Portraying a noble woman like Kate Lyon as a passionate but misguided fool broadens the scope of Milverton's power. He's quite an evil man, Watson, ensnaring the innocent along with his victims—all the while quite unconcerned with the damage he leaves behind."

On a lesser scale, Holmes might have been describing his own actions with the maid. Ignoring such thoughts, I asked, "And the women's trial?"

"There's nothing we can do. Both Miss Lyon and Mrs. Mills have committed the crime with which they are charged. I don't believe Aggie can make them look any worse. In fact, there's so much feeling against the two that a skilled barrister might even evoke enough sympathy to gain a jury's compassion. But for that we'll have to wait until the trial reaches its conclusion."

"Of course."

"In the meantime, old fellow," said Holmes with a final glance at the mirror, "allow me to change my clothes. Then, perhaps, the two of us might enjoy a fine piece of beef at Simpson's. I never realized how courting develops the appetite."

Allowing this last observation to hover in the air, he untied the red bandanna from his neck and replaced his workman's clothes in the cupboard he maintained for disguises.

I returned to the sitting room to put on my coat, and a few minutes later, Sherlock Holmes and I were seated in a hansom rattling down Baker Street on our way to a sumptuous meal.

* * *

Kate Lyon and Athalie Mills were released on bail shortly after their arrest at the inquest, and opening arguments for the actual trial were scheduled to begin on Monday, 21 November. While preparations were being made for the legal proceedings, other significant developments related to figures in the drama were also taking place.

Earlier in the month, Cora Crane had come to see us. It was a blustery fall morning, the kind of chilly day in November that presaged a cold winter. Holmes and I were concluding a late breakfast when Mrs. Hudson announced her arrival. We both rose; but while I donned my jacket, Holmes remained in his mouse-coloured dressing gown.

"Come in, Mrs. Crane," said he, "and join us by the fire."

In a thick wool coat and small round hat, she appeared much more in control of herself than she had on her previous visit. "Thank you just the same," Cora replied, "but I'll only be stopping for a moment or two."

She remained standing, and so did we.

"Any word of your husband?" I asked.

Cora shook her head. "Only those infernal rumours about Stevie that other writers feel compelled to bring across the Atlantic to me: He's ill again. He tried to kill himself. He's reigniting an old passion. He's romancing a general's wife old enough to be his grandmother."

Mrs. Crane took a deep breath. "Though you may not believe it," she said, reaching into her reticule and producing a folded sheet of paper, "I didn't come here today to talk about Stevie. In fact, I'm soliciting funds."

My word! Had her tenuous financial state reduced her to begging? I wondered.

Holmes arched his eyebrows as we both examined the page she'd given him.

I was wrong about Cora Crane. The paper proved to be a printed letter on behalf of Harold Frederic's "legal" wife Grace, asking friends and other interested parties for money to help the widow with her living expenses in raising the Frederics' four children.

"I didn't realize you were a supporter of the *other* Mrs. Frederic," said I with genuine surprise.

Cora shook her head. "Hardly. I offer this letter by way of illustration. From what I've been told, it's going to be distributed to a number of important people and a number of daily newspapers. While I have no objection to money being sought for Grace, I do believe that Kate deserves the same opportunity Grace does to receive such funds—actually, a *greater* need what with the legal obstacles Kate has to confront."

Holmes passed the circular to me, and I read it more closely. Signing the appeal for Mrs. Grace Frederic on behalf of the other prominent citizens on the fund-raising committee was the editor of the *Daily Chronicle*, W.J. Fisher, the self-proclaimed "Honorary Secretary and Treasurer" of the fund. Amongst the other members were such noted figures as Henry James, J.M. Barrie, Arthur Wing Pinero, James McNeill Whistler, Henry Irving, and George Bernard Shaw. I was surprised to find the name of Arthur Conan Doyle also included, having heard nothing from my literary agent about his involvement in Mrs. Frederic's defence. In addition, the circular contained a list of influential individuals who, like those on the committee, were slated to receive the letter directly. This list included such distinguished writers as H.G. Wells, George Gissing, Rudyard Kipling, and Joseph Conrad.

"Kate thinks asking for money is in shocking taste," said Cora, "but with the help of Mr. Stokes, who'd worked for Harold, I plan to form a committee on behalf of the *other* family. I'm going to write to each and every name on this appeal for Grace and make equally known to them the plight of Kate and her three children. Whatever you think of the arrangement, Kate's family is Harold's just as much as Grace's is. And all those moneybags ought to know it."

"You are a true friend indeed, Mrs. Crane," Holmes observed. "And just where is *your* Mrs. Frederic right now?"

"At Ravensbrook. First, I took in her children; and then, right after she was released on bail, I gathered her in as well." There was no sense of bravura in her voice or of her earlier resentments. Cora spoke as if inviting an additional four people to stay in one's home—even when one is constantly short of funds—is the expected model of behaviour. "Kate's been with me—and, more importantly, with her children—ever since the inquest."

For a few awkward moments, the three of us stood in silence near the door to the hallway. As the mantel clock ticked off the seconds, Cora held her green eyes on Holmes and then on me. There seemed no end to the hushed tension. At last, it dawned on me. Cora was waiting for us to offer donations. Flushed with the relief of figuring out what was expected, I was only too happy to oblige. Putting down the handbill, I reached into the breast pocket of my coat where I kept my wallet and fumbled with however many bills my fingers could gather. In the end, to avoid further embarrassment, I simply handed over to her all of the money I could find. I didn't bother to count it, and I don't know to this day whether I gave her too much or too little.

Holmes watched the proceeding with his jaw tightly locked. Not only had he no intention of contributing, but I'm certain that he also disapproved of the cavalier manner in which I was giving my funds away—no matter how altruistic the cause. As uncomfortable as I felt, I cannot deny that he had the moral right to judge. My inability to oversee money went back many years. In fact, I'd been too free a spender since the early 80's when I first arrived in London. Indeed, it was the necessity for inexpensive diggings that led me to sharing Baker Street rooms with Holmes from the very start.

Nor did the passage of time alleviate my propensity to spend unwisely—especially, as I have noted elsewhere, in conjunction with horses and the turf. So much discipline did I lack that I eventually asked Holmes to serve as my financial overseer, and he agreed to accept responsibility for my chequebook. Today, however, not even his stern mien could undermine the appeal of Cora Crane.

Thanking me for my generosity, she placed the money in her reticule and then resumed staring at Holmes. He simply returned her look.

The two of them stood there exchanging defiant glares for what seemed like minutes but in reality had been mere seconds.

"You're a hard man, Mr. Holmes," Cora Crane said at last.

"Mrs. Crane, my contributions come in the line of my work. Perhaps, I will have the opportunity to reveal to you my own form of charity."

Mrs. Crane pursed her lips quizzically. "I certainly hope so," she said coldly and departed our lodgings.

Holmes picked up his violin case, stalked up to his room, closed the door and began scratching out some angry tune on his fiddle.

* * *

The crime with which Kate Lyon and Athalie Mills had been charged sounded dreadful—officially, it was "being concerned together in feloniously killing and slaying one Harold Frederic, by neglecting to supply him with proper medical attendance". The wintry weather mirrored the icy days of the inquest, but more than just the cold evoked my sense of *déjà vu* at the trial. Besides the fact that I attended and Holmes did not, the testimony at the Croydon Police Court covered the same ground as had the preliminary enquiry. Once more, we heard of the struggle between faith-healing and modern medicine. Once more, we heard of Frederic's sporadic distaste for physicians who forbade smoking and drinking. Once more, we heard of Kate Lyon's encouragement of Mrs. Mills and her Christian Science philosophy.

Both defendants sat silently in the dock listening to the familiar testimony. Mrs. Mills, draped in a stylish and expensive long winter coat with fur collar, displayed the latest in *haute couture*. Atop her head rested an eye-catching flat-brimmed, ornately-dressed black hat. Kate Lyon was clad in a traditional dark frock with puffed up shoulders. Her wire-rimmed glasses rendered her stern and insensitive, seemingly older than her years. Aloof and impassive, they remained an unsympathetic pair.

Fortunately, the trial was not without its brief moments of humour. Cora Crane testified to prosecutor Horace Avory that, yes, it was she who had telegraphed Dr. Freyberger about Frederic's worsening condition.

"Harold looked weaker every time I saw him," said she.

Avory then took Cora back in time to the carriage accident the Cranes had suffered the year before on their way to Homefield, the same accident Cora had told Holmes and me about on the drive to Ravensbrook. Just how, Avory wanted to know, had the faith-healing Miss Lyon treated the practical challenge of Stephen Crane's broken nose?

"She thought," replied Cora, her expression deadpan.

The courtroom exploded into laughter like a music-hall audience.

All the while, Cora remained seated quietly in the witness chair, hands clasped in her lap, wide-set green eyes innocently scanning the room. Buttoned to the chin in a burgundy dress with a collar of delicate lace, she appeared the picture of innocence. Knowing her feisty nature as I did, however, I'm certain she'd intended just the sort of robust reaction she got.

Adoni Ptolemy was next. The Greek butler reported how he'd been asked by the Cranes to provide additional care for Mr. Frederic at Homefield—how he'd helped get Mr. Frederic dressed and undressed, how he'd enabled him to get into bed and out, how he'd taken him for walks and drives, and how—with the defendants' expressed approval—he'd driven the ill Mr. Frederic to hotels where the writer had enjoyed smoking cigars, eating beef, and drinking champagne or ale.

"And do you even know the difference between champagne and ale?" Kate Lyon's barrister asked.

"Oh, yes, sir," Adoni replied eagerly. "I learn the difference when I give him these drinks in his own house."

A crescendo of laughter accompanied Adoni back to his seat.

Such light-hearted displays during the trial were rare, however, and not much else stood out. Not a whit of new evidence presented itself after more than two weeks of testimony, and no one seemed particularly surprised when the charges against Kate Lyon and Athalie Mills were dismissed. Citing a lack of evidence as well as a citizen's right to his own beliefs, the court released the pair. In the end, the judge concluded, it would seem that Miss Lyon was simply acting out of her affection for the unfortunate victim; she was not—or so the court decreed—either intentionally or otherwise trying to kill the man.

Our involvement with Kate Lyon and Harold Frederic may have ended with the conclusion of the trial, but our dealings with Charles Milverton, which had begun with Frederic's visit to Baker Street, clearly had not. On more than a few occasions following my day in court, I returned to our rooms only to find Holmes's armchair empty. Hours later, he would appear in the clothes of Escott the plumber. As Holmes' continuing relationship with Agatha made clear, whatever stratagem he was cultivating to undermine the foul business centred in Hampstead, he was obviously going to great lengths to make certain that his plan had a solid foundation.

Chapter Nine

Behold, the grave of a wicked man,
And near it, a stern spirit.
There came a drooping maid with violets
But the spirit grasped her arm.
"No flowers for him," he said.
The maid wept.
"Ah, I loved him."
But the spirit, grim and frowning:
"No flowers for him."
Now, this is it—
If the spirit was just,
Why did the maid weep?
—Stephen Crane

Sherlock Holmes answered the clang of the bell himself. With Christmas but a few days away, the two of us had been downstairs sampling Mrs. Hudson's holiday cakes. The open outer door revealed a messenger boy in the retreating light of a late Tuesday afternoon. He was standing in the snow wearing a great blue coat, black scarf, red mittens, and military-style hat.

Snow flurries were constantly visiting the city in the winter of '98. More's the pity if your occupation forced you outside in such bitter weather. The poor boy faced just such a challenge. A telegram to be delivered to us that afternoon had driven him into the chilled air; and not all his protective clothing could prevent him from shivering on our front steps as he nobly completed his charge.

Holmes was reaching into the pocket of his dressing gown to offer the lad a gratuity when Mrs. Hudson spoke up.

"You, boy," she said. "I won't be letting you go out in that cold again without some sort of fortification."

"Ma'am?" he questioned.

Mrs. Hudson had already prepared a large mug of spiced hot cider, which she now offered the lad.

"Much obliged, I'm sure," he said, removing his mittens and wrapping his fingers round the warm glass.

"Happy Christmas," we all wished one another. Then Holmes, after giving the boy a coin, joined me, and we proceeded up the stairs to examine the message the boy had brought us.

It was from Cora Crane, and it proved to be as warming as the cider: *At last!* [it read] *Stephen cabled me that he got the money. He and a friend are returning to England.*

Holmes and I knew nothing about the financial arrangements that must have precipitated Crane's return, and Cora mentioned no date for his arrival. Yet I could picture the joy in her flushed face, the twinkle in her green eyes, the smile on her red lips as she consumed the news. Perhaps her golden hair was already down as she danced through the rooms at Ravensbrook. She would spread the word to Adoni and Mrs. Ruedy, to Sponge and the other dogs—to anyone who'd listen. Her Stevie was coming home—what a marvellous Christmas gift his arrival would be!

Later, Cora offered us the details: how Jack Stokes, who'd earlier worked for Harold Frederic, had sent Crane enough money—furnished from an advance by Crane's English agent Heinemann—to book passage for England via New York. How Stokes had cleverly not sent the money directly to Crane but to General Wade in Havana, so the general himself could hand Crane the sum and the writer couldn't deny receiving it. How Crane and his "friend", presumably the man named David, had sailed from Cuba on the steamship *Vigiliancia* that arrived in New York on 21

November—the same day that the trial of Kate Lyon and Athalie Mills had begun in Croydon. How, after suggesting to others that it might be simpler for Cora to return to the States, Crane had spent more than a month in Manhattan with his friend before booking their tickets to England.

New York had been the last straw for Crane. The local authorities had neither forgot nor forgiven his defence in court a few years before of a mistakenly arrested prostitute called Dora Clark. "The policeman flatly lied," was how Crane had put it. Slapped with so blatant a charge, the constabulary would have liked nothing better than to beat the tar out of Crane with their billys and run him out of town. Instead, he left of his own accord.

* * *

The following afternoon Mrs. Hudson announced another messenger.

"Mr. Adoni Ptolemy," she said with the stiff upper lip she reserved for all persons of foreign origin who she didn't believe were royalty.

Adoni marched into our sitting room, snapped to attention, and after removing the old Trilby from his head, bowed quickly. The young servant made no offer to remove his long coat, so we presumed his stay would be short.

"Message for doctor," he said in his broken English and handed me a small, pale-blue envelope with my name written across the front in a tiny, cribbed script.

"From Mrs. Crane, I deduce," quipped Holmes.

"Obviously. Who else but Mrs. Crane would be sending Adoni with a message?"

"I assume that it is addressed to you alone since my last meeting with the woman—when she tried to solicit funds for Kate Lyon—was less than cordial."

Unmoved by our banter, Adoni patted his thick black hair and inched towards the fire. "Mrs. Crane," he said, "she tell me, wait for answer."

The missive from Cora Crane required no lens for one to discern the word "Ravensbrook" inked in large, bold letters at the top of the pale-blue vellum. Clearly, she had ordered the stationery for her future residence prematurely; Crane hadn't even seen the house. The handwritten word covered the printed identification: *Brede Place, Brede, Northiam, Sussex, England.*

I perused the letter (the underscorings are hers) and then handed the page to Holmes.

Dear John [it began boldly],

As you might expect, it's been difficult to remain too happy about Stevie's homecoming without knowing precisely when he plans to appear. What's more, following a night's sleep, I also began to wonder about Stevie's "friend." Just who is he? I know that you've told me about Stevie's letter to Harold in which the man is mentioned. Is there anything you remember that could shed more light on him? I was hoping there might be.

In the spirit of the season, I convey to you (and to Mr. Holmes) my sincere Christmas greetings. Joseph Conrad, whom you talked with at Brede, sent me the following message, which I happily forward: 'May the Xmas be a season of joy indeed and the new year a year of peace to you. Amen.' I should also add that he wished he could hear good news regarding Stevie's arrival date. So do I! Not knowing exactly when Stevie's set to return, I haven't begun telling people that he's coming back—except for you and Mr.

Holmes. (Conrad somehow learned the news through his literary connections.) To tell the truth, when anybody asks, I just say, "Stevie's still in Havana." If I can spare the time, maybe I'll go meet the low-down skunk when he finally does get here.
Sincerely,
Cora Crane

"'Hell hath no fury like a woman scorned', eh, Holmes?"

"No, indeed, Watson, and yet I think that young Mr. Crane has given the lady ample reason for being vexed. He presents the perfect model of the prodigal son who shows no inclination to return to his home."

While the two of us bantered, Adoni, hat in hand, swayed nervously from one foot to the other on the hearthrug before the fire. It was clear we should compose an answer to Cora's letter as quickly as possible. With the wave of a hand, Holmes motioned the servant to a seat and offered him a cigar from the coalscuttle.

Adoni shrugged. He took the cigar and, after removing his coat, which he hung on a nearby hook, sat down, and struck a match. Soon, with his hat in his lap, he was enjoying the smooth draw of the panatela.

Once able to relax, however, he began casting his servant's eyes round our sitting room, absorbing all the chaos in which he'd found himself—the clutter of books, the mix of test tubes and newspaper cuttings, the knife pinning the mail to the mantelpiece, the bullet holes in the wall. I knew exactly what he was thinking, and his frown simply substantiated the point.

But we had a letter to compose. I looked at Holmes to see whose undertaking it was to be.

"*You're* the writer, Watson," he charged. "And let us not forget that the note you're answering was addressed to you."

I sighed, pulled out the chair at my desk and eased myself into it. "Shall we be blunt and tell her what we know?" I asked.

Holmes smiled mysteriously, and I picked up my pen and wrote the following:

My Dear Mrs. Crane,

Sherlock Holmes and I are greatly pleased to hear that the Christmas season will be enriched by the return of your husband.

As you correctly note and as we have previously informed you, Holmes and I have read the letter from Mr. Crane to Mr. Frederic, but even so we can't be certain that the man in that correspondence is identical to the person who will be accompanying your husband to England.

If he is indeed the same individual, he is called David. He and your husband were sharing a room in the Gran Hotel Pasaje in Havana, but seemed about to move to a less costly boarding house. As you are aware, your husband was planning to write a book about David to be called (rather oddly, it seems to me) "Flowers of Asphalt." And that's really all the information that the letter contained about the man. As Holmes has already told you, while the precise nature of the relationship between the two went unstated, it has nonetheless been the cause of your husband's payments to a notorious blackmailer here in London who feeds off the misadventures of others. Whether Mr. Crane deserves being considered such a victim is something that only he can explain to you.

I feel confident in repeating our general knowledge of so delicate a matter because I have come to trust your own self-description as a woman accepting of all sorts of human behaviours. What's more, we can be strengthened by the reassuring news that in the end your husband is coming home.

Please alert us of the exact time and place of Stephen's arrival in England; for should you be so inclined, Mr. Holmes and I would readily consent to accompanying you to meet his ship. In that manner, we might provide you with the moral support that, with all due modesty, I believe your letter to me is seeking.

In the meantime, we share the warm sentiments of Mr. Conrad in wishing you a season of joy and peace.

Sincerely,

John H. Watson

I blotted the ink and handed the letter to Holmes.

"No 'doctor' in your title, old fellow? Simply 'John'?"

Feeling the colour come to my cheeks, I attempted to fend him off. "If that's your only comment, Holmes, I accept your approval." I then folded the letter and placed it in an envelope, which I sealed and addressed with Mrs. Crane's name.

Despite the hodgepodge surrounding him, Adoni seemed to have settled in nicely with cigar and hearth; but once he saw that we were ready to send him on his way, he tossed the cigar into the fire, donned his coat and hat, and placed the letter inside a breast pocket.

Bowing as he had done upon his arrival, he said, "Thank you." Then, scanning the room once again, he added, "I help you clean."

Holmes shook his head and ushered the man down the stairs.

* * *

In the afternoon following Boxing Day, we received a letter by post from Cora Crane. In it she reported that she'd heard through Cooks Tourism (not from Crane himself) that her husband was set to sail for England aboard the *S.S. Manitou* on Saturday, 31 December. The steamship was scheduled to arrive at Gravesend on Wednesday, 11 January 1899.

"Because I'm afraid of how I might react [she wrote], *I was hoping you two gentlemen, <u>as you so graciously offered,</u> would indeed be kind enough to travel with me to Gravesend. The <u>Manitou</u> departed two years to the day after Stevie set out for Cuba on the <u>Commodore</u>, and we all know how disastrous that trip turned out to be. The coincidence makes me very nervous. I will stay in London on the night of <u>Jan 10th</u>, so that, if it suits you, we can travel to Gravesend together the next morning as we did when you joined me for our trip to Brede Place."*

Naturally, Holmes and I accepted her proposition.

* * *

The second day of the new year, a brisk Monday morning, found me about to exit our rooms in Baker Street just as Holmes, dressed in the togs of Escott the plumber, was returning. While he had been advancing his relationship with Agatha in Hampstead, I'd been preparing to attend the patients of Dr. Verner in Kensington.

"You're leaving, Watson?" asked Holmes. Once again, it was strange to hear the voice of my friend issuing from the dark, bearded face of the plumber.

"Dr. Verner and his wife are spending the holiday weekend in Paris," I explained, "and I agreed to act as *locum tenens*. I'll be gone all morning."

A furrow creased Holmes' swarthy brow. "'Tis a pity," he replied. "At 11:00 I'm expecting a visit from the Lady Eva Brackwell. I was hoping you'd be able to join us."

Holmes didn't need to identify the young woman in question. Anyone who followed the activities of the finer social classes in the public prints knew of the charming young *débutante* set to marry the Earl of Dovercourt in a few weeks' time. How I regretted not being present! Not only was I losing the chance to meet a renowned beauty; but more importantly, from a historian's point of view, I was missing the opportunity to hear a case from the start. But patients were waiting for me, and so I was forced to bid Holmes a quick *au revoir*.

When I returned to Baker Street not long past noon, Holmes was pacing the floor of our sitting room, a sure sign that he was agitated about a case. He was still clad in the coat he'd worn for his client; and as I sat in the armchair before the fire, I had to watch him march to and fro before he felt ready to describe his consultation with Lady Eva.

Sherlock Holmes frequently undertook different cases at the same time, and so I naturally had regarded his reference to the *débutante* as a fresh assignment, an unfamiliar challenge that would send him off in new directions—certainly in directions leading away from the chaos that surrounded Stephen Crane. Yet before Holmes had progressed much beyond describing the anguish exhibited by the morning's visitor, I discovered that the problem confronting Holmes' latest client was nothing new at all.

"The situation may be different, Watson," announced Holmes, halting his perambulation, "but you may rest assured that Lady Eva faces the same plague as Stephen Crane. Charles Milverton has paid a gentleman's valet quite handsomely for some imprudent correspondence that she had sent a country squire not so long ago."

"'Imprudent'?"

Holmes smiled and took to pacing again. "That's how Lady Eva described the letters. 'Not damning,' she said, but 'imprudent' enough so that the Earl, her *fiancé*, could easily misunderstand them. She has assured me that, although the letters are in no way compromising, they would, if seen by the Earl, be enough to cause significant distress."

"Surely not sufficient enough to terminate a wedding with so charming a creature?"

"Sadly, sufficient enough—or so she believes." Once more Holmes halted his marching about, this time to add, "Which is why Milverton paid so much for the letters in the first place."

"Just as he paid your friend Agatha."

"Worse, actually. The Earl has employed this valet much longer than the Frederics had employed Aggie. But loyalty be damned; Milverton's offer was generous enough to turn the valet's head."

Holmes settled into the armchair near the hearth and reached for his briar.

"And if Milverton fails to get the money," I asked, "what do you reckon he'll do with the letters?"

"I'm sure that you can guess, old fellow," said Holmes, lighting his pipe. "Milverton has told Lady Eva that, if he is not remunerated by Saturday, the fourteenth of this month, he will show the letters to the Earl in plenty of time for the wedding on the eighteenth to be cancelled. From Milverton's mistreatment of Frederic and his hiring of Aggie—not to mention his connection to the Greenwich incident—we can believe his threats are anything but idle."

"The swine," was all I could think of saying.

Holmes nodded grimly. "Lady Eva has commissioned me to negotiate with the man. I'm authorized to offer him two thousand pounds in exchange for the correspondence."

"Two thousand pounds!" I exclaimed. "That's quite a handsome sum."

"Higher than that I am not allowed to go; she doesn't have the funds. Yet as certain as there's tobacco in this briar, Watson, that two thousand will not be enough."

"Does the transaction require another trip to Hampstead?"

"No, Milverton will come to me if he thinks there is money to be collected. I have already sent him a telegram to meet here tomorrow afternoon."

Holmes exhaled a cloud of blue smoke and placed the briar in the ash-stand. He proceeded to exchange his coat for his dressing gown and disappeared into his bedroom. A few minutes later, I heard the cry of his violin from beyond the closed door. With the strains of Mendelssohn as background, I unfolded the copy of *The Times* that was lying on the settee, sat down, and began to read. For the rest of the day, neither one of us discussed the odious actions of Charles Augustus Milverton that lately seemed to be haunting our every mood.

* * *

The villain of the piece made his appearance at Baker Street at a time of his own choosing, two days after the date Holmes had suggested. The weather remained cold, and Milverton wore the same astrakhan coat in which I'd seen him during the Frederic inquest.

I have previously furnished the details of that volatile evening in our sitting room. Suffice it to say that, as expected, Milverton would not accept Lady Eva's generous offer for the return of her correspondence. Instead, as Holmes had predicted, the villain demanded more—seven thousand pounds!—to prevent the letters from being given to the Earl of

Dovercourt; and no matter how much Holmes argued, my friend could not budge Milverton from his position.

Readers will recall that so enraged with Milverton's recalcitrance did Holmes become that he actually attempted to wrestle the letters away from the man. But Milverton was not such easy prey. A quick dash to the side of the room, the display of a revolver inside his coat, and the smug boast not to be foolish enough to have those letters on his person in the first place—all cooled Holmes' temper. Besides, had Milverton actually shot Holmes in the course of such an assault, the blackmailer was quite right about having the law of self-defence on his side.

"You have till Saturday, the fourteenth," Milverton spat out before leaving. "And not a day after." The slam of the door preceded his heavy footfalls as he stormed down the stairs.

"Ten days from now," I remarked, "not a lot of time."

"No, Watson. Especially with so much still left to do. The fourteenth is just three days after we go to Gravesend to meet Stephen Crane. It's all quite macabre."

"Surely, there must be some way to stop the rogue."

"That's my goal, Watson!" Holmes shouted. And he banged his fist down on the table. After a beat, he added more calmly, "It's time to activate the plan I've been cultivating for weeks. I hope it will not only save Lady Brackwell, but—if all goes well— actually put an end to Milverton's entire wretched enterprise."

* * *

I saw little of Sherlock Holmes for the next few days although I couldn't help noting the increased appearances of "Escott the plumber", who entered and exited our Baker Street rooms at odd hours of the night or early morning.

Although my original account of the Milverton case recorded the heights—or depths, depending on one's point of view—that Holmes was willing to reach in his pursuit of justice, his involvement with Agatha Rimes continued to nettle. I shared his desire to bring the evil Milverton to justice, but nonetheless I was particularly incensed when he proclaimed, "I have asked Aggie to marry me."

"Really, Holmes!" I cried in disbelief. "Have you no shame?"

He dismissed my question with the wave of his hand. "What's more, the young lady has accepted my proposal."

I could only shake my head.

"When one fights a war, Watson, one cannot stop to question every minor distraction along the way."

"And since when in British history has a proposal of marriage been regarded a 'minor distraction'? Are the dreams of Agatha Rimes any less important than the future of the Lady Eva Brackwell?"

"Don't be foolish," Holmes chastised. "This is a practical matter. From my time with Agatha, I have gained much intimate knowledge."

"I'm sure you have. Let's just hope that while you're compiling your precious data, the young woman in question has not reported your matrimonial plans to anyone who might take exception to them."

"One must keep one's eye on the ultimate target, Watson. Agatha Rimes is a most important resource. In arranging our trysts, I have not only learned such details as Milverton's sleeping habits and the time his beastly dog roams the grounds, but I have also established enough trust in the young woman that she is willing to keep the gate and house open for me—a trust, I might add, that I have already put to the test. As you shall come to realize, these details will play key roles in my plan to help Lady Eva preserve her marriage date as well as to liberate Stephen Crane from the clutches of the villain who has been tormenting him. If I succeed, a parlour maid's sentiments are a small price to pay."

What could I say? Without more facts, I merely shrugged at his explanation. Once again, Holmes was asking me to trust him. And once again, I saw no connection between his behaviour and the intended outcome. I'm certain it was clear to Holmes, but I myself couldn't fathom how the facts he'd gained in implementing his dalliances would help bring about the grand destruction of Charles Milverton and his sinister network of decadence.

Part III

The Baron of Brede Place

Daniel D. Victor

Chapter Ten

A naked woman and a dead dwarf;
Wealth and indifference.
Poor dwarf!
Reigning with foolish kings
And dying mid bells and wine
Ending with a desperate comic palaver
While before thee and after thee
Endures the eternal clown—
—the eternal clown—
A naked woman.
                    –Stephen Crane

Gravesend. Does the word not ring like a death knell?

In fact, the town at the end of the sea-reach of the Thames is a prosperous commercial centre with trains pulsing to and from the heart of London on the most frequent of schedules; yet in Baker Street, on a storm-ridden Sunday evening peppered with lightning and thunder, it required little imagination to link the dead to such a name.

Most travellers disembark at Gravesend for one of two reasons: to avoid the chaos of London a good twenty miles west or to reach some location more convenient to the outlying port. At the time Stephen Crane had booked his passage, he had every reason to believe he would be travelling back to Ravensbrook, which is nearer to Gravesend than to central London. Disembarking at the former made good sense. But then he hadn't reckoned on Cora's bringing along two gents from the city, who would have to return to the same Charing Cross Station where they'd begun their trip. Logic had pointed Crane to the port at the eastern end of the Thames, so to Gravesend we too would have to go.

Whatever fantasies the name might conjure, I cannot utter "Gravesend" without recalling the very real encounter Holmes and I had experienced there some ten years earlier that almost cost us our lives. As I described in *The Sign of Four*, we had been racing up the Thames in a river-police launch in pursuit of the *Aurora,* the boat containing the murderous Jonathan Small. With Gravesend as the destination, we coursed the river at breakneck speed closing the gap between us with each tick of the clock. The chase itself was frightening enough; but all the while that Holmes and I were on deck during the mad ride, we had to remain ever mindful of the blowpipe and poisonous darts of Tonga, the bloodthirsty dwarf from the Andaman Islands. ("Fire if he raises his hand," Holmes had warned me, our pistols at the ready.) Small's goal was to reach the anchored *Esmeralda,* a vessel on which he hoped to make an escape to the Brazils. Fortunately, we thwarted the plan, but not before Holmes had shot and killed the grotesque little savage. After the case was resolved, Holmes carefully mounted Tonga's one remaining dart in the T-section of his case-book, a keen reminder of the horrific danger to which we'd been exposed. The recollection still makes me shudder.

"Gravesend does indeed evoke distressing memories, old fellow," my friend suddenly proclaimed.

It never failed to surprise me when Holmes seemed to read my mind. Not that his intrusions into my private thoughts were unexpected after so many years together; but each time he revealed his deductive prowess, I was amazed anew. On that particular night, I had mentioned nothing to him about my morbid associations with Gravesend. So far as Holmes could see, I was simply sitting by the fire catching up on my reading. For my part, I assumed that Holmes, staring off into space as he was, had in all probability been reflecting on some pertinent issue—like the fate of Lady Eva or the demise of Charles Milverton. After all, time was running out.

Instead, Sherlock Holmes was invading my thoughts.

"But—but, Holmes," I sputtered, "I have said nothing all evening about Gravesend. How could you possibly know that I was thinking of the place just now?"

"Elementary, my dear chap. On the table beside you lies your Bradshaw, open approximately one-fifth of the way— quite consistent with the railway times for our upcoming trip to a destination beginning with the letter "G". And your quick glance from behind the newspaper toward my files lettered "T," followed by a tremble or two, could only mean that you were recalling our narrow escape from Tonga's poisoned darts."

I smiled sheepishly.

"Let us hope," he added, "that this trip to Gravesend will be less harrowing than our last."

Yes, I thought as thunder rumbled in the distance, *let us hope.*

A lightning flash illuminated a window as Holmes removed a folded telegram from the pocket of his dressing gown.

"Although I'm preoccupied with Milverton," he said, "I too must confess my worries about Crane and Gravesend."

"Why? He'll be there on Wednesday."

"I hope so, Watson—for Mrs. Crane's sake. But, you see, old fellow, I took the liberty of telegraphing Mycroft to compliment him on his success in rousting Crane out of hiding. When I told him Crane was expected here on a steamer from New York arriving Wednesday, he sent back this message."

Holmes handed me the following telegram: *Hope Crane's arrival plans are correct. But American informant*

Daniel D. Victor

confirms Crane wired Willis Hawkins for $50 from Jacksonville on 28 December.

"Jacksonville," explained Holmes, "is a great distance from New York, where Crane's ship to England was to depart three days later. Worse—at least, from Mrs. Crane's point of view—Jacksonville's only a short boat trip from Havana."

"But what possible reason would Crane have to risk missing his ship? Or to return to Cuba, for that matter? And who is Willis Hawkins?"

"What reasons indeed, Watson? Perhaps we shall find the answers to those questions on Wednesday—if our man actually appears."

I threw the telegram down on the table. If Crane didn't show up—if, say, he had found some thing or some one more attractive in Cuba—I could only imagine how broken-hearted Cora would feel—let alone what vengeance she'd wreak upon him should she ever lay eyes on Crane again.

* * *

On Wednesday morning, the day of our trip to Gravesend, the rain fell intermittently, but the cold remained steady—near freezing.

Similar to our excursion to Brede Place, Holmes and I hired a hansom and retrieved Mrs. Crane at the Queen Anne's Mansions. We then drove to Charing Cross where we caught an eastbound morning train. Today, however, we were prepared for the dreary weather—Holmes in his cape and ear-flapped travelling cap; I, in woollen scarf, derby and mac; Mrs. Crane, in a man's broad-shouldered khaki overcoat and white, broad-brimmed, western-style cowboy hat.

"They belong to Stevie," she said of her unique attire.

For a little more than an hour, the train rattled through the ever-increasing rain, generally paralleling the

152

Thames into Kent instead of following the line further south towards Hastings, as the railway had done on our journey to Brede Place. Water washed against the windows as the railway skirted churning tidal creeks as it cut across sodden farmland and forest. In the final few minutes, we traversed a wasteland of malodorous marshes that announced the outskirts of Gravesend. Between foul pools of standing water and the twisted remains of washed-out vegetation, the train clattered over the various points that marked the entrance to the railway yard.

Soon enough, we found ourselves trudging along the boardwalk beneath a sluicing rain and into a bitter ocean-wind. Pulling down hard on our hats, we bent into the pelting sheets of water and pushed ourselves to the wooden docks. No comfort there. Like bullets spat from a Gatling gun, rain continued to pummel the decking. With breakers slamming into the support pylons again and again, the very floorboards trembled as if preparing to splinter. The same churning waters rocked the flotilla of ships anchored near the middle of the river. A haphazard collection of wood sticks, their masts jerked madly back and forth.

No matter how treacherous the weather, it is at Gravesend that embarking and disembarking passengers, as well as the river pilots who guide the vessels along the Thames, alight from the ships that are outward bound or join the vessels that need to be navigated up the river to London itself. On a stormy day like this one, the tenders ferrying the hearty souls leaving the larger crafts were in for a rough go. Wave after wave marched in on them from the great roiling sea, white caps grasping for the sky, then tumbling back, only to rise again.

In point of fact, by the time we had arrived at Gravesend, the *S.S. Manitou* had already moored. Though it lay a good distance from the dock, even in the downpour it was clearly visible. Too large to be tossed about, she rolled to and fro in rhythm with the powerful waves, a stately steamer with her one smokestack angled rearward to give a sense of speed.

At first, Cora feared we might have missed Crane's arrival, but a port official wrapped in an oilskin waterproof checked his watch and told us it was still close to an hour before passengers would be able to disembark. To avoid the wind and rain, Holmes suggested cover in the nearest *café*.

"As long as I can keep an eye on the ship that's carrying my dear one," Cora said.

With the rain tattooing the roof above our heads in a near-empty, tea room, we seated ourselves at a table that offered a large window onto the port. From such a vantage we could enjoy hot drinks and still watch the *Manitou* as it bucked the waves. Holmes and I settled for a pot of tea between us; Mrs. Crane, a cup of coffee. Neither Holmes nor I had spoken to her of the latest concerns delivered to us via Mycroft's telegram. It was clear that Crane had been in Florida; whether he'd got back to New York in time to board the *Manitou* was not. But Holmes and I agreed that there was no need to upset Cora with newly unsettled prospects. If Crane didn't make an appearance, we'd all know soon enough.

Cora spoke incessantly. For someone supposed to be angry with her husband at having cut off correspondence for so many months, she talked eagerly of the plans she would institute once her Stevie arrived.

"Tomorrow—or Friday at the latest—I'm going to take Stevie to see Brede Place. He's going to love it. I've already sent three hundred rose bushes there to be planted. Mr. Mack, the old-timer with the white beard, will get it done. He's staying on along with the couple of others I told you about, but the additional staff will be new—not the servants from Ravensbrook. I don't mean Adoni and Mrs. Ruedy, of course. They're coming along. But I'm only paying Mrs. Bryant, my current housekeeper, till the end of this month. I even told her she could leave a week earlier since I'm hoping we'll be all moved out of Ravensbrook by then."

Cora seemed to have finally run out of nervous talk, and the three of us sat, cups in hand, listening to the wind whipping across the broad river and the rain pelting the roof. Sometimes the windows in the *café* would rattle; but though the rain clouded our view, we still managed to see that so far no small boats had left the *Manitou*'s side.

To Cora, the entire situation must have been frightening. In addition to the storm, the moment she'd been anticipating for so many months was almost upon her. Certainly, the reunion with Crane would be joyous. Yet at the same time all those plans she'd been making were about to demand fulfilment. What if her Stevie wanted no part of them?

Happily, the rain began to lighten. Once the mist dissipated and the maritime scene before us became clearer, we could actually make out people milling about on the *Manitou*'s deck. A group were walking towards a gangway that led down to the little shore-boat bobbing in the restless waters while still lashed to the side of the large ship. It was time for us to return to the dock.

With the rain having eased, we found it much easier to traverse the wooden decking. It took only a few minutes to reach a spot nearest the *Manitou*. No sooner had we positioned ourselves than Cora shrieked, "There he is!" She was pointing with one hand and covering her open mouth with the other.

From such a distance and through so lingering a mist, I didn't believe it possible to identify an individual among the some-twenty passengers preparing to disembark; yet when I looked at the figures lined up to leave the ship, I could see what had so excited Cora. Under darkened skies, a solitary apparition stood brightly illuminated on the *Manitou's* gloomy deck.

Or so it seemed. Cloaked in a long white raincoat—no doubt the same gleaming duster that he'd been reported wearing in the face of Spanish gunfire at San Juan Heights— Stephen Crane looked for all the world like the ghost so many people thought he'd already become. He'd stood erect calmly smoking a cigarette—or so the story ran—while bullets from Spanish Mausers magically failed to strike him.

Soon the white coat joined the group as in a single-file they carefully made their way down the gangplank and into the dancing shore-boat. At the very least, Holmes and I could lay to rest our concern that Crane had missed boarding the ship in New York.

We followed Cora towards the top of the gangway that the passengers would be ascending once the shore-boat reached the dock. She stopped well short of the dock's end, however, and we halted a few paces behind her. With the wind in our faces, the three of us waited, marking the progress of the small boat as it increased in size amidst the rolling waves.

And then it was there; and the passengers, helped along by the blowing wind now at their backs, trudged slowly up the gangway.

Cora stood watching.

The man in the long white coat was the last to mount the dock. With the group well ahead of him, he stood by himself at the end of the wooden platform, a tiny figure, isolated, alone. From this distance, he looked no bigger than a finger. A white handkerchief went to his mouth, and his body shook for a moment. But in the whistling wind, we couldn't hear the cough.

Cora stood watching.

Stephen Crane was not a tall man, and his various illnesses had obviously taken their toll. Because of the long coat, one couldn't sense how shrunken he really was. On his head rested a crumpled dark fedora. Even as he began the trek towards us, he kept the hat tilted forward so that the front brim concealed his eyes and kept his face in as much shadow as a sunless day can create. One could barely discern the untrimmed moustache drooping down at the sides of his mouth. His left hand held a battered leather valise; his right still clung to the handkerchief.

Cora stood watching.

As the travellers drew closer, Crane caught up to the man directly in front of him. Clearly they knew each other, and they now walked a few paces together, Crane moving slowly, the other lagging in his gliding gait to allow Crane to catch him. Moments later, having stuffed the handkerchief back in his pocket, Crane marched ahead of his companion, last no longer.

Cora stepped forward, then ran directly at him. As soon as he saw her, Crane dropped his bag; and she fell straight into his arms. In her delight, she knocked his hat to the wooden decking, and a dark-blond shock of hair fell across his brow. But that's all that I could see because the brim of Cora's wide hat immediately eclipsed my view, and the two of them locked in a kiss that could have lasted for eternity.

At last, they broke apart, and she held him at arm's length.

"Let me have a look at you," said she with concern as she eyed him up and down. "No bullet holes or missing parts?"

Crane smiled sheepishly. "Nope, Hon', I'm all here."

Cora's small lips grew straight and her green eyes narrowed. "Then I can tell you how I really feel." She took a deep breath and shouted, "I hate you!" and struck him on the shoulder. But immediately she began to choke back tears and pulled him towards her again. Another long kiss followed.

When they concluded their second embrace, Crane stooped to pick up his fedora and motioned with it for his companion to come forward. One couldn't help noticing the round, tinted glasses the newcomer wore on so dark a day. With a smooth, olive complexion that seemed at odds with the grey overcast, he appeared quite young, perhaps in his teens or early-twenties. His sharply chiselled features included an aquiline nose and a strong chin. Blue dungarees and a navy-blue pea coat covered his short frame, and a canvas bag rested on his shoulder. The black knit cap hugging his head and the blue bandanna round his neck made him look ready enough to manage at sea.

"Hon'," said Crane to his wife, "this is David Bergman, the friend I told you I was bringing along." Crane put his arm around the stranger's shoulder, guiding him even closer to Cora. "I met him in New York last spring. We've sort of been travelling together."

"Hey," the stranger said by way of introduction. His full lips managed a brief smile.

"Welcome to England, gentlemen," said Holmes before Cora could respond. Extending his hand to each of them, he announced, "My name is Sherlock Holmes."

Crane nodded, a quizzical look in his almond-shaped eyes of blue and grey.

I introduced myself as well, and Cora told Crane that Holmes was a consulting detective there to help them and that I was his colleague.

"Consulting detective?" Crane eyed both of us up and down; then he turned to his friend. "Look like plain-clothes coppers to me, David."

His friend smirked in apparent agreement.

"Anything but," Holmes replied.

Crane shrugged, and Cora took the opportunity to say it was time to get back to London.

"A good idea, Mrs. Crane," Holmes said. "But let me insist that we all share a first-class railway carriage so we may talk in private during our return."

Aided by the wind that was now blowing from behind us, we hastened Indian file to the train station. Holmes, the tallest, led the way; I came second; Crane and Cora, hand in hand, were next with young Bergman bringing up the rear. Thanks to Cora's broad-shouldered coat, she and Bergman looked similar in stature.

Our walk took but a few minutes, and soon we were ensconced in a railway carriage rattling along wet rails back to London.

*　*　*

The rain formed little bubbles on the window. As the train coursed through the drenched countryside, the bubbles inched their ways to the edge of the glass and then disappeared into the mist.

Crane, Cora, and Bergman sat opposite Holmes and me. Like a metronome, the methodical clacking of the rails kept time with the sway of the carriage.

Stephen Crane removed the white handkerchief from his pocket. At the same moment, Sherlock Holmes leaned forward and spoke directly to him. "We have only a brief opportunity to talk, so we must take full advantage of this trip to London."

"OK," Crane agreed, obviously unclear about where the conversation was headed.

"I assume," said Holmes, "that you know of the death of Harold Frederic."

Of course, Crane knew. It was common knowledge printed in all the papers. He nodded his head and coughed deeply, quickly covering his mouth with the handkerchief, a practice with which he was obviously quite familiar.

"You'd be better off not smoking all those cigarettes you roll," Holmes offered.

Good advice, but how he knew Crane's habits on such short notice was beyond me. Crane's suspicious look revealed it was beyond him as well.

"Your fingers," said Holmes. "They're stained with nicotine."

Crane took the linen from his mouth and examined his brown-tinged fingers. Satisfied, he nodded for Holmes to continue.

"What you probably *don't* know is that, before Frederic died, he shared with Dr. Watson and me the fact that you were being blackmailed by a man called Milverton. Charles Augustus Milverton."

Brow furrowing, Crane glared at Holmes; but Bergman sat up at the name, his coloured glasses concealing whatever thoughts his eyes might have revealed.

Cora took her husband's hand. "I know too, Stevie," said she. "And whatever you're being blackmailed about, I don't care."

The train whistle screeched as we approached a station.

"I'm writing a book about David," said Crane. "*Flowers of Asphalt* I call it. It deals with men who love other men, men who perform sex with other men. But just 'cause I'm interested in the subject doesn't mean it's about *me*."

He flashed a defiant look in Cora's direction.

"Still," Crane said, "people get wrong-headed ideas. That's why I had to keep this Milverton fellow quiet. And I'll admit it, Hon'," he added, looking at Cora, "I didn't want you to know anything about it either."

Cora shook her head. "Oh, Stevie, you're so thin-skinned. The things I've seen in my life—nothing shocks me. I love you is all."

"Mr. Bergman didn't accompany you to New York last November, did he?" asked Holmes.

Behind the glasses, the expression of Crane's friend seemed passive.

"No," said the writer. "I left him hidden back in Havana."

"At Mary Horan's boarding house?" I asked.

"Let's just call it Havana," Crane said. He obviously appreciated our knowledge, for he added with a nervous smile, "Say, you fellows really are 'tecs, aren't you?"

Holmes ignored the compliment. "Am I correct in assuming," he asked Crane, "that you returned to Havana late last month to bring David Bergman back with you to New York, so the two of you could leave for England together?"

"That's right. But how did you know I even went back down there?"

"Your telegram to a Mr. Hawkins asking for fifty dollars. You sent it from Jacksonville on the twenty-eighth of December."

Crane let out a whistle. "You really *are* good. I won't ask how you know all this; but Willie's a friend of mine, a fellow writer. I did return to Havana, picked up David, and the two of us took a boat back to Jacksonville, and then a train up to Manhattan. When it was time to leave New York, my brother Edmund escorted me to the dock—I guess, he wanted to be certain I actually boarded the ship. He's always looked out for me. I bought David a ticket too, but he had to sneak on so my brother wouldn't see the two of us together. Right, David?"

"Yeah," was all the young man said.

Cora was not so calm. "You spent *our* money on an extra boat ticket?"

In response, Crane simply stared at her.

Holmes, however, continued to press. "Once Milverton discovers you're back in England, I'm certain that he'll come hounding you in person. He'll stop at nothing to get as much money from you as possible."

A smirk crossed the writer's face.

"Trust me, Mr. Crane," Holmes warned. "Milverton can't be frightened off."

"I hear you, Mr. Holmes. That son of a bitch ruined our life down in Havana. And that was *after* he'd started playing his little game with us up in New York. I figure he must have had some two-bit flunkies following us around over there. I don't want him doing the same to us now that we're here in his own backyard. What did Henry the Fourth say of the king he replaced? 'Have I no friend will rid me of this living fear?'"

The quotation was greeted with silence, yet Holmes flashed a concerned glance in my direction. Since Crane was a writer, his familiarity with Shakespeare shouldn't have surprised me. Yet with his rugged Western persona, it did. Not only was he a journalist, but also an American.

At the same time, Cora interlocked her arm with his, and David Bergman squirmed in his seat. I could see Bergman's fingers at his side clenching into a fist.

Holmes broke the tension with an offer of hope. "As Watson can attest, I recently acquired a client—a young woman, who, in order to keep her life intact, must be saved from this man Milverton by Saturday. *Saturday!* The deadline is Milverton's, and it leaves just three days to thwart his scheme."

"Not much time, is it, Mr. Holmes?" said Crane.

Holmes smiled. "I have devised a plan to extricate the lady from Milverton's clutches. Watson knows a little something about it. But what is important to *you*, Mr. Crane, is that if everything goes well, my plan will also free countless others, including yourself."

"I'm telling you, Stevie," said Cora, squeezing his arm tighter, "this man is someone you can trust."

"Thank you, Mr. Holmes," said Crane, stifling another cough.

"In the meantime," Cora announced, "we're staying the night in London. We'll find a place for David in our hotel. Then tomorrow we'll be back in Ravensbrook—for as short a time as possible."

"Why, Hon'?" Crane asked her. "What do you have planned for me?"

"Just you wait," she said with a smile. It would be her only smile on the trip back to London.

* * *

We hired a growler at Charing Cross. Two small, well-behaved white horses stood waiting for instructions from the coachman seated atop the four-wheeler. Dark lacquer on the doors covered some prior heraldic emblem, the obliterated device hinting at a previous upper-class existence for a vehicle now fallen to the level of hackney coach.

As a rule, such carriages usually seated four. But as we five began our journey through the rush of hansoms and omnibuses to Petty France, Cora was more than pleased to sit on her husband's lap. Driving along muddied roads and slick pavements, we passed St. James's Park and rolled to a stop before the Queen Anne's Mansions, its lofty pinnacles disappearing into the low-hanging mist and lightly-falling rain.

Before they exited the carriage, Holmes addressed the Cranes: "Do you mind if Watson and I borrow Mr. Bergman for awhile?"

We all turned towards Holmes at the unexpected question.

"Why?" asked Stephen Crane, his voice tinged with suspicion.

"I want to provide him with more background on the Milverton case," answered Holmes. "I'm sure Cora will do the same for you."

"That so, Hon'?" Crane asked her.

"Just you wait," she purred and kissed him full on the mouth.

"OK with you, Dave?" Crane asked.

"Suppose so," the young man said. He stared for a moment at the couple nuzzling before him, then added, "Guess I don't want to be a third wheel anyhow."

We watched Cora and Stephen scramble out into the rain and head for the entrance to the red-brick hotel. In an instant, a porter brandishing an umbrella opened the outer door and ushered them inside.

No sooner had they disappeared than Holmes knocked on the front window for the coachman's attention. "Drive anywhere!" Holmes shouted. "Till I tell you to stop."

The carriage lurched forward, and Holmes and I both fell back into our seats. To avoid tumbling forward, David Bergman steadied himself with a hand on our leather cushion. Almost immediately, the horses found a steady rhythm, and soon the roll of wheels on cobblestone was producing that low rumble that earned the "growler" its sobriquet.

As we jolted along, Bergman removed the tinted glasses and the knit cap. Now that I could see his face more clearly, I realized that he was older than I had first guessed. Originally, I had thought him to be quite young—almost a boy, really. In fact, he must have been closer to thirty. His hair was short and black, but it was his tired eyes that revealed a man who appeared no stranger to the brutalities of life. Suffering seemed to have permeated his entire being.

"So what do you want to talk about, Mr. Holmes?" he asked.

Till now, Bergman had spoken very little, yet with these words I could clearly discern his accent. Like Kate Lyon, Bergman spoke with a New Yorker's inflection; but because she more properly enunciated her letters and syllables, her pronunciation reflected a higher class. Bergman's speech—with its broadened vowels, dropped final *r*'s, elided consonants, *th*'s sounding like *d*'s, and *d*'s like *t*'s—seemed more rudimentary or primitive. The flat American tones take some getting used to in general, but Bergman's dialect was particularly grating to the ear of an educated Englishman. Rather than the way I rendered it in print, for instance, Bergman's previous question to Holmes sounded more like "So whadda ya wanna tawk abowt?"

No matter how he verbalized it, however, I admit to having harboured the very same query.

"I wished to speak with you alone, Mr. Bergman, because, without alarming Mrs. Crane—or Stephen, for that matter—I want to impress upon you the real danger that your friend is facing"

"Danger?" he repeated, his dark eyes flashing his concern.

"We've already talked about this man called Milverton who's been blackmailing Crane."

"Yeah?" Bergman's eyes narrowed, hardening his features. His olive skin looked even darker in the shadows of the carriage.

Holmes and I both suspected that Bergman was well acquainted with the general operations of Charles Milverton. Although the letter we'd read from Crane to Frederic contained no specific details, it certainly suggested that Bergman had somehow helped Crane avoid whoever had been following them in Havana, probably in some violent fashion.

"You seem to be a man who takes matters into his own hands," said Holmes.

Bergman shrugged, too modest or suspicious to enjoy the compliment.

"Let me explain what it is that you're up against," Holmes offered and then proceeded to lay out the case against Milverton with which we both were already too familiar—how Milverton blackmailed his victims so ruthlessly, how he paid off people's trusted associates for compromising information, how he always carried a loaded revolver. But Holmes went even further. Citing the bomb outrage at Greenwich, he suggested that Milverton was cold-blooded enough to threaten murder to cow victims into paying for his silence.

At first, Bergman said nothing, the staccato beat of the horses' hooves ticking off the passage of time.

Finally, he said, "OK, I consider myself warned."

"Good," Holmes replied and then surprised me by venturing in a new direction altogether. "Mr. Bergman, I have no intention of prying into your personal behaviour. You and Mr. Crane are both well passed your majority, and how you dispose of your lives is your own concern."

Bergman folded his hands in his lap. "At last," he sighed, "the moral lecture."

"Not at all. But I do feel I must emphasize the obvious. In New York and in Havana, you and Crane were on your own. Here, there is a third party; and while Cora

166

Crane can be a bit trying, both Dr. Watson and I have worked diligently to reunite her with the man she now calls her husband."

Nodding his head slowly, Bergman stared grimly at Holmes. "Look, it's not that I don't appreciate what you're doing. But Stephen and I have been together for almost nine months. He found me lying bloody in the street. The pimp I worked for beat me and worse—said I hadn't earned him enough money. Stephen took me in, fed me, eventually got me to talk."

"Was that what he was writing about?" I asked. "About your life?"

"Yeah. A little anyway. I guess you know he wrote a book about a whore called Maggie—put up the money himself to get it published. I suppose *my* story made it a matched set—you know, first the woman, then the man."

"You're talking about 'Flowers of Asphalt,' said I.

"Right, again. Yeah. Well, he did find me on the 'asphalt', and I guess he considered me his 'flower'. Go figure. He did a lot of writing when we were together; but, you know, he didn't really write about *me* that much. He was working on a novel about the Greek war with the Turks. *Active Service,* I think he called it. And he was always writing those funny little poems. Being at Mary Horan's in Havana— which you already seem to know of—he also wrote about his time in Cuba. You know the kind of thing I mean—the killing, the blood, the stupidity."

Bergman paused to take a breath. What was obviously a warm memory lit up his face. "You know, when Stephen wasn't sick with fever, those were good times we had at Mary's place. She used to get him to take late-night walks to relieve his tension. Down those narrow cobblestone streets in Havana. During the daytime, he'd sit under the orange tree in her patio. That's where he did his best thinking. He liked to write on those long sheets of lined paper he carried all over. When he was out there in the patio holding a pen, I knew enough not to bother him. Do you know that lots of times when he was writing, he'd wrap a wet towel around his head. He said it cooled his brain. And he'd talk to himself about his work. "'That's great!' he'd shout out if he wrote something that he really liked."

'Writers," I muttered, shaking my head.

"Stephen got me to read *Maggie*, so I can assure you he knows a lot about how tough life is on the streets. He also knows a lot about women. But you know what? He doesn't— or didn't—know much about men. I mean—about men being with other men—not until he met me—if you see what I'm driving at."

"I'm afraid I don't," I was quick to say. Suddenly my face reddened and I blurted out, "I-I didn't mean that 'I'm, I'm *s-sorry* that I don't know more'. . . ."

David Bergman leaned forward and put his hand on my knee. "Relax, Doc," he said softly, all the while, looking into my eyes in the most mesmerizing manner. "I get what you're trying to say."

For his part, Holmes was staring out the side window, his hand covering his mouth. If I was reading him correctly, he seemed to be stifling a smile at my expense.

"And what about the two of *you*?" Bergman asked.

Holmes turned back to look at him while I exploded. "See here," I barked, "I'm a widower. I'll have you know—"

"No disrespect," Bergman offered. "But do the two of you live together?"

"Why, y-yes," I stammered, "but—"

"Relax, Doc," he said again. "All I'm trying to say is that nobody really knows what goes on behind closed doors. Stephen likes to open those doors and show people."

Holmes nodded in obvious approval. "But better to open those doors oneself than to let someone else do it for you, eh, Mr. Bergman?"

"You're right about that, Mr. Holmes. I appreciate your advice. And let me add this: Stephen told you how I had to sneak aboard the *Manitou* back in New York, so his brother wouldn't see us together. I knew what I was getting away from in the States; I *don't* know what I'm getting myself into here in England. But I'll tell you one thing." Here he raised his forefinger to emphasize the point. "I do know how Stephen was always inventing ways to avoid writing to Cora. He had no problem asking his agent or his editors for money; but when he had to tell *her* where he was or, for that matter, when he was planning to come back to England—well, he found it too tough to write her."

"Believe me, Mr. Bergman, when I tell you that anyone here in London who knows the woman at all has been made very much aware of Mr. Crane's—how shall I put it?—lack of enthusiasm for contacting his wife."

Bergman nodded. "'What the hell,' I thought when Stephen offered me a boat ticket. I'll go to England and see for myself. He was paying, after all—not that I know where the money came from, but he wanted me to go along. I figured he was trying to tell me something, so I decided to come here and learn once and for all what was or wasn't going on between him and his wife."

"I realize that you've only seen them together for a few hours," said Holmes, "but I must ask: Is it too early to inquire whether you've already reached a conclusion?"

David Bergman rubbed his hands together as if he was washing them. "I've seen enough, Mr. Holmes. *'Es suficiente,'* as they say in Cuba. All the time we've been taking this little carriage ride, I've been thinking—if *you* hadn't invited me along, I probably would have gone off somewheres on my

own. To a bar maybe. Or to that Buckingham Castle where
the Queen lives. We passed a sign back near the hotel that
said it was just down the street. And you know what else?
After seeing Stephen and Cora together today, I sure as hell
have no plans to go with them to their house tomorrow."

"To Ravensbrook?" I asked.

"Yeah," he said. "Ravensbrook. That's the place. I'm
no fool. I can see what the two of them have together. And it
sure doesn't include *me.* Stephen and I had some good
times, but it's obvious he belongs with Cora. Nobody should
get between them." He leaned back in his seat and put on his
coloured glasses once more. "Is that a good enough answer to
your question, Mr. Holmes?"

"Yes," said my friend with a sigh of relief that
surprised me. Holmes may have been a stoic, but Cora Crane
had obviously evoked a sympathetic response he seldom
displayed. Holmes really did seem to desire that her
relationship with Stephen Crane be all that she wished for.

I knew that Holmes still had his scheme against
Milverton to get straight; but following these words with
Bergman, he allowed himself a satisfied grin. Then he
knocked on the front window of the carriage again and
shouted up to the coachman: "Buckingham Palace, if you
please!"

Chapter Eleven

A man feared that he might find an assassin;
Another that he might find a victim.
One was more wise than the other.
--Stephen Crane

Time was moving quickly. It was now the afternoon of Friday the thirteenth, a date I hoped was more coincidental than ominous. Holmes had only one day remaining to resolve Lady Eva's dilemma, and as yet he had not revealed to me even the most general nature of his stratagem—let alone my own presumed responsibilities as part of it. While it is true that I continued to witness the entrances and exits of Escott the plumber, it wasn't until later that same evening that Holmes finally announced his plan, the entire execution of which required completing within the next few hours!

The plot Holmes laid out to me was exactly as I'd explained it in my original narrative—and just as desperate. With no other alternatives, he had concluded quite simply that the only way to protect Lady Eva—as well as Stephen Crane and the other poor wretches under Milverton's power—was to burglarize the villain's safe—that is, to rid it of all the incriminating letters, which Milverton employed for leverage.

At last, I could understand Holmes' need for cultivating the attentions of Agatha Rimes. While I was deploring his trifling with her fancies, he was surreptitiously gaining vital knowledge of Milverton's life: how the household was run, how the man's day was scheduled, how the grounds were laid out. The stakes were very high indeed if Holmes was going to succeed in gaining access to

Milverton's house, breaking into his safe, stealing his most valuable possessions, and—most significantly—making good an escape.

Naturally, I tried to talk my friend out of such an illicit scheme. In the first place, it was dangerous. There was that gun of Milverton's. Then there were the laws Holmes would be breaking; Scotland Yard would like nothing better than to charge their premier rival with some sort of crime.

In the end, however, Holmes and his pragmatic reasoning brought me over to his side. "Think in terms of surgery, Doctor," he said. "Consider my burgling an operation to cut out a cancer that's threatening the body."

He'd made his point—for Holmes, an uncharacteristically altruistic point. He might indeed be breaking the law, but as long as it was only the incriminating letters that were taken, I had to agree that the goal was noble. It was principled. It was virtuous. In fact, so convinced of the righteousness of Holmes' foray into crime did I become that I insisted on accompanying him. I demanded to go along even though he protested against jeopardizing my own well-being.

"Putting myself at risk is one thing, Watson. Including you is quite another."

His argument may have been logical, but it remained unconvincing. On not a few occasions, we had placed ourselves in jeopardy together—"The Speckled Band," "The Empty House," "The Copper Beeches" to name a few. Were we suddenly to change our *modus operandi*? Holmes might feel confident that he could open Milverton's safe on his own; but I pointed out to him that, despite his safe-cracking skills, he was no expert in breaking the law.

"Neither are you, old fellow."

"True," said I, "but even you must agree that two heads have to be better than one."

He raised both hands in the posture of giving up and, having acquiesced, proceeded to share the details of his plan. Entry to the grounds of Appledore Towers later that night depended on the romantic *rendezvous* he'd already scheduled with his "*fiancée*". Her passions enflamed by the expectation of seeing her suitor, Agatha was to arrange with the groundskeeper to keep Milverton's brute of a dog chained up. Leaving the gate unlocked was no problem at all for a young woman charged with desire. Escott the plumber could thus advance unmolested to her window. At least, that's what Holmes assumed she was expecting him to do. The "plumber" in question, of course, had decidedly different intentions.

* * *

Later that cold winter's night, two well-dressed gentlemen, sporting silent shoes and harbouring black silk masks in their pockets, made their way by cab to Hampstead Heath. In deference to the chill, I wore my overcoat; Holmes, his cape.

Thanks to Agatha, we knew that Milverton retired at 10:30 every night. So deeply did he slumber, she'd told Escott, that the servants joked about how difficult it was to wake him in the mornings. Holmes' plan required us to leave for Hampstead at 11:00, so that by the time we reached Appledore Towers, we could expect Milverton to be sound asleep.

Some short time after half-past eleven, we slipped through the gate that Agatha had left open; donned our masks; and, unmolested by the dog, tiptoed along the veranda past a door Holmes knew to be bolted. Soon enough we arrived at the locked entrance of the greenhouse.

"The greenhouse," whispered Holmes, "leads to the drawing room; from there, we can find our way to Milverton's study."

Employing a glasscutter, which he'd brought along with his other burgling tools, Holmes produced a circular hole with a diameter of some eight inches in the window of the door before us. Pushing aside his cape, he pulled the right sleeve of his jacket tight with his left hand and carefully inserted his right arm through the newly-cut aperture. From the inside, he unfastened the lock, withdrew his arm, and opened the door. He then took my hand in his and led me through the darkness from one room to the next until we reached Milverton's study.

Dancing flames in the fireplace illuminated the familiar scene: the red-mahogany desk with its turning chair at the centre; the book-lined shelves; the heavy curtains before the window; and our target, the large green safe—all still presided over by the white bust of Athene.

Holmes tiptoed to the entrance of Milverton's bedroom to listen for the man's snores. At the same time, I checked the door leading directly outside, the same door we had passed on our way to the greenhouse. Surprisingly, it was unbolted.

"Strange," Holmes whispered when he returned to my side. "I hear nothing from within Milverton's chamber." There was a touch of concern in his voice.

"The door to the outside is unlocked," I reported.

"I don't like it. Something is amiss."

Such concerns did not prevent Sherlock Holmes from beginning the task for which we had come. Transforming himself into master thief, the master detective crept to the safe and opened his burglar's kit on the floor in front of it. After sorting amongst his drills and keys and jemmy, he commenced to crack the combination lock.

In the original account of this escapade, I admitted my fears of being found out, and I see nothing to gain from confessing them all once more. But I will re-emphasize the sense of exhilaration I discovered in breaking the law for a greater good. What I'd anticipated to be a feeling of revulsion became instead a mind-clearing rush of excitement. The forbidden fruit we were sampling was proving to be quite the heady meal.

After some thirty minutes, the muffled snap of the lock startled me out of my reverie. Holmes gently opened the large door and, producing a dark lantern from under his cape, lit the flame and began to peruse the letters, packets and files he'd found within the safe. At one point, he paused to examine a particular envelope and, after having done so, slipped it inside his coat. No sooner had he stashed it away, however, than he froze, head tilted in a listening posture.

In the hallway, soft footfalls were approaching the room.

Immediately Holmes was all action, shutting the lantern, closing but not locking the safe's door, scooping up his tools, and darting behind the window curtains—all the while, motioning for me to join him as quickly as I could.

Holmes drew together the heavy drapes, leaving only the slightest of gaps between the two sections. It was the best we could hope for. The cloth was thick enough so we couldn't be seen, but neither could we discern anything going on beyond it—though various sounds did offer an indication. Someone had entered the room and, after switching on the central electric light, had seated himself at the desk and begun to rustle some papers. We heard the strike of a Vesta, and within moments the room was engulfed in the pungent aroma of cigar smoke. A stifled cough was noise enough to reveal that the perpetrator of these events was Milverton himself.

What's this then? The man's supposed to be asleep. I knew Holmes was harbouring the same thought. I could only wonder if that large revolver was now lying on the miscreant's desk.

The next few minutes passed by as slowly as any I can remember, offering me ample time to envision one of two terrifying prospects: spending years in prison for breaking and entering or being shot dead through the curtain by Milverton as intruders in his house.

Recalling the Danish prince just then was a logical leap. Concealed behind a curtain, who wouldn't think of Hamlet's deadly sword-thrust that killed Polonius in the queen's chamber? The blade had pierced the arras behind which the old man had hidden. Were Holmes and I to suffer a similar fate? Was Milverton posturing on the other side of the drapery, shifting his papers as a dodge while aiming his revolver at our hearts?

To preserve my sanity, I needed to know what was taking place in the room. Thus, I dared peep through the tiny space between the two curtains before us.

Despite the precariousness of our position—the safe's door remained ajar—relief flooded over me. So far, we remained undetected. Milverton was seated at the desk a few feet to our left, his back turned to us. For the moment, he was involved with reading what looked like legal papers while puffing clouds of thick smoke into the air. There was also no sign of the revolver.

My relief was short-lived, however. Noises from elsewhere in the house began penetrating the room, and soon we were able to detect footsteps on the veranda as well. At last it dawned on me: Milverton was working at his desk so late at night with the side-door unbolted because he was expecting a visitor, someone no doubt directed to the side-entrance by the butler at the front door.

Holmes squeezed my hand in a gesture of confidence, then gently attempted to pinch closed the curtains.

A knock on the door followed, and we heard Milverton rise. "You're late," he said amidst the rustling of a woman's skirts. "Our appointment was for midnight."

Milverton went on complaining about his visitor's tardiness, and during his rant my curiosity again got the better of me. Defying all sense of reason, I carefully ventured once more to separate the curtains and peer into the room. Bending low, Holmes too gazed through the tiny space.

In front of the red-mahogany desk, a strange woman stood looming over Milverton. A veil shielded her face though jet-black curls peeked out at the sides. She was breathing heavily as with one hand at her neck she held closed a dark cloak, which concealed a small but sturdy frame. In point of fact, excluding her hair colour, the unknown visitor put me in mind of Cora Crane.

Milverton continued to growl. "You couldn't have come earlier?"

She merely shook her head. Perhaps she was too upset to speak; her whole body seemed to tremble. And yet there was defiance in her posture.

Milverton leaned forward. "You telegrammed that you wish to sell me some letters. You said that they incriminate your mistress."

The woman nodded

Milverton put out his hand. "Let's see what you've got then."

She offered him nothing.

Though the veil's netting was thick, I could distinguish a heavily made-up face behind it. And while it might have been my imagination, I thought I could also discern a look of fury: the furrowed brow signalling anger, the piercing eyes flashing hatred, the painted lips emoting rage. I knew of no new cases involving letters stolen by a maid, yet there remained something oddly familiar about this female informant.

Perhaps Milverton sensed a mystery as well; for after receiving no letters, he put down his cigar and leaned back to scrutinize his visitor more closely. The chair groaned with his movement.

At the same time, the feminine hand that had been holding the cloak together now reached beneath it. When it emerged, it was holding a long-barrelled revolver.

"You'll ruin no more lives," the woman hissed, pointing the gun at Milverton's chest. They were the last words uttered in the room that night, and they were voiced in the shards of a whisper.

She squeezed the trigger, and the loud report must have echoed throughout the house. Then she fired again and again and again. Only after all six bullets had penetrated the vile creature's body did she stop.

Following the first shot, Milverton had gasped. Following the second, he'd fallen forward onto the shiny red desktop, his gold-rimmed glasses shattering when his forehead banged onto the mahogany. The remaining bullets accompanied his descent as he tumbled to the floor, a swipe of scarlet marking the trail. The woman kicked at his head to make certain there was no more movement and then, rushing to the door that led outside, completed her escape.

Of course, there was nothing we could have done to save the wretch; but even as my Hippocratic instincts were shouting at me to make some sort of attempt, I felt Holmes grab my wrist. I knew what he was thinking; and as much as I hated to admit it, I knew he was right: a world without the likes of Charles Augustus Milverton was a better world indeed.

No sooner had the woman left the room than Holmes sprang for the door that communicated to the rest of the house and locked it. Although we could hear movement somewhere beyond—servants no doubt alarmed by the gunshots—Holmes rushed over to the large safe. Its door was still ajar, and in great handfuls he removed the bundles of paper residing within. He grabbed every one of them—the countless incriminating, embarrassing, humiliating letters that had haunted all nature of people, from aristocrats like Lady Eva to commoners like—well, like Stephen Crane. Holmes tossed them all into the fire.

Then, black masks still in place, we were through the side door ourselves and out onto the veranda. A footman and under-gardener took up the chase, the latter momentarily grabbing hold of my ankle as we mounted the garden wall. With a sharp kick, I extricated my foot, and both Holmes and I scrambled over the top to freedom. With the great expanse of Hampstead Heath before us, we ran blindly into that cold night, energized not only by the horror we had just witnessed but also by the joy that accompanied the destruction of the damning contents of Milverton's safe.

"Who was that woman?" I gasped when we finally came to a halt. "The woman who shot Milverton?"

"Ah, Watson," said Holmes between deep breaths, "what makes you think that the person with the gun was a woman at all?"

* * *

We flagged a hansom in Hampstead High Street, and soon we were back in our rooms sipping brandies to calm our nerves.

A few minutes of silence passed, and then Holmes placed his glass on the table. "I have something to show you,

Watson," said he and from an inner pocket removed the envelope I had seen him pluck from the others within Milverton's safe. Now that I was closer to it, I could clearly read the name scrawled across its front: "Captain Donald William Stewart."

"What does this mean?"

"It means that amongst the papers Milverton employed as leverage in his blackmail schemes was some sort of correspondence pertaining to Cora Crane's legal husband."

"Of what sort?"

Holmes flashed a quick smile. "Unless we open the wrapper, my dear chap, we'll never know."

The flap wasn't sealed, so Holmes simply slid it out from the envelope and withdrew the two sheets of paper that had been folded inside. The first was an official-looking document with tiny print, a number of signatures, and dignified scrollwork at all the margins. Closer inspection revealed that it was, in fact, a bill of sale dated 21 March 1895, for a parcel of land labelled Lot 6, Block 124, in the city of Jacksonville, Florida. The property included miscellaneous furniture and a boarding house, and it was signed by the purchaser, one Cora E. Taylor.

"What does this mean?" I was forced to ask again.

"I'm sure that Mrs. Crane will be able to offer a more complete explanation; but unless I am very much mistaken, this document is the original bill of sale for what was to become the business establishment of Cora Crane—Cora Taylor in 1895—the place she called the 'House de Dream'. The disorderly house she owned and ran. In short, a brothel."

"My word!" I gasped.

"You may recognize 'Taylor' from the list of Mrs. Crane's surnames I cited when Harold Frederic called on us last summer; it is a designation she seems to have inherited from a suitor prior to Captain Stewart."

"A previous husband?"

Holmes shrugged.

"And the relevance of such a document?"

"Let us examine the other page."

The second sheet contained a brief letter. At the top was Milverton's name; at the bottom, Captain Stewart's signature. The message was short and to the point:

Enclosed is a draft for the 1000 pounds you demand annually. I trust that neither my family nor the British people will ever come to hear of my wife's association with that vile place in Jacksonville. I understand that should I divorce her, the terms of my agreement with you will be voided and that you will make public my wife's sordid past.

"It does appear," Holmes said, "that we have finally discovered the answer to the question I put to Harold Frederic last July—why would Cora's distinguished husband not want to rid himself of so annoying a wife? Obviously, we now learn, because Captain Donald W. Stewart, the distinguished husband in question, was himself a target of Milverton's blackmail. If the captain ended his marriage to Cora, Milverton would lose significant income. Thus, the rogue threatened Stewart with scandal were the marriage ever to end."

"And we had no idea," I said in amazement. "But surely in America people knew of Cora's activities. Crane himself met the woman in her own establishment."

Holmes nodded. "But the ocean between our two countries is vast, Watson—as vast as the gulf between the manners of our aristocracy and those of America's common people. There is also quite the difference between actual

Daniel D. Victor

proof in the form of a bill of sale and what otherwise might be dismissed as idle gossip. Remember that Crane himself always referred to Cora as his wife—and never offered a hint of her prior employment. Besides, I should imagine that Donald Stewart has been quite adept at keeping Cora's shadowy past from his family—from his father, the Baronet, in particular."

Suddenly, a new implication of Milverton's death dawned on me. "Wait a moment," I exclaimed. "With Milverton dead, there's no more threat to Cora's secret. Stewart is now free to divorce her. She and Crane can marry legally, and he can make an honest woman of her."

Sherlock Holmes held high his brandy. "To everyone who will be freed as a result of tonight's dark business."

"Especially, to Cora and Stephen Crane," said I. "For their sake, let's hope the remedy is simple."

Holmes took a sip. "One may hope, Watson," he sighed as put down the glass, "but like everything else in this case, something tells me that such a resolution won't be simple at all." With a final smirk, he slipped the two papers back in their envelope, which he proceeded to place in the pocket of his dressing gown.

* * *

Despite Inspector Lestrade's search of Milverton's study and the grounds of the estate, I can announce with complete confidence that the two mysterious figures seen escaping from Appledore Towers were never discovered. As we had expected, Scotland Yard remained unconcerned about Milverton's female caller. The police assumed that the two thieves who'd robbed Milverton's safe of whatever was in it were also the rogues responsible for the man's murder.

It was at this point in my original account of Lestrade's investigation that Conan Doyle, my literary agent, encouraged me to include a bit of comic relief. Humour, he reasoned, would provide a needed lightening of the mood following so intense a description of murder. Since he knew the vagaries of the market place far better than I, his advice was easy to follow, especially since actual events had handed me a situation to embellish.

It so happened that the gardener who'd grabbed my ankle was able to furnish the police with a partial description of the man he'd almost caught. Though masked, the intruder was said to be "middle-sized and strongly built," featuring a "square jaw, thick neck, moustache."

Conan Doyle insisted that I should have Holmes observe to Lestrade that the report was so general "it might be a description of Watson". Predictably, Lestrade would respond to Holmes' seemingly preposterous suggestion "with amusement."

"Have no fear," Conan Doyle told me. "Your readers will perceive the humour in the dramatic irony."

The scene was fiction and heartily enjoyed by the public. In reality, however, had Holmes volunteered the similarity between the alleged murderer and me, I would have no doubt betrayed enough genuine agitation for Lestrade to arrest me on the spot.

It was Conan Doyle I also had to thank for the so-called "red herring" that concluded the original story. At the time, I'd wanted to draw my readers' attention away from the true perpetrator of Milverton's murder. Conan Doyle suggested that false business at the end when Holmes shows me the photograph of a "regal and stately lady" who he believed had been wronged by Milverton and who he suspected had subsequently shot the blackmailer. Introducing the *faux* portrait, Conan Doyle explained, would establish an imaginary aristocrat as the murderer rather than the mysterious figure we actually saw commit the crime.

With Milverton dead and the incriminating letters burned, Lady Eva's marriage to the Earl of Dovercourt took place as planned on the eighteenth of January, just five days after our hair-raising experience at Appledore Towers. Newspapers' accounts described the wedding as a glorious affair. Of even greater significance, I firmly believe, was the fact that once news of Milverton's death and the destruction of the contents of his safe were circulated, many troubled people throughout the land besides Lady Eva Brackwell would sleep more soundly.

Of Milverton's true veiled assassin, Holmes and I spoke scarcely another word.

* * *

It was the rare occasion that Mycroft Holmes paid a visit to Baker Street. Until this time I had recorded such an event only twice—once, as readers may recall—in the case dealing with the Greek Interpreter, the other revolving around the stolen plans for the Bruce-Partington submarine. Yet on the day following our meeting with Lestrade, the generous bulk of Mycroft Holmes filled the stairwell as he climbed the seventeen steps to our sitting room.

He spent a moment standing on the hearthrug before our fireplace to catch his breath. Then he lowered himself into his brother's favourite velvet-lined armchair. Waving away our offers of food or tea emphasized the serious nature of his visit.

"Knowing you as I do, Sherlock," said he to my friend, "I can only conclude that by now you have come to the realization that a most important figure in our global plans was being blackmailed by the late Charles Augustus Milverton."

"But how—?" I was about to ask.

Mycroft's raised his hand to stifle my question.

"Captain Donald W. Stewart currently plays a vital role in our efforts to colonize the tribal people of Africa—most recently in the Gold Coast. So important a figure is he that I have it from the highest of authorities that knighthood is not far off. Not only can we ill afford to jeopardize his personal reputation, gentlemen, but we can also ill afford to expose the vulnerability of the defenders of the British Empire."

He underlined the certainty of his conviction by fixing us both with his steel-grey eyes. The fire crackled in the background.

"Let me be clear," said Mycroft with finality. "The government do not want Captain Stewart's awkward relationship with Milverton made known to anyone. *Anyone.* Including past relations. *Especially* past relations. Full stop."

The large man pushed himself to the front of the seat and, with the same dexterity I'd seen before, rose from his chair. He nodded at us both, then marched down the stairs, and out to the awaiting government carriage.

Holmes' wry smile suggested his suspicion that some sort of caveat like this would be coming. With a deep sigh, he got up and slowly walked to the coat hook where his mouse-colour dressing gown was hanging. From a side pocket he extracted the envelope he'd placed there the night before. Shuffling over to the hearth, he shrugged and tossed the incriminating evidence into the fire.

Daniel D. Victor

Chapter Twelve

There was a man with tongue of wood
Who essayed to sing
And in truth it was lamentable
But there was one who heard
The clip-clapper of this tongue of wood
And knew what the man
Wished to sing
And with that the singer was content.
                    --Stephen Crane

One might think it would have been difficult for
Holmes and me to honour Mycroft's request—that keeping
quiet about the blackmailing of Cora's legal husband would
have gnawed away at the two of us. Not only did we both
think she deserved to know, but we also shared a sense of
sympathy for the woman. What's more, in his inimitable
fashion, Sherlock Holmes envisioned Cora's divorce from
Donald Stewart and subsequent marriage to Stephen Crane
an eminently logical untangling of a legal skein.

Yet weeks passed and then months, and still Donald
Stewart made no move to end the marriage. There seemed
little to be gained from telling Cora how close she'd come to
freedom with nothing to suggest that Stewart's hatred of her
had diminished or that any desire for legal separation had
taken root. Providing her with such news, Holmes and I
agreed, seemed tantamount to cruelty. Not seeing the lady for
most of the next year made our silence all the easier.

We did communicate by post, however—or rather
Cora did. The first of two letters from her arrived a few weeks

after Mycroft's visit. It was written on the same pale-blue vellum that she had sent us before; only on this occasion there was no handwritten "Ravensbrook" blotting out the full address of Brede Place.

Dear Dr. Watson and Mr. Holmes [the letter ran],
 I am pleased to tell you that, while Stevie and I did not get to our new home during his first week back in England as I had hoped, I did take him the following Tuesday. He <u>loves</u> the manor house, and making use of train and wagons, we moved in last Sunday—February 12, to be exact. Despite all the house's challenges, which you already know about, we've settled in nicely, and Stevie has come to like the idea of being an English squire. In fact, I've taken to calling him "<u>The Baron of Brede Place</u>." In particular, he's quite pleased with his study above the entry hall and plans to do all of his writing there. We've painted it red and given him a long table for all his manuscripts. As only Stevie can, he's already named the stronghold his "lonely prison of happiness." I think he'd actually like to fortify the room to prevent anyone—<u>except the dogs</u>—from getting inside and disturbing him, but you can bet that from time to time I'll follow Spongie in there to check up on him.
 In case you were wondering, we haven't seen David Bergman since that first night in London when the two of them arrived. Perhaps, they had some sort of row that Stevie won't tell me anything about. Although he's always on the lookout for David, Stevie seems to have given up on the novel he was writing about him, the one called <u>Flowers of Asphalt</u>. In fact, Stevie tossed the manuscript into one of those big fireplaces we have here at Brede. The pages burned so quickly that it didn't take long for the fire to consume the whole thing. To be honest, judging from its brevity, I don't believe he'd written very much anyway.

As far as finding out who killed that awful Milverton is concerned, we don't really care. Stevie said it would take a detective like "Sherlock Doyle" to untangle the crime. Let sleeping dogs lie is my attitude.

We both thank you for all of your help.

Best,

Cora Crane

I was pleased to learn that the transition to Brede Place had gone so smoothly for the Cranes, but *"Sherlock Doyle"*? I could understand such a misstatement from a general reader, but not from a writer who was supposed to understand the difference between a literary agent like Conan Doyle and the chief actor of the drama. Based on Crane's reference to "untangling crimes," I suppose I should be flattered that the man had read some of my narratives. But at the very least, what we writers all crave is proper recognition.

* * *

The next correspondence from Cora Crane arrived near the end of the year. Holmes and I were sitting in our armchairs before the fire one afternoon in early December when Billy the page brought up to us the second missive from Brede Place. Actually, it was more of an invitation.

"Do be a good fellow," Holmes sighed upon hearing of the sender. "Read the letter to yourself and then summarize its contents for me. The human brain is too small an attic to be cluttered by the excess lumber so often supplied by Mrs. Crane."

I allowed myself a chuckle and, picking up the letter, began to read her pinched script. Once I'd finished, I furnished Holmes with the highlights. Cora was pleased to announce that Stephen, despite some bouts of coughing and a generally weakened condition, had spent much of the year writing productively. With Cora doing his typing, she reported that he'd completed *Active Service,* his novel about the Greco-Turkish war, as well as various poems, numerous tales, and much of an Irish Romance he called *The O'Ruddy.*

On the other hand, she confessed to hosting countless parties at Brede that she knew interrupted her husband's focus. Thanks to a plethora of social columns regarding the pair, I'd already learned of such goings-on. Indeed, the Cranes' reputation as reckless party-givers seemed well established in the public prints; and during the past few months in particular, the pair had reportedly hosted many wild affairs. Apparently, countless writers, actors, and other such exalted personages couldn't consider themselves truly accomplished until they'd spent a raucous weekend at a garden-party or *soirée* with Stephen and Cora Crane.

"Cora says that Crane refers to his guests as 'Indians'," I reported to Holmes, "and it seems that you and I are being invited to join the powwow. The Cranes are planning a major celebration at Christmas time and would like us to join a large group at Brede for three days of holiday revelry. Cora writes of high-toned holiday entertainment—some sort of play—to be put on at the end of the month."

"'High-toned', Holmes observed dryly, "is not a term I associate with those two."

"If that isn't entertainment enough," I continued, "she says that on the evening of the final day, they are planning a sumptuous feast and ball—musicians and so forth."

The next bit I read verbatim so Holmes would not miss Cora's exact wording: "'I'm afraid you'll have to bring your own bedding, and anything extra will be appreciated.'"

My friend raised an eyebrow, and I was already anticipating the reasons he would cite for turning down the invitation—an invitation, I must confess, that to me felt oddly appealing.

"Although such a celebration may sound tantalizing, Watson," said he in his most sarcastic tone, "my idea of a proper Christmas involves sitting in this soft chair before the hearth, smoking my pipe, and slowly imbibing one of Mrs. Hudson's hot toddies." No doubt to conjure the image in his fertile brain, he leaned his head back and closed his eyes.

Part of me was inclined to agree. "'Bring your own bedding'?" I repeated with a smirk. "And what about the weather? Why, the foul weather alone could ruin such an excursion. Do you remember how cold it was last winter when we were closing out the Milverton case? I'll send our regrets."

Holmes didn't move, but he did reopen his eyes.

"My dear fellow," said he, "just because *I* might prefer Mrs. Hudson's spiced wine is no reason for *you* to decline attendance at the bacchanalia. Cora Crane's diversions have attracted your attention in the past. Recall the drudgeries of the Frederic inquest and Kate Lyon's trial that you seemed to thrive on. Now you are being offered frivolity that will actually be intended."

He made a good case.

"But the weather, Holmes," I replied weakly. "It would be quite a challenging excursion if the weather is bad."

"True, Watson, in all probability the weather *will* be bad. And yet every so often one feels an urge to flaunt the confines of reason and act on whim—at least, during the holiday season. Check your histories, old fellow, and I think you will see that sometimes even you and I have acted out of character at that time of year. In the case you recorded as "The Blue Carbuncle", did we not—quite uncharacteristically, if I do say so myself—offer Mr. Henry Baker a free goose at

Christmas? Rest assured, I will get along quite well without you."

The three-day festivities did sound inviting. And Holmes was right: I hadn't let the snow stop me from getting to the legal proceedings in Croydon the year before. Besides, for some exhilarating reason I really did enjoy the company of Cora Crane. What's more, there would probably be lots of other authors present—Crane's friends like Conrad, Wells, and James, fellow writers with whom I could share my thoughts.

"I'll go!" I concluded.

Holmes smiled, closed his eyes again, and seconds later, breathing deeply, exhibited all the signs of innocent slumber.

* * *

It was more than Mrs. Hudson's spiced wine that had put Sherlock Holmes in a jovial mood that Christmas Day of '99. As we toasted the holiday, I really did have reason to worry about the weather while he got to remain indoors. The carpet of snow under which London lay buried had easily convinced Holmes that he'd been wise to avoid the trip to Sussex upon which I was about to embark. In fact, those three days at the close of the year during which the Cranes' holiday party took place presented some of the most severe English weather that I can recall.

I set out for Brede on a rainy Wednesday, the twenty-seventh of December. Bundled in a heavy ulster, I was additionally equipped with kid gloves, woollen scarf, and black bowler, which I'd pulled down over my brow. I had no use for an umbrella since both of my hands were already occupied. Each was carrying a large brown-leather valise—one filled with my clothes; the other, as requested by Cora Crane, with whatever extra bedding Mrs. Hudson could spare—a few linen sheets, two down pillows and three woollen blankets.

There wasn't much to observe from the railway windows during the trip to Hastings, lots of wet slate and smoking chimneys in London and rain-drenched hills and sodden farmlands throughout the countryside. And all of it under a sky painted dark by heavy, driven clouds. With all the rain and snow, I reckoned that getting from the train station to the manor house itself would be the major challenge of the later afternoon. The usual dogcart or trap would face rough going in weather like this.

As it turned out, I needn't have worried. Despite the deluge, four matching bays, reddish-brown mahogany in colour with black manes and tails, stood proudly at the front of a large omnibus just beyond the station. Through the downpour, one could discern on the vehicle's door a dark-coloured coat of arms. Cora had told us of her husband's British ancestry; I imagined that the insignia—featuring a large bird, presumably a crane, at the centre—to be some sort of proof.

Under a penetratingly cold rain, I boarded the bus along with a number of other travellers I didn't know, but who'd ridden the same train to Hastings as I. In the face of heavy snow, icy winds, and muddy roads, one could easily have believed that some divining force was trying to prevent our appearance at the celebration. But the horses pulled mightily, and despite the gods' wrath we reached the manor house in less than an hour.

* * *

Readers will remember that, due to the summer rainstorm that had interrupted my only previous visit to Brede

Place, I'd never got the opportunity to enter the house itself. Cora had warned that the structure, being in such a state of ill repair, would offer little protection from the elements. It was not without irony then that with conditions far worse on this icy afternoon than on that rainy day in August, I now sought shelter beneath its leaking roof.

"Mind the owls," warned a gnarled old man holding open the iron-studded outer door. This was not the servant called Mack, the ancient with the white beard I'd seen on my first trip to Brede; but rather, I would soon learn, the serving man called Heather whom Cora had told us came along with the rental of the house. He now worked as butler, and amongst his other responsibilities was to prevent us from standing directly under the large white birds that were nesting in the high beams of the entrance hall. Lifting our bags, however, did not seem part of his job.

At Baker Street, Billy the page had brought my two valises downstairs, and in the roadway the cabbie had hoisted them atop the four-wheeler. On the railway platform in London, a porter had loaded them onto the train, and at Hastings another porter had taken them off. From there, however, I had been on my own.

I now struggled with the clumsy suitcases up a set of smaller steps, through another oak doorway, and into a large antechamber. Festooned with all sorts of romantic regalia, it left little doubt as to whose domain one had just entered. Hanging on the walls were two crossed swords—relics (so Cora would inform me) from Stephen Crane's callow days of military training at Claverack College in New York—and red-and-green-striped blankets—souvenirs from his travels to Mexico in the days before he and Cora had met. The bright yellow and red of a tattered Spanish flag hung centre stage, a trophy Crane had acquired in Cuba.

Fortunately, I managed to carry my bags a few more paces to the Great Hall, an oak-panelled chamber running the length of the house. A number of log-fires made the room glow orange and red. In fact, within the largest of the fireplaces below a stone-carved over-mantel with Tudor rose and *fleurs-de-lys*, there burned what appeared to be an entire tree trunk. The huge blaze produced not only a most welcome warmth, but also a smoky sort of smell that conjured thoughts of well-cooked meats and rich cigars. With the crackling fires and the many inviting couches and armchairs, it seemed obvious that Cora had worked hard to render the Great Hall the social centre of the gathering.

In fact, Cora's enthusiastic—if not obsessive—hand was obvious everywhere. Silvery tinsel dangled from the Christmas holly-and-ivy draping the woodwork. Fat, white candles in black wrought-iron sconces hung from walls and ceiling-beams. Despite such noble efforts, however, one could scarcely avoid noticing the hot wax that threatened the dancers beneath the candles and the twisting shadows that enveloped them in a melancholy darkness. At least, I couldn't avoid noticing; and in the midst of all the revelry, I felt filled with sadness.

Fortunately, a liveried footman with ginger hair broke in upon my gloomy thoughts.

"Sir," said he, indicating my valises on the floor beside me, "I'll deliver these to the men's dormitory."

I should have felt relieved. But my first reaction was to say, "*Dormitory?* No bedrooms?"

"No, sir," he replied. "The men's quarters are in the attic."

"The attic?" I grimaced. "Then here," I said, removing my coat, hat, scarf and gloves and handing them to him, "you might as well take these too."

"Bedrooms were offered to the guests who arrived early, Sir," the footman explained, presumably not for the first time, "and the few individual rooms that were available are now already occupied."

"Already occupied"—just my luck! At least, I didn't have to make the journey with the bags myself, I thought, as I stood there watching the poor fellow struggle with my belongings on his way to the staircase.

"It's always the early bird that catches the damned worm, what?" I heard a high-pitched voice from over my shoulder say. "Bedrooms for the first guests only."

I turned and saw before me a rather slight gentleman whose thin, blond moustache and narrow face looked familiar.

"H.G. Wells," he said, eyes flashing. "My friends call me Bertie."

I clasped his hand, gawping at the thrill of meeting the author of such well-known romances as *The Time Machine, The Invisible Man,* and *The War of the Worlds.*

I introduced myself, but he seemed to have already recognized me. "I've followed your accounts of Sherlock Holmes' cases in *The Strand,*" Wells was kind enough to offer. "Your friend Mr. Holmes is not with you?" As he asked the question, his bright eyes peered round the room.

I explained that he was not.

"Pity to miss him. Do you know that there are some who think he should have tried his hand against my Martians? Would have rid the damned world of them all the sooner, they say."

"Perhaps with some help," I chuckled. "Why not throw Conan Doyle's Professor Challenger into the mix? Together, the two of them could save the world." Holmes, of course, would have ridiculed Wells' far-fetched concept—the invasion of the earth by creatures from Mars, indeed!

"On the other hand," Wells went on, "had Holmes actually been here, you no doubt would have required a room for the two of you, and then Jane and I might have been odd-man-out. As it is, not to boast, we've been given private quarters over the main gateway."

Why would Wells think Holmes and I would request one room for the two of us? What was he thinking? I suddenly felt the same anxiety I'd experienced in the growler when David Bergman misconstrued my words. I must have communicated my discomfort because, for whatever the reason, Wells took the opportunity to change the subject.

Actually, he began elaborating what the footman had just described. "The overflow crowds are divided into men and women," he said. "The women are to sleep in what Cora likes to call the Girls' Dormitory. The men, as you've heard, are consigned to the attic. You'll have to make do with truckle beds and cots. I hear they were hired from a nearby hospital. Not much heat up there either, I'm afraid. Nobody to keep you warm—if you know what I mean." He punctuated this last sentence with a sly wink.

"I'll manage," said I, ignoring his *double entendre* while appreciating the woollen blankets I had brought with me.

"Mind you," Wells cautioned, "one needn't be too envious of the lucky few who *have* got their own rooms. No one has any plumbing to speak of. A single ancient facility for the women, and we gentlemen have to literally make do with the great outdoors. And in this damned weather."

It was at this juncture that the host and hostess appeared, Cora in a velveteen frock of navy-blue, Crane dressed to the nines in formal attire, with only his dark-blond hair and drooping moustache left shaggy in some act of rebellion. That his clothes hung loosely on his small frame testified to the weight he had lost during the past year. Still, with a cigarette in one hand, a tall whisky and soda in the other, and a lock of that tawny hair falling casually over his right eye, he looked quite the sophisticate. The pair of them did.

They circulated throughout the hall. When they arrived before Wells and me, Cora took both of my hands. "Welcome, John," she beamed. At first, Crane didn't look at me. Instead, he continued scanning the guests that he and Cora had not yet approached.

I smiled at the hostess and nodded at her husband.

"Hey," Stephen Crane said when he finally fixed his sad eyes upon me. "I see you've already run into Bertie here. Alf Munroe's walking around somewhere as well. This place is getting to be pretty much like a writer's convention."

In point of fact, Cora told me later that some of Crane's most notable literary friends had sent their regrets; writers like Joseph Conrad, Henry James, Rider Haggard, Robert Barr and George Gissing had all been invited but apparently had other places to be.

"You two have really made quite a spectacle of the old place," I said.

Crane chuckled. "Would you believe that Cora here thinks that Sir Walter Scott designed the house just for her? Silly girl," he teased, hugging her round the shoulder.

All hostess now, Cora shook herself free. "We're sorry Mr. Holmes couldn't be here," she said, looking to Crane for agreement. But once more, the writer seemed distracted. He'd begun scrutinizing the crowd again. "Aren't we sorry Mr. Holmes couldn't be here, Stevie?" she repeated, jerking his arm.

"Yeah, sure, Hon'," he muttered. "Whatever you say."

"Did you enjoy your bus-ride from the station?" Cora asked me.

"Quite impressive. Especially your horses."

At the mention of the bays, Crane redirected his attention.

"The lead horses are my own," he said. "Hengist and Horsa. Named after the famous Jutes, who saved England from the Germans more than a thousand years ago."

"Indeed," said I, impressed by the American's knowledge. I for one couldn't have named a single leader of the Jutes, let alone two.

"If I'm not very much mistaken," Wells put in, ", the Jutes defeated the Britons as well—and ended up settling here in Kent." He paused for a moment and then added, "One can never trust those damned Jutes."

The couple smiled blankly at Wells' witticism as revellers often do at large affairs when they don't pay full attention. Then host and hostess moved on to greet still others. But even as Crane ambled along, he resumed his surveillance of the crowd. It seemed obvious that he was looking for someone in particular.

Wells broke into my thoughts. "Join me and Jane at dinner, won't you, Watson?" he offered.

How could one refuse an invitation from the creator of a Martian invasion and a machine that could travel through time?

"With pleasure," said I.

* * *

When the meal was announced, I had no trouble locating the table at which were seated Wells and his wife. Jane, an attractive, fair-haired young woman whose sharp brown eyes signalled a sense of independence, had been his student before they married. Her real name was Amy Catherine, but for some reason Bertie called her "Jane".

"I'm afraid I haven't seen much of the party," Jane apologized. "I'm the musical accompaniment for tomorrow's show." Holding up both hands, she waggled her fingers. "Piano. I've been in rehearsal for much of the day with the dramatic production."

"Sorry Conrad couldn't be here," Wells said. "You'd have enjoyed his company, Watson. The man's such a delight to provoke."

Jane looked disapprovingly at her husband while I explained how I'd already met the Conrads during our rain-shortened visit to Brede Place in the summer.

"You see?" Wells said to his wife. "Watson knows the man. I'm sure he'd agree that Conrad is forever cynical. He's forever finding much to be critical of."

I feared Wells was going to call on me for confirmation of his thumbnail of the man, but he seemed more intent on illustrating his own analysis.

"Do you know what Conrad would call these revellers?" Wells asked, arms outstretched as if embracing the entire crowd. "He'd call everyone a 'free-luncher'. He said as much at a dinner party here once before. Referred to all Crane's friends as damned 'free-lunchers'. Surely, you remember, Jane."

"My husband," Jane said shaking her head. "He just couldn't contain himself that evening." Chuckling a bit, she recalled, "Right after Joseph mentioned 'free-lunchers', Bertie told him it was too late for '*lunch*'."

"The man couldn't see the joke," said Wells, slapping his hand on the table. "Conrad's a smart fellow, don't you know? But he just couldn't see the joke. Turned red as a beet, didn't he Jane? 'For all your considerable talents,' I told him, 'humour is one of our damned English tricks you've never learnt to tackle'."

"I like his wife Jessie," said Jane.

"An English working girl many years younger than her husband," Wells winked. "Attractive, but a trifle large,"

"Cora and I find her pleasant enough," Jane explained in support of their friend, "although she generally lets her husband do the talking in social gatherings."

"He does rather insist on it," said Wells.

"I was also hoping to meet Henry James," I offered, trying to shift attention away from the poor Conrads.

"Couldn't make it, I'm afraid," said Wells. "Though I'm told he did bid hello from his front porch to some of these very pilgrims as they passed by."

"A pity," said Jane. "He's always so charming."

"I believe he looks down upon all this frivolity," Wells observed. "He does like conversing with Stephen, but I think his sensibilities are offended by the informality—Stephen walking around in riding breeches, puttees, and flannel shirts. Not the sort of attire James fancies. Not to mention when Stephen fires that long-barrelled Mexican revolver."

"Cora too," Jane added. "She shoots as well."

Cora and guns. Suddenly, my mind filled with images from that night in Milverton's study. I could hear the rapid gunfire blasting away the silence; I could see Milverton's body splayed across the desk, then tumbling to the carpet; I could feel Holmes' firm grasp of my wrist as the cloaked murderer bolted out the door. I'm sure my face mirrored my disgust.

"Some women are frightened by firearms," Wells went on, either not noticing or simply ignoring my discomfort, "but Cora's quite the marksman. During target shooting, she just takes that cannon and fires away. Hits every bottle Stephen sets up for her. Quite impressive, really—another Annie Oakley!"

Now I was remembering Cora's puckered red lips as she blew away the phantom smoke from the tip of her forefinger.

"But as I say," Wells continued, "with her eccentric dress and cowboy performances, Cora contributes to a casualness all too reminiscent of the America Henry rejected. I believe he finds her quite embarrassing."

"I must say," observed Jane, "that such concern has never stopped him from feasting on Cora's doughnuts."

"Remember what Harold Frederic once called him?" Wells said, eyes full of mischief. "An effeminate old donkey who insists on being treated like the Pope."

I let them go on talking like that without interruption. It gave me the chance to collect my thoughts and settle my pulse. Fortunately, the arrival of food at our table put an end to the gossip. Instead of guns and insults, we could turn our attention to more savoury matters—in this case, roast turkey with stuffed chestnuts, plum pudding covered in a rum hard sauce with a holly sprig at the centre, and lots of champagne. And none too soon, I thought, since I found Wells' comments regarding Henry James less than appropriate, especially with the man not there to defend himself.

* * *

Our host seemed reluctant to engage in the type of banter that guests like Wells and his wife had been exchanging. Actually, he seemed reluctant to engage in conversation with anyone. Following dinner, a worn-out and solitary Stephen Crane sat slumped in a chair by the hearth in the Great Hall. The huge fireplace seemed to dwarf him. When a passer-by asked the most innocent of questions, the renowned man of letters would answer in monosyllables like "great" or "gaw" or "good". I didn't believe it was the night's raucous chatter that had put him off, but rather the simple desire for time by himself.

Earlier in the evening, he'd invited anyone interested in learning the game of poker to join him in a side room; and Wells and I sat at the large oak table with a handful of others watching as Crane solemnly distributed the cards. I'm afraid, however, that no one took the game seriously but Crane. When Wells leaned over to say something amusing to me, Crane immediately noted his movement. "In any decent saloon in America," he shouted at Wells, "you'd be shot for talking like that at poker!" Instantly, everyone grew quite, and Crane slammed his cards down on the table and stalked out, leaving the rest of us with little else to do but sit staring at one another.

It was near two in the morning when Cora swept in to wish everyone a good night. She informed us that breakfast would be served until noon the next day, so there was no need for anyone to rise early.

"I hope you can all stay warm tonight," she added. Then she kissed her Stevie and adjourned to the cavernous first-floor drawing room, which she'd commandeered for her *boudoir,* the same large chamber in which Friday night's ball was scheduled to take place. When she opened the double-doors, I caught a glimpse of a single candle burning at the far end of the darkened hall. It illuminated a solitary bed, which was standing upon the dais intended for the orchestra. Save for the small table with the candle and a nearby bureau, the grand room remained vacant. Amidst the gloom, the bed looked like a tiny vessel adrift in a vast and empty sea.

With Cora setting the example, the rest of the women also began taking their leave. It was a good idea. Worn out from the exhausting combination of foul weather, railway travel, and exhilarating celebration, I concluded that it was time for me to retire as well. Some of the gentlemen had already begun the trek up the broad staircase to the attic. I must admit that the Spartan conditions in our so-called dormitory—the large, cold room and the stark accommodations—did nothing to encourage my progress.

And yet once the sleeping room began to fill, it took little time for a kind of camaraderie to develop. As I'd learned in the army, such is often the result of facing hardships together. It made more meaningful our offer of extra blankets to those in need. Being bound together as favoured guests proved to be an additional factor. I couldn't speak for the others, but I for one had never before been to a *fête* whose grand design required three days of dedicated entertaining by its hosts. I believe that it was this bond of empathy that helped allay our anxieties when the wind began to shriek and the rains washed into our room.

It was only much later that H.G. Wells would so accurately put into words the contradictory nature of those three days at Brede Place. "An extraordinary lark," he wrote of the festivities, "—but shot, at the close, with red intimations of a coming tragedy."

* * *

Had I been a writer of horror stories—Joseph Le Fanu, for instance—I could not have devised a more fiendish setting for a tale of terror than the men's dormitory on that first—and proverbial—dark and stormy night. Situated high in the cold attic, the large chamber at the top of the manor house served only to bring us nearer the angry agents of heaven. Though the windows were tiny, periodic bursts of lightning lit up the entire room. Each fresh flash, as if a bright new photograph, illuminated the grim faces of some twenty gentlemen in various stages of cold, covered by as many blankets as they could secure.

Curtains of rain and rumblings of thunder shook the dank walls, rendering the darkness all the more terrifying. The wind cut through irregular casements and whipped round our confines, its continuous howl in counterpoint to a drumbeat of raindrops within the room. Somebody had strategically positioned metal tubs and buckets amongst the cots and small beds, and the dripping water echoed percussively. There may not have been any glistening cobwebs drifting from the rafters—Cora had supervised the cleaning of the house—or rusty chains clanking from belfry; but in more ways than one on such a night, Brede Place was destined to give anyone the shivers—and not only from of the cold.

Fortunately, by late the following morning, the rain had ceased. Although the countryside remained drenched, we male guests, a frozen band of brothers, could attend to calls of nature without worry of the heavens opening up. As the trails of mist dissipated, one could discern any number of relieved men returning from the sloped gardens on the eastside and the slippery pathway to the river on the west.

I managed but a single glimpse of our host that morning. Stephen Crane emerged from the outer door at the entrance to Brede Place with a white baseball in his hand. He tossed it in the air, caught it, and then surveyed the wet grounds. With a disappointed frown, he tucked the ball in the pocket of his Norfolk hunting jacket and ambled back into the manor house.

Meanwhile, in the two-storey-high kitchen, staff had prepared a breakfast of scrambled eggs and rashers of bacon, sweet potatoes from America, and various assortments of cakes, beer, and ale. All this we would eat in the large dining room, a medieval-like chamber complete with long refectory tables and wooden benches. Rather than costly carpets, the floor was covered with matting of fresh rushes picked from meadows near the river.

"Enjoy the damned plumbing?" Wells greeted me as I joined him at table.

"Indeed," was the only comment I could muster though I do confess to harbouring a thought or two about Holmes' disguise as Escott the previous year. Although he had merely pretended to be a plumber, I was convinced that my friend could still offer some pragmatic suggestions for improving the water pipes in the old place.

Yet all I said was, "Without your wife again, eh, Wells?"

"Yes," he managed between forkfuls of egg. "She's down at the village school making final preparations for this evening's performance of Crane's play. On the day of your arrival, there was actually a dress rehearsal put on for the children—although between you and me, I'm sure some older gawpers made their way inside as well."

"You mention the day *I* arrived. When exactly did you and Mrs. Wells get here?"

"Jane and I were amongst a select few invited for Christmas Dinner." Wells produced a small white card from inside his jacket. "Here's the menu—hand-lettered by Cora herself. The foods are all Stephen's favourites."

I reproduce the bill of fare exactly as Wells presented it to me:

> *Xmas Dinner 1899*
>
> *—Stephen Crane—Author—8 People.*
>
> *Roast Turkey, Stuffed Chestnuts, Giblet Gravy,*
>
> *Sweet Corn, Stewed Tomatoes, Cranberry Sauce.*
>
> *Plum Pudding, Hard Sauce,*
>
> *Mince Pies, Pumpkin Pies,*
>
> *Nuts, Raisins, Apples, Oranges, Figs, Dates.*
>
> *Coffee, Champagne, Claret, Green Mint.*
>
> *Brede Place, Sussex.*

"So," I observed as I handed the card back to him, "by arriving first, you and your wife gained not only a private bedroom, but also a delicious meal—not to mention the details you've learned regarding the festivities."

"Right," Wells said sarcastically, "all the *important* information—like how Stephen and Cora procured the servants, hired the horses, and commissioned a small orchestra for the ball."

Thanks to Jane's participation in the rehearsals, Wells had also gained background on the play itself. For instance, he had learned how the initial concept of the dramatic presentation—"actually, more of a farce, as I understand it," Wells said—had begun months earlier at the same time Crane had come up with the idea for the party. As it turned out, he and Cora had needed all that time to allow for composing a script, writing the music, constructing the omnibus, painting the scenery, and negotiating with the village to appropriate a suitable venue. To grease the wheel, as it were, the Cranes even agreed to donate to the Brede Hill school the additional stage they were having built within its walls.

"Quite a project!" I exclaimed.

"Indeed," Wells said. "As a writer yourself, Dr. Watson, you might particularly appreciate Crane's inventiveness." Wells took a pull of beer from a brown bottle. "Although Stephen created most of the dialogue himself, he did ask a number of his literary friends to contribute a line or two or even just a basic word—the shorter the better, in fact. It was all meant to be tongue-in-cheek as he was soliciting only simple words like *it* or *they* or *you*. But that way, you see, with even the smallest of offers, he could claim as additional authors of his grand production such noted writers as James, Gissing, Conrad, Rider Haggard, Mason, and—with all due modesty—myself. Most everyone cooperated. In fact, not only did Alf Mason contribute—in his case, 'collaborate' is probably a better term—Crane got him to agree to serve as stage manager and director. He's also playing the part of the Ghost of Brede Manor."

"*A ghost,*" I thought. Here it was again. However light-hearted Crane intended the play to be, he still couldn't avoid his flirtations with death.

Wells turned to the American potatoes.

"And Cora's role?" I asked. With her husband having created the script, I could easily picture her as a featured thespian.

"How does Milton put it?" Wells asked between bites. "'They also serve who only stand and wait.' Cora's the prompter. A minor functionary, to be sure, unless, of course—as is quite likely—people forget their lines."

Wells had so aroused my curiosity that I found myself eagerly looking forward to the dramatic spectacle. It sounded like a grand comedy, and yet I wondered what more it might reveal about the uniqueness of the Cranes.

I had only to wait a few more hours for the answer. When one begins breakfast near noon, the remains of the day appear significantly shorter.

* * *

The heavy rainfall resumed during the late morning of the second day; by early afternoon it was snowing. How right I had been to worry about the weather! At some point I feared that the performance might be cancelled, but Wells assured me that there was no chance of Crane's being denied his playwriting debut.

With nowhere to go, I found myself perusing the bookshelves scattered round the house, eager for some reading to keep me occupied. *What sort of authors might the young writer admire?* I wondered. Certainly, there was no scarcity of poets. Amongst the more familiar names were those of Shakespeare, Burns, Dryden, Longfellow, Browning, Rossetti, Swinburne, and Shelley. I also saw novels by Kipling and Henry James.

In the end, I sat down with an American magazine containing a piece called "The Monster" written by Crane himself. As one might suspect from the title, it proved to be a most unsettling tale. While saving a young white boy in a fire, a Negro man has his face horribly disfigured. The ironic result of his heroism is that the rest of the town now shuns him. The story seemed another example of Crane's sympathy for those who fall outside of society's traditional parameters— like the prostitute, the homosexual, the coward.

Though the sombre tone of the piece matched the gloom of the sky, I didn't want the oppressiveness of the story to colour the rest of the day. After all, despite the foulness of the weather, there was still Crane's play to enjoy—provided we could all get to the Brede Hill schoolhouse to see it.

It was the author himself who, when confronted by the continuing snowfall, decided on an early start. Some three hours before the curtain was due to rise, the single omnibus began ferrying guests the few miles into town to the schoolhouse, the site of the theatrical production. It fell to Hengist and Horsa and the other stalwart bays to haul the bus through the slurry of snow and ice and mud. Some four excursions were required to accommodate everyone, and what some regarded as Crane's overly cautious departure times proved to be very wise indeed. On my trip, the second of the four, the conditions on the roadway were so daunting that the male passengers disembarked mid-journey to help free the large vehicle from the slush.

In the end, despite being a trifle wet and dirty, everyone arrived on time; and the performance of "The Ghost"—written by Stephen Crane and others—began more or less promptly at 7:45.

Chapter Thirteen

"I have heard the sunset song of the birches
A white melody in the silence
I have seen a quarrel of the pines.
At nightfall
The little grasses have rushed by me
With the wind-men.
These things have I lived," quoth the maniac,
"Possessing only eyes and ears.
But, you—
You don green spectacles before you look at roses."
--Stephen Crane

One need not be a drama critic to recognize that Stephen Crane intended his play about the supernatural to be light-hearted. Why else set it impossibly in the future? Why else embellish it with a bouncy melodic score? Why else encourage Jane Wells' spirited performance on the piano? Her renditions of dances and songs that echoed the mincing notes of Gilbert and Sullivan's *The Mikado*—"Three Little Maids from Rye" comes to mind—could only be expected to evoke the audience's amusement. Why else accommodate the musical talents of a hot-blooded young female performer with a rousing dance accompanied by castanets? A local newspaper review got it right when it labelled the theatrics "a combination of farce, comedy, opera, and burlesque."

And yet even in humour Stephen Crane seemed unable to resist his obsession with the transitory nature of life. Permeating his script of "The Ghost" were musings on how the present so quickly recedes into the past, how life's treasures fade so quickly.

Although the play features Sir Goddard Oxenbridge, the eponymous spirit and actual sixteenth-century resident of the manor house, the action itself begins at Brede Place in the year 1950. A group of sceptical tourists is listening to Sir Goddard lament the demise of belief in the supernatural. Prompted by the ridicule of the insensitive sightseers, the ghost relates to them his own legendary and tragic history, including how in days of old he used to eat little children, an admission that drew good-humoured hisses from the audience in the schoolhouse.

Unfortunately for Sir Goddard, on one of those occasions, he was rendered insensible from drinking too much; and the villagers, recognizing the opportunity to rid themselves of the child-eater, killed him. Actually, they sawed him into halves, resulting in the two-part ghost that he now is (or is supposed to be—since Alf Mason, who was portraying the spirit, demanded that his body remain intact). At the conclusion of his macabre narrative, the ghost, who has frightened none of the tourists, is reduced to begging for a couple of bob.

Death, doubt, disbelief—certainly, Crane must have sensed by play's end that his staged holiday merriment was verging on the depressive. Why else but to reinvigorate his audience would he have concluded the production with a lively dance and chorus that bring together unhappy ghost and doubting tourists?

The audience responded with wild and enthusiastic applause. Amidst calls of "*encore*" and "author," Crane, who'd been sitting off to the side of the stage, pushed back the shock of hair falling over his forehead, and joined the cast to take their bows. The cheers echoed for many minutes; and before the participants could exit, the audience rose and served up their own rendition of "For they are jolly good people". During the chorus, Crane blushed. At the same time, he persisted in scanning the crowd.

I too joined in the singing, yet I couldn't shake the gloom that had overwhelmed me at the play's conclusion. I couldn't rid myself of the notion that Crane's drama, so obviously intended for holiday merriment, seemed built on a foundation of melancholia.

Not that I regarded the play as entirely dark. I didn't infer the spiritual "emptiness" of the entire house in the programme's description of the setting as "an empty room at Brede Place"—though I must confess that some part of me did construe the phrase in that manner. How could I not after having heard the solitary footfalls echoing through Cora's enormous bedchamber?

Nor did I infer that the borrowing of characters invented by his friends indicated a loss of Crane's creativity. I suspected that he was probably just honouring his fellow authors. Yet with all the pressure on Crane to amplify his income, such figures in Crane's script as Dr. Moreau (appropriated from Wells' horror tale, *The Island of Dr. Moreau*) and Peter Quint (taken from Henry James' ghost story, *The Turn of the Screw*)—not to mention Rufus Coleman lifted from Crane's own *Active Service*—reveal a simplistic shortcut in the creative process.

The role of the ghost raised similar issues. While the historical Sir Goddard was supposed to have been a kindly old man, the interpretation of the legend by a heavily made-up Alf Mason, was in reality quite terrifying. Mason's skull-like brow, his pale face-paint with its darkened eye-sockets, his silver strands of thinning hair—all rendered him the epitome of those ghastly beings we've come to label the "undead". At the same time, the entire point of the opening scene was to present "Sir Goddard" as a ghost that couldn't scare anyone. Is it not too far a stretch to discern in Crane's impotent phantom the kindred spirit of an author fearing the loss of his artistic power?

I realize that I must have been alone in my philosophizing that night. For everyone else, neither the frightful weather nor the darkness of the play seemed to lessen the high spirits generated by Crane's theatrical production. Yet despite all the good cheer—the singing, the laughing, the backslapping—I couldn't seem to lose my feelings of depression.

Perhaps it was a case of knowing too much about the author, of having too much information about the struggles of this young man who loved to wander and about the worries of his devoted wife who cared so deeply. Perhaps it was a case of watching the two hosts try too hard to entertain. Or perhaps I was simply being churlish, jealous of my friend Sherlock Holmes who, at that very moment, was no doubt enjoying our warm quarters in Baker Street. While I remained hostage to my dark visions and the biting cold, I could envision my friend ensconced in his armchair before the fire, smoking some strong black shag in his favourite clay pipe.

Whatever the cause, it seemed that the longer I lingered amongst the revelry, the more melancholy I became. Even now, after so many years have passed, it remains difficult to accept the scene I witnessed from my rickety bed later that night. Haunted yet again by howling winds and flashes of angry lightning, I had to ask myself how so many of my fellow play-goers could fall asleep with smiles on their faces. Like myself, hadn't they not also just witnessed Stephen Crane's veiled testimony to the evanescence of human life?

* * *

Daniel D. Victor

They were enigmatic people, Stephen and Cora Crane—they entertained and then retreated back into their own wild fantasies or desultory bickering or whatever it was that kept them together and let people like me wonder about the nature of their relationship. Yet there was little wonder about the generous spirit of their merry-making. However they got the money to finance their parties, the celebrations were first-rate.

The ball highlighted the third day.

It was probably for the best that the heavy snows had kept most of the local neighbours away—the Great Hall was crowded enough with the wild revellers from the guest list. The small orchestra that the Cranes had hired from London provided toe-tapping music, and amidst a group of beautiful young American women—some friends, some related to friends—guests whirled and twirled throughout the night. Not to be outdone by the dancers, H.G. Wells involved a number of enthusiastic celebrants in a game that included racing on broomsticks across the waxed tiles.

Nor was Stephen Crane averse to shaking a leg. Early in the evening, the orchestra struck up "Run Away Girl," and he joined in a lancers and then a barn dance and, fittingly, a last waltz with Cora. Later, after the dancing had ended, he sat before a small group of friends, strumming his guitar in accompaniment to some Spanish songs he'd no doubt learned in Cuba.

By midnight, however, he seemed to have disappeared. He hadn't joined Cora at the door to bid good-bye to those not staying overnight, nor did he come to offer *ave atque vale* to those of us trudging off to the dormitories.

Later, after the trouble, a trembling woman would recall having seen Crane seated on a wooden settee in one of the side rooms. She said he'd been leaning against a stranger who was short in stature and dressed in black.

214

"I-I think Stephen's head was resting on the man's shoulder," she said haltingly.

Whoever the dark figure was, the woman reported that she'd seen the man's shirt mottled with blood as he exited. Although I didn't understand the meaning of such a tableau, it was my speculation that, as intimate as the two men appeared to have been, this mysterious stranger must surely have been the person whom Crane had been seeking for the past three days.

While it seemed much longer, it actually took only a few minutes to find the missing author. Crane was discovered unconscious in another side room, stretched out on a hard-backed settee—apparently placed there after falling into unconsciousness.

"We need a doctor!" someone shouted; and I immediately answered the call. From then on, of course, everything was different.

In medical terms, Crane had suffered a haemorrhage from the lungs and passed out. He had coughed up blood, no doubt the origin of the stains on the mysterious visitor's clothing. Perspiring freely when he came round, he tried to conceal his condition from Cora who'd come running to the scene just a few moments after me.

"I'm fine, Hon'," he whispered as she tenderly kissed his forehead. "Just get me into a chair."

But Cora was smarter than that. Sending everyone off to bed, she cleared the room of gawping spectators, allowing only Wells and me to remain. It was the two of us who lowered Crane onto the soft cushions of a nearby armchair. Carrying so light a burden made me realize how thin and frail the poor fellow actually was.

Cora planted herself on one of the chair's wide arms and stroked Stephen's lank hair. "This isn't the first time, John," she said to me quietly over her shoulder. "You and

Mr. Holmes have seen him coughing. He's been like that ever since he returned from the States."

"Without doubt *before* he returned," said I. "Has he had a diagnosis?"

She shook her head. "No. But whatever he's got is probably why the navy turned him down in April of last year."

It was Wells who offered the explanation. "Tuberculosis," he announced definitively. "I had it as a child." Better prepared than I, he produced a thermometer from a breast pocket.

It took but a few minutes to document a low fever, and then Cora resumed charge and ordered Stephen to bed.

"I don't want to bother anybody," Crane murmured; but Cora hushed him, and Wells and I managed to guide the young man to his room.

Moments later, she approached me with a letter.

"I got this report last September from a doctor in New York. I wrote to him after I'd heard that Stevie had gone to see him last summer. It was about a month or so after Stevie left Cuba. He sailed to Virginia on a transport that flew a yellow flag. He told me he was all right—even though I learned later that the flag meant the ship was carrying soldiers with Cuban Fever."

The letter she handed me had been posted by Dr. E.L. Trudeau, the lung specialist known round the world for his impressive work in treating tuberculosis. "Your husband had a slight evidence of activity in the trouble in his lungs," Trudeau had written, but he had added that Crane "has improved steadily" and that "he looked very well." In light of the letter, it seemed obvious that it was after Crane's return to Havana that the dreaded Cuban fever—no doubt, some form of malaria—had brought the author to his current state of deterioration.

While Cora and I had been examining Trudeau's note, Wells had ventured out in the rain to rummage about in some outlying sheds. Mack, the caretaker, joined him; and between the two, they were somehow able to discover in the darkness one of those old bicycles called "penny-farthings", the kind with the large front wheel and a much smaller back one.

"With all due respect, Watson," said Wells, "I feel I must somehow reach Stephen's personal doctor in Rye. From my own damned experience, I know full well that tuberculosis is not an illness to be trifled with."

Despite the lateness of the hour and the continuous drizzle, Cora and I both encouraged Wells to attempt the trip. Securing a doctor familiar with the patient's specific history would be particularly helpful.

"I'm afraid," added Cora, "this won't be the first time Stevie's doctor's been called in."

It would have made a striking image in its own right— H.G. Wells, noted author and social critic, riding off into a night full of rain on an old-fashioned bicycle along muddy trails and unknown roads. But on a mission of mercy, Wells' determination to cover the seven miles to Rye in such foul weather and the blackness of night seemed downright heroic.

Enveloped in a mac, scarf, and chequered deerstalker, whose flaps he'd pulled down over his ears, Wells kissed Jane good-bye, placed his foot on the peg above the back wheel, grabbed the handlebars, and mounted.

"Do you know, Watson," he said to me before departing, "I first took Crane to be sulky and reserved. I now recognize that he was profoundly weary and ill."

Then, equipped only with the address that Cora had furnished him, Wells pedalled off. He wobbled some at the start as the bicycle fought for traction in the mud, but within moments he had straightened up and, without turning round, raised a gloved hand in farewell. That brave man disappearing into the rain and darkness has remained a sight I shall not soon forget.

Chapter Fourteen

A man saw a ball of gold in the sky;
He climbed for it,
And eventually he achieved it—
It was clay.
Now this is the strange part:
When the man went to the earth
And looked again,
Lo, there was the ball of gold.
Now this is the strange part:
It was a ball of gold.
Aye, by the heavens, it was a ball of gold.
--Stephen Crane

"And for whom do you think Crane kept so sharp an eye during those three days?" Sherlock Holmes asked me following my return to Baker Street.

"I can't be certain," I offered weakly. "More guests, I suppose."

"Your account of the affair tells me that it was well attended. Why would Crane be seeking more guests? And who was the stranger in black? You reported that someone said Crane had been leaning against him before he became ill."

"That's true."

"Come, Watson. Do you see no connection between a search at the start of the festivities and a scene of comfort at the end? Crane's wife was already there. Of the major players in this drama, which one was not in attendance?"

I suppose that given the severity of Crane's illness, a more imaginative writer than I—Edgar Allan Poe comes to mind—might suggest that the mysterious visitor upon whom Crane had apparently laid his head was in reality the personification of Death—uninvited, perhaps, but certainly not ignored.

I chose, however, to furnish a more practical answer. "There is David Bergman, of course, but he has returned to America."

Holmes cocked a questioning eyebrow.

I hadn't immediately thought of Bergman because I had assumed he'd left the country. But what alternative could there be? Beyond him, I for one had no suspicions. Perhaps, he hadn't left England after all. And if it was a look of optimism I'd detected in Crane's eyes as he scanned the guests, perhaps Crane too believed—or hoped, at least—that Bergman had hidden himself away in some corner of the islands for the previous eleven months and had not actually gone back to the States.

Holmes' grey eyes flashed with certainty. "Don't you see, Watson? Crane intended that this three-day gala, along with all the other parties he'd hosted during the year, would attract Bergman's attention wherever he had gone and, as the casual moth is attracted to the flame, bring the errant young man back to centre-stage."

"But, Holmes," said I, remembering my friend's suspicions about the murderer at Appledore Towers, "if Bergman really *is* nearby, surely he must be found and questioned regarding the death of Charles Milverton."

"Watson, you forget. Were we to bear witness regarding the murder, we would be forced to confess our own criminal activities in Milverton's house."

I could only nod in response.

"Recall, Watson, that just after the shooting, we agreed that in the long run—with the death of Milverton and the destruction of his letters—justice had truly been served."

A knock at the door put an end to our conversation. It was Mrs. Hudson come to give me a telegram. The message was from Cora Crane thanking me for attending to her "Stevie" at Brede Place. In addition, she was happy to report that, with the help of the doctor in Rye who'd been successfully roused by Wells, Crane recovered his strength almost immediately and was up and about in no time.

* * *

Fate teases in cruel ways. However reassuring Cora's early news of Crane's good health, a mere five months later we were destined to learn that his recovery had been short-lived. Literally.

It was on Wednesday, the sixth of June, 1900, that I opened the morning *Times* and cried out, "Good God!"

At my exclamation, Holmes looked up in concern. He'd been brewing a muddy concoction in a retort over the high blue flame of a Bunsen burner. To catch the condensation, he'd placed a litre measure next to the burner.

"What is it?" he asked.

Thunderstruck, I managed to utter, "S-Stephen Crane. He died of tuberculosis yesterday in Germany. He was just twenty-eight."

Holmes stopped his work and turned off the flame. "Once again," said he in his most serious tone, "I am forced to ask how nature can play these cruel tricks on such poor creatures as ourselves? We spend all our time on earth seeking more from life, and in the end we discover too quickly that all we are left with is nothingness."

How could one disagree with so pessimistic a philosophy when the life of Stephen Crane could be offered as confirmation? I responded to Holmes with the conclusion of *The Times'* report. The early death of Stephen Crane, the newspaper observed, "removes from the ranks of letters a man of real ability, from whom not only the public, but his fellow-craftsmen, expected a good deal."

Crane had suffered numerous relapses. As we were to learn later, Cora, having struggled for months with his debilitating illness and their continual need for money, had finally secured enough funds in the name of her dying husband to arrange their journey to a sanatorium in Badweiler. Even though the institution specialized in tubercular illness, by the time they got to Germany, her "Stevie" was too far-gone for any treatment to be of help. In the end, all Cora could do was to return his body to London on its journey for burial back in America.

* * *

The casket carrying Stephen Crane arrived in London by way of Dover on Saturday, 9 June, the same weekend Holmes and I were in the middle of the singular case involving the broken busts of Napoleon. Still, we made it our business to be on hand when Cora Crane came to see us at Baker Street that Saturday afternoon. Brief as her visit was, her appearance in black rendered the tragedy all the more real.

"I don't know my way around London," she confessed. "Then again, who ever would have imagined that I'd need to inquire about a mortuary?" Did we know of any, she asked.

As luck would have it, we did.

"There's a small establishment just across the road at Number 82," Holmes said; and immediately Cora left to take care of the sad details.

Two days later, still savouring Holmes' solution to the problem of the six Napoleons, we received a card bordered in black. It came from the Queen Anne's Mansions where Cora was staying once again. Announcing the scheduled viewing of the writer's remains on 14 June 1900, it read: *Mrs. Stephen Crane has arranged that friends of her late husband may see him to say goodbye, at the Mortuary, 82 Baker St., on Thursday between the hours of 3 and 5 o'clock.* (I learned later that the cards had been hand-lettered by Crane's niece, Helen. His brother William's daughter, she attended school in Switzerland and had previously stayed with Stephen and Cora at Brede Place.)

* * *

Clad in mourning black and top hats, Holmes and I crossed Baker Street at precisely 4:00 Thursday afternoon. Dodging the usual carriages that came at us in all shapes and sizes and sidestepping the slurry of mud and horse droppings, we made our way to the other side of the road not far from our destination, a low-slung building of brown-brick fronted by fluted white columns.

Suddenly, Holmes touched my arm. "Observe," he said.

Exiting the mortuary and turning away from us was a short, stocky woman wearing black. Although her face was veiled and a broad-brimmed hat concealed the remainder of her features, she looked decidedly familiar. At first, I thought it was Cora, but then I recognized the broader shoulders and more strident gait.

"Holmes," I said with alarm, "surely she is the person we saw shoot Charles Milverton. Shouldn't we—"

"Come, Watson," commanded Holmes. "There's nothing left to be said upon the subject. Now we have condolences to pay." Then he took me by the arm and fairly pushed me towards the door of the mortuary. Little did I realize it at the time, but those words effectively marked the end of any further discussion between us concerning the murder of Charles Milverton.

The sombre foyer contained a table on which stood a simple white vase full of red roses. Next to the vase, a brass plate had been set to receive the name-cards of people who had attended the viewing. At the time of our arrival, only a handful of cards lay upon it.

"We're here for Stephen Crane," said Holmes to the dour woman in black standing by a wide archway that led outside.

In fact, she directed us toward to the stables, a dusty open courtyard surrounded on three sides by horses' bays. Two of the bays were occupied by a pair of restless chestnut mares whose occasional snorts were the only sounds to interrupt the silence. Save for the watering trough and bales of hay that were off in a corner and a jumble of carts that occupied the centre of the yard, the area looked deserted.

"Where are all the people?" I asked. "They used to go to Brede Place by the hundreds."

Holmes didn't answer.

On a wooden trestle perpendicular to the small entrance of the single empty bay rested the coffin containing the body of Stephen Crane. A stable was certainly not the most formal of visitation cites for the so-called "Baron of Brede Place"; but for an American writer who liked to fashion himself as some sort of cowboy, complete with six-shooter, holster, and spurs, maybe it was not so outrageous a resting place after all.

A movement on the left caught my attention, and I turned to see Cora Crane standing motionless in the shade of a black awning. Next to her was Jessie Conrad. Both ladies wore mourning dresses; and Cora's face, like that of the woman we had seen outside the mortuary, was veiled. Holmes and I touched the brims of our hats in the direction of the ladies and walked slowly to the casket, which had a glass lid to allow for viewing. Only when we stood before it did I notice an ashen-faced Joseph Conrad standing in the shadows of the bay a few feet behind the coffin. He was mumbling to his departed friend in an undecipherable language that might have been Polish or French.

Holmes and I joined him and escorted him the few paces back to the coffin.

"Mr. Holmes, Dr. Watson," said Conrad in his heavily-accented English. "It is comforting to see you both. A few others have come and gone, but it is especially comforting to see you here." Then he placed both of his hands on the coffin and added softly in French, "*Quel dommage.*" Pointing at Crane, he asked, "Did you know that we had bought a sail boat together?"

We did not.

"'*La Reine*' we called it."

One of the nearby horses stomped in the dust as I peered at Steven Crane's diminished form lying beneath the glass—his dark-blond hair combed to the side, his moustache neatly trimmed, his dark-blue cravat tied smartly beneath a white celluloid collar. Though his pale brow and hollow cheeks suggested the turmoil he'd undergone in the weeks before his death, he appeared quite the distinguished author now, not the dishevelled vagabond in the long white duster emerging from the *Manitou* on the day we'd first seen him.

"In the autumn of '97, Stephen and I used to walk the streets of London," Conrad said. "Despite my stick. In the fog. In the rain. On carpets of mud. It made no difference. We'd begin after lunch, and many times we'd walk through the night. Until the next morning. We learned London together."

Conrad allowed himself a brief smile. "Like many writers," he said, "Stephen saw visions; but unlike the others, Stephen could brood over them to some purpose."

A tribute to Crane's writing from a master.

"Stephen was a good man," Conrad said slowly. "It was the rotten crowd with whom he surrounded himself that stifled his freedom."

"'Indians' he used to call them," I offered, remembering how Bertie Wells had told me Conrad labelled them all "free-lunchers."

Conrad nodded. "Stephen was, as the French say, *mal entouré*. I believe he was worth the whole bunch put together."

I thought of all those parties at Brede that the Cranes had hosted—and their extravagant cost in manuscripts never completed.

"Before he was ill," said Conrad, "I used to think that Stephen had a quiet sort of smile that was both frightening and charming. What made it so? I wondered. Until I realized that his was the smile of someone who knew that he had not long to live."

Holmes and I simply listened.

"Do you know the one sentence I contributed to Stephen's Christmas play?" asked Joseph Conrad.

Our silence confirmed that we didn't.

"'This is a jolly cold world.'" He paused for a moment, then said it again: "This is a jolly cold world. Who could have foreseen that the poor man would be dead six months later?"

We nodded grimly.

"*Quel dommage*," he repeated, slowly shaking his head.

Sombre-faced, Holmes and I nodded to Conrad and slowly walked off in the direction of Cora Crane. She raised her veil and looked at us with her deep-green eyes. Then she shook hands with us both.

"God's speed, Mrs. Crane," I said.

"Thanks to your husband's writings," added Holmes, "you can take comfort that Stephen Crane is a name that will not extinguish any time soon."

"Thank you, gentlemen," she said. "You've both been too kind."

Holmes and I tipped our hats and were about to take our leave when Cora Crane called to me.

"May I have a word with you in private, John?" she asked.

Unaccustomed as I was to hearing my Christian name in public, I was slow to offer her my arm. But once I collected my wits and nodded at Holmes, she moved to my side and guided me to an empty corner of the courtyard.

"I have always found it easier to speak with *you* than to your friend," said she, resting her hand on my arm.

All I could do was gaze into those mesmerizing eyes. Sullied by recent tears, they still had the power to penetrate

"Before I leave for America, I wanted to share some information that has recently come my way. I leave it to you to tell Mr. Holmes."

I looked at her quizzically.

"A few weeks ago," said she softly, "I received a letter from Sir Norman Stewart, Donald's older brother."

She spoke so low that I had to lean towards her to hear her fully. Upon doing so, I was immediately engulfed in her flowery scent.

"Norman's been serving in India, and the mail can take months to get here. Apparently, some time back in February, he came to learn through his channels in the government that Donald had also been a victim of that wretch Milverton who was bringing so much grief to my Stevie."

At her mention of Crane's name, her eyes welled up, and she dabbed at them with a white handkerchief she'd kept inside the sleeve of her dress.

"Norman has always been very kind to me," she went on. "Of course, he knew that Donald and I had never legally divorced; but once he learned that I had become 'Mrs. Crane', he was kind enough to abet my deceit."

"Rejecting scandal in the name of the family honour," I put in.

She shook her head. "No, John. Even though I'm certain Sir Norman has that in mind, I believe he genuinely wishes me well. In his letter, he called himself my friend and said how he appreciated my kindness, my lack of bitterness. He said that he would keep my secret and wrote, 'God bless you'. No, I feel he is quite genuine."

I saw Holmes waiting for me near the exit, but I knew that Cora had not yet got to her point.

"Norman told me that Milverton was blackmailing Donald as well as Stevie. Apparently, Milverton had some proof about my life at the Hotel de Dream, which he threatened to make public if Donald ever divorced me." She chuckled. "If the idea of *divorce* was scandalous to the Stewart family, imagine the calamity that proof of my wicked past would produce."

"Indeed," said I, not needing to inform her that Holmes and I had already imagined the calamity.

"With Milverton dead and no evidence remaining, you see, Donald could have divorced me, and I could have married Stevie legally before he died. But only if Donald would have made so gracious a gesture—which I don't believe he ever would."

She dabbed at her eyes again.

"I suspect that you and Mr. Holmes had some role in bringing Milverton down. How deeply you were involved and how much you learned, I really don't want to know. But I wanted to tell you both that freeing myself from Donald doesn't matter anymore. I've spent all these months just trying to keep Stevie alive. Neither one of us ever felt bound by rules. We were happy together, and that's all that mattered. So I thank you and Mr. Holmes for your help. I have no regrets. I hope that's equally true for the two of you."

She pulled me towards her and kissed my cheek. When she released me, she nodded in the direction of Holmes, and then walked back towards Mrs. Conrad.

I re-joined Holmes, and together we slowly exited the grounds. On our way out of the stables, we had occasion to pass one of the mares. She bobbed her head in my direction, and I stared into her round, sad eyes. Perhaps it was the empty courtyard or the death of so promising a writer or simply the nature of horses, but what came into my mind just then was the Houyhnhnms of Jonathan Swift, the wise, philosophical horses in *Gulliver's Travels* that could think and speak. While I pondered such a fantasy, the mare suddenly emitted a shrill whinny. How that horse's neighing coincided with my dark thoughts! To me, the sound seemed a sardonic laugh, a sarcastic chortle at the accuracy of Conrad's singular contribution to Crane's play. In the end, it was indeed a "jolly cold world" in which we all lived.

Epilogue

At the end of the account I called "The Adventure of the Six Napoleons," I mentioned that Sherlock Holmes wanted to turn his attentions to the problem of the Conk-Singleton forgery. In addition to solving the mystery, he had hoped that the new challenge would distract us from thinking about the untimely death of Stephen Crane. Since there has never been any documentation of the Conk-Singleton case, it has always been assumed that Holmes never brought the matter to a successful close. I hope someday to correct the omission in the historical narrative. Let the record show that it was I who lacked the strength to tell the story of my friend's success.

In fact, during the period beginning with the terrible end to the party at Brede until well after Crane's death, I found myself so emotionally drained that I could no longer bring myself to document my friend's cases. It was not that Holmes lacked work or had lost interest in his criminal investigations during the year 1900. It was that his Boswell remained shrouded in melancholy.

* * *

Letters have propelled this chronicle from the start, and thus it seems fitting to conclude with one more. In late 1910—by which time Sherlock Holmes had long been comfortably retired in his cottage in the South Downs and I, happily set up with my new wife on Queen Anne Street—a letter arrived from America that had been forwarded to me from Baker Street. I didn't recognize the sender's name, a Mrs. Forman of Chicago—or so it was written on the outside of the envelope. In point of fact, the letter-writer proved to be none other than Harold Frederic's common-law wife, Kate Lyon, who had left England with her three children some six years before. This is what I read:

My Dear Dr. Watson],

> *I have heard that Mr. Holmes has retired and moved outside of London, and I trust that you will convey the contents of this letter to him. I am writing to you both because I know of the kind service you provided to Cora Crane in freeing her and Stephen from the clutches of that evil man, Milverton.*
>
> *Cora was as true a friend as ever there can be—she stood by me in court, took in my children, and gave me a place to live when I needed one. That is why I am doing her the service that she would have wished—to tell both you and Mr. Holmes of her passing on September 5th of this year.*
>
> *Cora had returned to America in need of money; and when various friends and family turned her away, she went back to Jacksonville where the more dubious side of her life had begun. As only Cora could, she called in a number of debts, made a few threats, and ended up, I'm sorry to say— although she herself would obviously not be—running a new house of ill repute called The Court. I have been told that it was even grander than her establishment in which she'd met Stephen. Cora married again—briefly and unhappily—but eventually lived for a short time with another man whom she found much more compatible. Then one hot summer day, after trying to help a stranger push his car out of the sand where it had gotten stuck, she felt dizzy, lay down, and died.*

Cora was the kindest person whom I have ever known.
　　Yours sincerely,
　　Kate (Lyon) Forman

Of David Bergman, we never again heard anything at all.

One final note: In 1907, Joseph Conrad did indeed complete his novel about the bombing of the Royal Observatory at Greenwich. He called it *The Secret Agent* and, true to his word, wrote nothing that could specifically be traced back to Martial Bourdin, the perpetrator, or to Charles Milverton, the sponsor. It is needless to add that Conrad was much more than a simple storyteller. In his many novels, he found various ways to present his vision of how people create the veneer we call civilization in order to conceal the sordidness of their daily lives.

Some literary critics with much greater insight than I possess have suggested that Conrad's "Stevie", the innocent lad in *The Secret Agent* who is blown to bits while carrying the Greenwich bomb, evokes the young St. Stephen, the first Christian martyr. I respectfully disagree. I see in that poor victim another young "Stevie" taken from us before his time was due, the Stephen whose death left Conrad muttering so desolately at the side of his good friend's coffin.

I'm certain that Conrad and Crane must have had many a philosophical disagreement during their strolls together in London. On one issue, however, I'm sure they would have agreed: the personification of human vileness that both of them depicted in their fiction was readily apparent in the actual figure of one Charles Augustus Milverton, the primary engine in this sad tale of so much human misery. As I've maintained from the start, I had for many years felt that I couldn't do proper justice to the story while so many of its subjects still lived; I trust that this second time round I have succeeded in illuminating the causes of much of their pain. At least I hope so. I owe it to the memories of Cora and Stephen Crane. *Requiescant in pace.*

THE END

Editor's Selected Reading

For further biographical information on Stephen Crane, I recommend R.W. Stallman's *Stephen Crane: A Biography,* Christopher Benfey's *The Double Life of Stephen Crane,* and Linda H. Davis' *Badge of Courage: The Life of Stephen Crane.* For information on Cora Crane, there is Lillian Gilkes' *Cora Crane: A Biography of Mrs. Stephen Crane.* The life of Harold Frederic is discussed in Bridget Bennett's *The Damnation of Harold Frederic: His Lives and Works.* Stanley Weintraub's *London Yankees: Portraits of American Writers and Artists in England 1894-1914* contains substantial chapters on both Crane and Frederic. Biographer Thomas Beer presented evidence that Crane may have begun a novel about a boy prostitute whom Crane had allegedly met, but the facts in Beer's story have never been substantiated.

It seems hard to believe that Crane's adventurous life could engender embellishment, and yet a number of authors have submitted the biographical facts to fictional interpretations. In his novel *Cora Crane,* Paul Ferris writes of Cora's dilemma in dealing with her missing husband. In *A Mouthful of Dust,* Douglas Savage suggests what Crane might have been up to in Cuba when he'd gone missing. In *Hotel de Dream* Edmund White has invented his own version of the completed text of *Flowers of Asphalt* (which White has renamed "The Painted Boy"). And in *Dark Rider: A Novel Based on the Life of Stephen Crane,* Louis Zara has dramatized virtually all of Crane's major experiences.

As an interesting historical footnote, Benfey, among others, reminds us that Charles Becker, the officer who arrested Dora Clark the prostitute whom Crane wound up defending in court and whose real name may have been Ruby

Young, would go on to earn his own brand of infamy. In 1915, he became the first American policeman executed for murder. The murder itself is described by fictional gangster Meyer Wolfsheim in F. Scott Fitzgerald's *The Great Gatsby* in which Becker is referred to by name.

Readers interested in more information regarding Joseph Conrad and the Bomb Outrage in Greenwich must, of course, begin with Conrad's own *The Secret Agent.* Excellent analyses of the novel appear in Norman Sherry's *Conrad's Western World* and Ian Watt's collection of critical essays in MacMillan's Casebook Series of *The Secret Agent.*

Although none of the aforementioned books makes use of Watson's narrative (its discovery became known only after those other works had been published), Benfey's biography hints at the trouble Milverton caused for Crane when Benfey suggests that Crane's constant need for funds in Cuba "has given rise to speculation about gambling debts or even blackmail." Stallman locates the mortuary in London where Crane's body temporarily rested as "opposite the house where Sherlock Holmes was supposed to have lived."

One final note: While reminiscing in 1907 about the investigation into the Greenwich bombing of 1894, Sir Robert Anderson, then Assistant Commissioner of the CID at Scotland Yard, described his methodology as follows: "I set myself to investigate *à la* Sherlock Holmes."

D.D.V.

Also from Daniel D. Victor

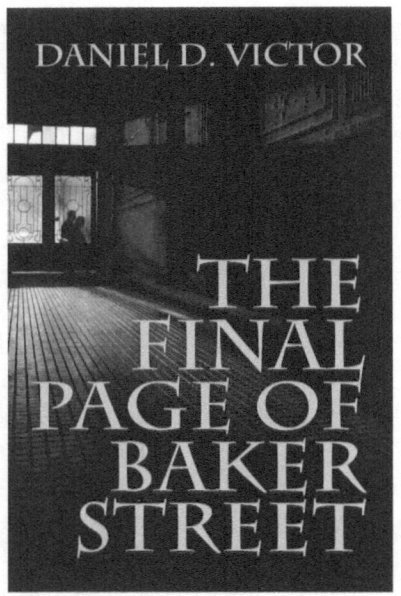

When misadventure led a schoolboy in London to employment at Baker Street, few could have guessed where his introduction to Sherlock Holmes would lead. But as the lad matures and he finds himself caught in the middle of a murder investigation, his friendship with Holmes and Watson lures him into the role of detective. "Billy" documents his experiences, and soon his sleuthing skills not only bring him to another murder, but also lay the foundation for his metamorphosis into a famous mystery writer, the novelist the world now knows as Raymond Chandler.

www.mxpublishing.com

Also from MX Publishing

MX Publishing is the world's largest specialist Sherlock Holmes publisher, with over a hundred titles and fifty authors creating the latest in Sherlock Holmes fiction and non-fiction.

From traditional short stories and novels to travel guides and quiz books, MX Publishing cater for all Holmes fans.

The collection includes leading titles such as *Benedict Cumberbatch In Transition* and *The Norwood Author* which won the 2011 Howlett Award (Sherlock Holmes Book of the Year).

MX Publishing also has one of the largest communities of Holmes fans on Facebook with regular contributions from dozens of authors.

www.mxpublishing.com

www.ingramcontent.com/pod-product-compliance
Lightning Source LLC
Chambersburg PA
CBHW022040240626
47154CB00007B/2493